"There is an aching beauty woven into the lyrical prose of this novel that lingers with the reader beyond the last page. Against the richly drawn canvas of a landscape rendered vividly and with meticulous detail, a story unfolds of a family and community faced with both outward and inner desolation. Compelled to untangle the difficult questions of what it means to be both human and humane in the face of unspeakable cruelty and horror, one is drawn in and held by their resilience, courage, vulnerability, and tenderness and the inimitable power of the ties that bind."

—Colleen van Niekerk, author of *A Conspiracy of Mothers*

"*Such a Beautiful Thing to Behold* is a stark, powerful novel about family, resilience, and survival in the face of nearly insurmountable odds. Turaki's engrossing storytelling will draw you in from the very first page, and the siblings' determination to escape their grim fates is as harrowing as it is hopeful, reminding us that even when faced with all matters of adversity and tragedy, humanity will still seek a way to forge ahead and prevail."

—Kirthana Ramisetti, author of *Dava Shastri's Last Day*

"Grim, beautiful—a stunning novel."

—T. L. Huchu, author of *The Library of the Dead*

SUCH A
BEAUTIFUL
THING TO
BEHOLD

SUCH A BEAUTIFUL THING TO BEHOLD

A NOVEL

UMAR TURAKI

Little
a

This is a work of fiction. Names, characters, organizations, places, events, and incidents are either products of the author's imagination or are used fictitiously. Any resemblance to actual persons, living or dead, or actual events is purely coincidental.

Published by Little A, New York

www.apub.com

Amazon, the Amazon logo, and Little A are trademarks of Amazon.com, Inc., or its affiliates.

ISBN-13: 9781542034661 (hardcover)
ISBN-10: 1542034663 (hardcover)

ISBN-13: 9781542034678 (paperback)
ISBN-10: 1542034671 (paperback)

Cover design by Kimberly Glyder

Printed in the United States of America

First edition

For my mother,
Esther Kisitmwa Turaki.

You carried my dreams so far.
Now may they carry you.

Your eyes are windows into your body.

If you open your eyes wide in wonder and belief,

your body fills up with light.

—Matthew 6:22, The Message

I

THE FIRST EIGHT DAYS

1

DUNKA

The Grey-ridden neighbor, Nana Ritdirnen, licked her lips and parted them to continue speaking. Dunka sat on the floor at her feet, his whole spirit leaning in so he could hear her when she spoke. His body, however, he held back. Hope was an easier burden to carry if you did not put your all into it.

They were in her bedroom. She sat on a white plastic chair with flimsy arms that folded like paper if you put too much weight on them. The name he was waiting to hear was like a secret too heavy to leave her tongue. Nana Ritdirnen's eyes were already black and void, like two holes inside her head. Her strength had all but failed, and Dunka was certain she was blind, even if she would not admit it. Rit, his sister and Nana Ritdirnen's namesake, would bring her what tiny meals they could spare and help her clean. Nana Ritdirnen was the closest thing they had to a mother, as she had liked to remind them back when she could still walk from her front door, across their backyard, past their father's sky-blue pickup truck and the place where their mother was buried, and into the kitchen. Once inside, she would call out the children's names and wait for them to emerge from their rooms. If she came with some food, she would place it on the countertop and order them to get to eating. If she had nothing, she would ask them whether they needed anything before turning around and going back home. It had taken several months for the Grey to reduce her to this point, where she had just enough strength to migrate between her bed and the white chair, and barely enough to speak a string of words.

"Fifteen Goma Street. Pagak, but they call her Matyin," Nana Ritdirnen said at last. There it was: the name and address of the woman who lived in the next village. The woman who might save Dunka and his siblings from the Grey. Nana Ritdirnen had stressed *might*, saying there was nothing to lose in trying. As though reading his mind, she added, "It's too late for you and me. But if she can help the others, it will be a good thing."

Back in his room, Dunka studied his eyes in the knife-size sliver that was all that remained of his father's mirror. He had first seen the Grey lodged in them two days ago. There had been more relief for him than fear at that moment, because he had been waiting for it, but the waiting had been its own kind of terror. He looked around his room. It had been his father's room first. He was seeing the objects in the room, but at the same time not seeing them: his gaze had been rendered a monochromatic silver by the Grey. The Grey did that: it stole the color from your eyes as it killed you quietly. He stared at the toneless room and its profusion of belongings—clothes, a handful of schoolbooks, furniture, the paper ceiling—failing to differentiate between what had been his father's and what had always been his, and how the two had become one. With the Grey now inside him, nothing mattered any longer. Not even Nana Ritdirnen's words and the fleeting hope they had puffed into him.

He took a long walk in no particular direction, paying little attention to his surroundings. It had rained about four weeks ago, and that initial single rainfall had been so brief that it had barely soaked the ground and had failed to make the fields come alive. When the rain ended, he had stood by the flame tree near the house, gazing toward the five-kilometer stretch of wilderness that lay between their village, Pilam, and the next village, Pishang, wondering how long it would take to see green fields again. That had been before he'd gotten the Grey, before he had lost all hope of ever seeing color again. Now everything was drab and leaden, like in those old black-and-white films that had sometimes aired on television in the afternoons when their lives had been normal and they'd had electricity. He grew tired of walking and circled his way back home, collapsing on his bed and falling asleep.

He was roused by Rit. The frozen look on her face made him sit up, even though his body felt like a deadweight. Ashen morning sunlight was splashed everywhere.

"What is it?" he asked.

"It's Nana."

He found the older woman dead in her chair. The knife she had used to cut her wrist was still in her hand. The arm with the slashed wrist hung outside the chair, letting her blood fall to the ground. Rit stood by the door, crying.

"Go back to the house," Dunka said, not turning to look at her.

After she left, he watched Nana Ritdirnen for a long time, breathing the silence in and out. He carried her to the mouth of the grave that had been dug for her husband a year before, after he had gone missing, after they had searched and searched the surrounding area, after Uncle Golshak had left to look for him among the hills and also never returned. Dunka's father had dug it alone, telling them he was still strong, even though they could see how the Grey crouched over him like a black storm waiting to break.

Dunka retrieved an old, faded wrapper from Nana Ritdirnen's room and covered her with it. He laid her in the hole and filled it with the hard, caked earth. Then he sat in their living room, tired all the way through, and waited for Panmun to come in.

If there was going to be any righting of things, if they were all going to learn to live together as a household, then he needed her, as the second born, to be aligned with him. As a united front, they could convince Panshak to not be away so much without saying where he went. Rit was already doing more than her fair share of things, and how old was she? Barely fifteen? He could not remember. It was time for him and Panmun to take the weight off her shoulders. Apparently, Nana Ritdirnen had to die for him to see that much. And he needed Panmun's cooperation.

He waited several hours, eventually falling asleep on the sofa. When his sister stumbled in, her dreadlocks wild from wind and abandon, he awoke.

"Panmun, sit down," he said. Panmun gave him an acidic look, but he kept going. "Nana Ritdirnen is dead. I buried her this morning."

Panmun sank into the closest seat. She bent her head and began to cry. Dunka listened to her sobs for a while before moving closer and placing one hand on her shoulder. Panmun shook it off without looking up. Dunka wondered whether any of his siblings had noticed the Grey in his eyes over the last two days. No one had said anything. Were they pretending to not have seen it because acknowledging its presence would mean accepting that he was going to die? Or did they just not care?

"Nana and Baba aren't here anymore. We have to take care of each other."

Panmun looked up. Her eyes were enflamed with rage. "Our parents have been dead for six months. Did you just notice?"

The words stung, but Dunka remained straight-faced.

"If I hadn't met Zumji," Panmun continued, "we would have all starved to death."

Dunka tried to contain his growing frustration as she spoke. He forced himself to be still, to not betray any emotion.

"And you, you just sit there and wait for food to come. You've never done anything except sit and wait for food to come. You're actually the most useless person in this house. Even Panshak goes out there and tries to bring something home. But you . . ."

The rage welling up inside him did not wait for her to finish. It pushed him aside and raised his arm as though it were attached to a string. His hand fell, aiming for Panmun's cheek, but she moved her head just out of reach. She leaped to her feet and stood her ground, staring at him with her red, red eyes. She did not seem like his sister just then; she looked like a ferocious, indeterminate creature, bristling and ready to inflict damage.

Dunka stood, breathing hard. He was already hating himself for even thinking of hurting her, let alone trying. He had thought the Grey would deaden all his emotions. Clearly not. He turned away and hurried to his bedroom, where he locked the door and stretched out on the bed. He felt so tired. Maybe death would come to him if he remained still long enough. It began to grow dark outside. He closed his eyes and opened them again. Now, he could feel the heat of the sun drenching the floor all the way from his place on the bed. He went to the living room and saw no one. As he was about to go out through the front door, he heard his name.

"Dunka."

It was Rit. She stood with a wrapper tied over her flat chest and a scarf covering her hair, like a miniature version of their mother. It broke his heart.

"You didn't eat anything yesterday."

Dunka frowned. "I had some mun."

"That was the day before."

Dunka stared at her. She was not making sense.

"You didn't come out of your room yesterday," Rit said.

The realization that he had slept through an entire day settled over him softly. Time was slipping through his fingers, his life leaking away like drops of water that had no better use.

"Where's Panmun?" he said.

"In her room."

One part of him wanted to go to her, though he did not know what he would say. The other part needed air. "I'll be back," he said, before heading out.

He walked until he found a small hill, climbed it, and faced east. More hills and great baobab trees were scattered across the undulating, rocky landscape like a crew of sad, lonely monsters. Abandoned terrace farmlands decorated the stone-crusted hillsides. Beyond them, he could glimpse the outskirts of Pishang and the barricade that had been erected after the Grey had come to Pilam. He had only ever seen it from a distance. It did nothing to change the idea that had taken root in his mind.

Early the next morning, Nana Ritdirnen's words still rang in his head. Fifteen Goma Street. Ask for Matyin. Nothing to lose. It was true that a dreaded vigilante group patrolled the perimeter between the two villages, looking for trespassers from Pilam, but it did not matter. He was dead anyway. Picking up the shirt he had worn the day before, and countless days before that, he sniffed it. It did not smell so bad after all, he decided, pulling it over his head. He did not remember the last time he had washed. Or desired anything. Or dreamed of anything. As he stepped out of the bedroom, it was with an overbearing sense of finality.

Panmun was lying on the living room sofa, wearing sunglasses in the dim light. Her dreadlocks were scattered about her head like a halo. The sight of her lying there, still as death, made Dunka catch his breath for a moment. He wanted to reach out, to touch her, but he was afraid of waking her up if she was sleeping. Would she hurl more barbed words at him? A part of him wished he could stay and talk with her until he was out of words. Talk about all those hurtful things she had said to him after their parents' deaths, and on and on afterward, hurts he had stored up like savings even though he told himself he had forgiven her. Had he really forgiven her? He wanted to make her suffer. And what better way than to leave without saying goodbye, go missing, and be lost forever to mystery? She would carry the guilt of having made him go out there to prove his worth. He would die, and she would blame herself for it.

Outside the house, he turned to look back only after he had cleared the small rise that led toward the flame tree and, beyond that, toward Pishang. Their house was an unpainted, crumbling block of concrete, topped by an old, sagging zinc roof weighed down with rocks. Dunka remembered coming home with his father from the farm and seeing the column of smoke rising from their backyard. He had always anticipated the way the maize they roasted during harvest would explode in his mouth, filling it with sweet juice and tiny chewy particles. He had dreaded seeing his mother's stooped figure by the kerosene stove they used sparingly. He remembered how the stove would fill the kitchen with the smell of burned carbon while thunderstorms raged outside. One time, such a storm ripped their roof right off, and this was the most they could do: pin it down with rocks and hope for the best.

In his hand was the longbow stick he had converted into a staff. It bounced and bent lightly as he walked. In his pocket was a coil of hemp twine that had served as the bow's string. Within minutes, he could assemble these items into an effective weapon—the arrows were wrapped in an old cotton shirt and tucked into his boot beneath his trouser leg. Under his shirt, he had tied his long hunting knife around his waist. It had been a gift from his grandfather. Perhaps, if he was lucky, he could steal a goat or a chicken on his way back. He walked mechanically, placing one foot in front of the next, using the stick as a third leg. The farmlands he trudged across lay useless and dry and overgrown. There was some fruit to be found in the trees, and though the parentless, emaciated children who straggled across Pilam subsisted on it, it was not nearly enough. Nobody had the strength to farm anymore, and dried bushes that were a faint green in only his imagination had burst forth and reclaimed what had once belonged to men. The Grey had felled so many farmers that the skill of knowing when and how to work a field had become trapped in the amber of memory.

Memory. His was still intact. And remember he did, in full color. There really had been nothing to warn the people of Pilam that a strange sickness was about to unfurl across their lives with impunity. A sickness that had no seeming cause, no purpose, and therefore, no meaning. It had simply risen with the sun of a new day and changed everything forever. The strangest thing about the situation, though, was not the nature of the sickness itself, or the way it mowed perfectly healthy people down, or the fact that children alone seemed to be immune to it—it was the viciousness with which the world around them had responded. After the residents of Pilam realized that the Grey was spreading without any logic, and that their village was the sole site of the mysterious epidemic, many people tried to leave. They packed their belongings and loved ones into vehicles, those who had the sickness and those who did not. Somewhere between the settlements, they met a wall of soldiers sent by the government. The refugees ignored the commanding officer's instructions to turn back and tried to barge through the perimeter of wire mesh and barrels. Dunka did not witness the massacre, but the explosion of firearms and the cries of the dying flew across the distance and tore into his being like shards of glass. That had been two years ago, when he was eighteen.

Dunka forced himself across fields and bushes, over hills and around them, until he found himself standing in front of the infamous barricade. Seeing it so close had the desired effect on him: he wanted to turn back and go home. It was made of slashes of barbed copper wire and splotches of concrete, rocks, metal pieces of furniture, carcasses of vehicles, rusted heavy-duty equipment, razor-sharp sheets of zinc and aluminum, old doors, and window bars, all twisted and raised as a barrier to make passage painful for the desperate. It was the embodiment of an entire nation's terror.

Dunka walked along the barricade, inspecting it. The copper wire, reams and reams of it, stretched to the right and the left, as far as the eye could see. Every few meters, cakes of concrete sealed what once had been holes in the ground, holes dug by others just like him. After the massacre, the people had become even more determined. They tried back roads and mountain passes; they tried the expanse of wilderness that stretched on and on to the setting sun. At every turn, they found a well-guarded military installation. They sneaked and fought and snarled and raged, until at last, it dawned on them that there was no escape from the quarantine. Defeated and exhausted, their spirits broken, the people of Pilam resigned themselves to apathy. Eventually, the major roads that led into Pilam were permanently blocked. Leadership groups of neighboring settlements took over from the military and erected obscene boundary fences, further hemming in Pilam and its inexplicable pestilence.

He had not gone far when he saw the first dead body strapped to the barricade like a scarecrow. He forced himself not to look at first, and not to count. One by one, as he passed them, he caught glimpses of the decaying masses out of the corner of his eye, until it occurred to him that any of these men could be his father. He stopped to look at the next one. The birds and the weather had been at the man long enough to make his face indistinguishable. He had short limbs and stout features, which disqualified him. Their father had been a tall man. But then, the corpse could easily have been Nana Ritdirnen's husband, or Uncle Golshak. They had all been middle-aged men, lumbering under the weight of the Grey. Dunka's father had left in search of Uncle Golshak and never come back. This chain of missing men had been replicated throughout Pilam. Fathers and husbands, going in search of each other and failing to return. These bodies may have belonged to such men, or to any other trespasser unfortunate enough to have been caught by the men who patrolled the barricade.

There had been a time when Dunka could not look at his father without judging him. When men around Pilam formed groups to sneak across the barricade in search of food for their families, Dunka's father had stayed back. Some missions were successful, others doomed to failure. One day, Dunka's father had picked up his long-nosed musket and made his way to the barricade. It did not matter to him that the weapon, a piece crudely forged from iron, had no bullets. He returned almost immediately, telling them that he had turned back at the sight of two dead babies suspended from the barricade, no doubt to discourage other desperate parents from abandoning their children at the foot of the fence. "There is only death on the other side," he had said. "Anybody that can build something like that will do anything to keep us here." There had been no shame in his voice, no shame in his body. Dunka had wrestled then with a quiet disappointment, telling himself that if the time ever came for him to cross that stupid boundary fence, he would be a man about it—yet it had taken Nana Ritdirnen's death and Panmun's harsh words to bring him here. His own hypocrisy rustled in his ears, but he pretended not to hear.

Dunka walked for nearly twenty minutes along the barricade until the cement-filled holes dwindled away. At some point, there were no more bodies. He kept walking until he found what he judged to be a perfect spot.

With the little hoe he had brought along, he began to dig a tunnel under the space where two rocks met. Anything could be waiting for him on the other side. The patrolmen may have studied the tactics of trespassers like him. Perhaps they could now predict his every move. What if they were hidden somewhere, watching him right now? Dunka stopped digging and looked around. When nothing moved among the rocks and bushes, he bent over and continued digging. His strength was already fading, and there was a chance he would have none left to make it back to Pilam—even if his mission was successful—but he did not stop digging.

2

ZUMJI

The sunset over Pilam was a glorious, bleeding death, the most stunning one Zumji had ever seen. The fact that he was standing on this ledge, staring at it, on what would be his final night in his village, felt significant. Tomorrow, he was going to run away with the girl he loved, away from this place and the miasma of despair that had overtaken it. There was nothing for them here. Sooner or later, like every adult in Pilam, they would also fall victim to the Grey. So they would go somewhere that they could find the hope that had forsaken this place. He would miss the sunsets, would miss this ledge, which was a watchtower or rampart of sorts to him, where he often stood to watch over the village. He sometimes wondered whether he might have seen the Grey coming like a dark cloud to descend over Pilam had he kept watch, but he had been only seventeen when the scourge began, fresh from losing his father, still finding his footing as a solitary man in the world. He did not know anything about standing on a ledge and weeping for his home, or a sunset.

As the last of the setting sun disappeared, leaving behind a crepuscular hue in the sky, Zumji wiped the tears from his eyes and began the climb down from his ledge. As far as he knew, he was one of few adults who had not been touched by the Grey. Yet. Every day he woke up, he looked in the mirror. Before the Grey, he had been something of a hermit, a trait he had inherited from his father, who had been a trapper. When Zumji accompanied his father to lay traps in the bush, he had watched the older man closely, how he waited for the creature to blunder into the trap, how he spoke to it and soothed it before drawing a knife across its throat. And how he let the tears run freely down his cheeks, never bothering to clean them until after the hunt had ended. The connection between his father and all of nature was something Zumji desired for himself. The older man had a habit of periodically disappearing for an entire night, only to drag himself back in the following morning, heavy with drink. Zumji had begun to question the true depths of his father's loneliness since the death of Zumji's mother—and he had his suspicions about how his father attempted to tame that loneliness. Before Zumji could summon the courage to ask him about loneliness and losing a wife in childbirth and how that could push you readily into the arms of a different woman each night, Zumji's father left one night and failed to stumble back in the next day. He never returned.

All that had been before the Grey. By the time it had finished settling its weight over the entire village, Zumji had become fully acquainted with solitude and self-sufficiency. He caught his animals alone, sold them and their meat at the market, and lived by himself in the house his father had built on the edges of Pilam. Zumji knew he had been a phantom, going and coming as he pleased, speaking to no one unless he had to, but the arrival of the Grey changed him in a way he would never have suspected. He stopped being a specter to the community and became, to them, a kind of anonymous savior. As Pilam slowed gradually toward death, Zumji found himself performing strange rituals of concern, like standing on his ledge and gazing over the entire settlement prostrated before him like a supplicant, his heart breaking, bleeding for the people, for each person. Or minuscule acts of kindness, like leaving small parcels of cured meat and herbs in front of houses in the dead of night. As time went by, he came to see himself as the settlement's protector, its defender, its last hope.

But then the burden of doing good began to grow heavy. How long could he keep it up? This path of altruism and self-sacrifice he had chosen stretched endlessly before him. And just as abruptly as he had begun, he stopped his acts of kindness, withdrawing into himself and his own concerns. This lasted about a day or so. Perhaps he might have continued in this manner longer, had what happened not happened. But it *had* happened, and now he had started leaving food on the doorsteps of the inhabitants of Pilam again, perhaps to assuage the guilt that shadowed him despite his best attempts to ignore it. And he had decided to run away.

As he ate his last supper in Pilam, he thought about Panmun and the way she filled his future with an inexplicable hope. Later, after he had put out what was left of the candle and was lying in bed, he could not sleep. A couple of days had passed, and he was still tussling with the weight of what he had done. Try as he might, he could not circumvent the monolithic presence of this single transgression, which stood erect and visible for miles in the plain that was his life. It was with him at every moment, waiting for him to turn away from the momentary distractions presented by the outside world, waiting to accuse him in the private interior of his existence. The charge was simple and carried with it the clarity of cold morning light striking a blade of grass: he had killed a man.

The following morning, he composed a note for Panmun, folded it neatly, and gave it to the girl who still looked hungry despite having just finished a meal of bananas and groundnuts. Her name was Tongrot. She was ten years old but looked younger, her hair a pathetic carpet of copper upon her head. The children were the true victims. The adults were dying and finding their peace in death, but it was the children who had to grapple with the problem of survival—until they too were old enough to die. As he watched her head out the door to deliver the note to Panmun, he had to remind himself that there was only so much he could do. At the same time, he had to resist the pervasive apathy that had gripped everybody, for they were simply waiting for their turn to catch the Grey and die. And the children . . . well, the children were left to their own devices.

In the early days of the Grey, after the electricity had been cut off and the world had shut them in, the daughter of the village head had created a communication system that involved the use of messengers to ferry missives across Pilam. For the most part, children were the only ones available to be employed as Runners in exchange for food. This kept them busy at first and gave them some semblance of purpose. But in time, even the village head's daughter succumbed to the Grey, and the system caved in on itself. The boys and girls who once had served as the village's communication lifeline found themselves idle, full of energy but with nowhere to direct it. They loitered about the streets and in front of their homes, playing games and staying out later than they should have, with no adult to supervise them. That was how a little girl spied Zumji leaving some food in front of her house one evening and followed him home, where she watched him warily. After he had given her something to eat, she returned the next day with her older brother, Tongzum. Zumji assumed they were orphans. He asked them why they did not go to Nana Kanke's house, where she took care of orphans, but Tongzum skipped over the question as though it were an obstacle in his path. Zumji had taken an instant liking to Tongrot. There was an intelligence in her eyes that unfurled and retracted like a whip, depending on who she was speaking to. Her small stature and pitiful appearance belied her understanding of the world. Zumji had initially tried to fit her into his escape plans. However, the decision to leave with her had other decisions attached to it, like bringing her brother along and raising the two of them. So, instead, he taught Tongzum a few survival tricks, like how to set traps, skin game, and grow certain things. He would have loved to teach him a bit of terrace farming, but there was not enough time and the ground was still hard from the lack of rain. He would leave the house to the two siblings and, perhaps, Panmun's siblings too. Time was a sure, steady river, an illusion that created a false sense of safety: it would carry them forward without ebbing, and they would blink one day and find that they had become grown-ups. Tongzum was a strong-willed boy. He would protect his sister. And if the Grey lifted by the time he grew up, he and the rest of them would have a real chance at living self-sufficient lives.

Zumji inspected the four sacks that were standing just inside the main door. One held a variety of animal pelts: antelope, goat, sheep. Another contained four watermelons he had harvested that morning, albeit prematurely. The last two sacks each held old guzuk and beans. Weevils had already been at his store of beans long enough for him to consider relinquishing it to them, but beans tasted the same in spite of weevils. Using thick lengths of rope, he tied the mouth of each sack and linked them in pairs, then carried them outside. He locked the front door and deposited the key under the doormat, where the children knew to find it.

Zumji left the house of his childhood carrying his sacks like a yoke. He was not abandoning his home; no, he was just taking a break from Pilam until things returned to normal. This, his leaving, was a kind of inverted bravery, because cowardice could be something as basic as sitting on a cold night and folding your limbs up for warmth instead of braving the chill to get wood and start a fire. He dared to brave the chill, find the wood, start a fire.

He walked for nearly thirty minutes to get to the cluster of bushes where he had concealed the auto-rickshaw to look like a part of the foliage. The portions of yellow paint on the vehicle were visible in swatches like tiger stripes. It carried an air of decrepitude that belied its true usefulness. Inside, tucked behind the roughly patched back seat, was a blue plastic jerrican that could hold at least nineteen liters of water. It had been similarly positioned in the rickshaw when he found it. Zumji made space in the back for the four sacks. When he was done arranging them, he walked out of the thicket carrying the blue container. He checked, as always, to make sure he was not being followed.

The route he took back toward the center of Pilam was one he had been avoiding for days now. It ran by a copse of great mango trees that had a stream passing through it. The ground there was soft because of the stream, the trees lush with dark emerald leaves. They towered high above him to his left as he passed, ominous and patient with the secret in their midst. Zumji did not look once in the direction of the great trees as he walked by, afraid that the secret may be there in their shadows, watching him.

The streets were all but empty. Children, reedy as sugarcane stalks, skulked in corners, watching him with hungry eyes. He ignored them and marched on. Various fruits were coming into season. There would be plenty for them to gorge on soon.

The man he wanted to see lived in the center of Pilam, in a house surrounded by a high wall topped with shards of broken bottles. Everybody knew him as Mister—nobody seemed to know his real name. There had been a time when Mister was not the sort of man anybody could just decide to go and see. Men who carried imported rifles had guarded the big black gate and searched you before allowing you into the compound, where you were made to stand in a corner and wait for Mister to confirm the appointment you had been given on the phone. Meanwhile, three giant dogs roared at you nonstop from their steel cage, their jowls quivering with each bark, commanding terror into every tissue in your body. Then the Grey came and changed all that. The stream of men and vehicles that brought containers of petroleum goods to Mister dried up. His guards were picked off by the Grey, shooting, hanging, or stabbing themselves; those who did not die left, until only his two sons remained to protect their father. Now the gate to the compound stood wide open in perpetuity.

Rumor had it that the three dogs had been eaten by their master. Zumji had no reason to doubt this, because there was no sign of them as he stood and surveyed the large compound. There was a warehouse to one side surrounded by all shapes and sizes of barrels. Two red pickup trucks sat in front of it without their tires, corpses in their own way. The stillness was so powerful he felt a tingle crawl up his spine. On the opposite end of the compound was the house itself, a big two-story building with ornate frontage and Greco-style pillars that seemed overwrought in the otherwise banal surroundings.

Zumji had two choices before him. He could go into the house and politely ask Mister for permission to get some gasoline from his storage, assuming Mister was still alive. Mister would more than likely refuse him. There was another rumor that some members of the community had come in the beginning of the quarantine, asking for help—a little oil, a little grain—and Mister had turned them away. All of them. They had returned under the cover of many successive nights, carting away what could be carted. Mister's sons had used up most of their bullets shooting into the air to scare them off instead of shooting at them, but the thieves feared hunger more than they feared the rain of ammunition. They left nothing except the fuel, and if that could have been drunk, it would have been taken too.

Or Zumji's other choice: he could simply go to the warehouse and help himself to some gasoline. What would that make him? A thief? He would not be stealing, in the pure sense of the word, would he? If Mister was already inside death's door, what difference would it make for Zumji to restrain himself from collecting a small quantity of fuel for his rickshaw and going on his way? It would not take the Grey away from Pilam. It certainly would not absolve him of any of his previous sins. None of his good deeds would.

Having convinced himself, Zumji walked over to the warehouse. Many of the barrels inside were either upturned or punctured, and their contents covered the floor, making it slippery and filling the air with pungent fumes. Zumji picked his way carefully to an untouched barrel and pried it open. Gasoline the color of dark beer sloshed gently inside, and a smell like two rough hands reached up his nostrils and into his brain. He took a step back, steadying himself.

Zumji found a hose, dipped one end into the barrel, and sucked on the other end once. He directed the flowing liquid into the blue jerrican. As he averted his face from the heady fumes, his eyes fell on a man standing in the gaping doorway of the warehouse. He froze, watching the figure. The man's face was harshly visible, his empty, lightless eyes fixed on Zumji. He had a full beard and a bald head. But it was not these features that jolted the terror of recognition through Zumji's skull; it was the hole in the front of the man's beige shirt, bordered by a wide bloodstain. The wound peered through the wide gash in the shirt, revealing pink layers of flesh.

For the last few days, Zumji had felt that he was being followed, but this was his first time seeing the confirmation. The two men regarded each other across the expanse of damaged, scattered barrels. Though the strange, wounded man in the doorway showed neither signs of malevolence nor goodwill, Zumji was slowly submerged in a rising tide of dread. He was attempting—and failing—to understand how the dead could have such a powerful effect on the living. The thing that had happened, that accused him when he was alone and unable to sleep . . . it would never stop haunting him.

This was what had happened. He had left the house without a plan, without locking the front door, with nothing but the desire to walk away forever, toward some other town, into some other valley, under some other sky. It was what his father had done, after all. Walked away. Panmun was at home, none the wiser. It would be easier this way, cleaner, kinder. He did not walk far before coming upon the rickshaw. It sat awry on the side of the road, like a piece of furniture out of place. When he peered into the rickshaw, he saw—on the other side, past the blue jerrican and pieces of cabbage littering the floor of the vehicle—the man stretched on the ground, squirming like a worm. Zumji moved to stand over him, watched him grip the hole in his stomach, watched him die. Nothing in all of growing up, in all of living, had prepared Zumji for this. He had seen animals in the throes of death, often because of his own traps; had seen firsthand the face-off between the willfulness of life and the inexorability of death; had seen how unbearable it was and had ended it quickly because suffering is a contagious thing, even between species. But what was one to do with a human being in the final stages of expiration, whose body was dying but whose eyes were alive—desperately alive—and trained on you?

"Help me."

Two simple words slipping out like fragments of his soul. A dazed, lucid whispering. Blood as copious as vomit gushing out of him. Zumji watching, frozen. This poor man was snagged in the doorway between life and death, trapped in the process of dying. He could not go back, but it seemed he could not go forward either. Zumji waited, and the man went on squirming. Should he end his suffering the way he had ended the suffering of wild pigs and antelope? Was that the kind of help the man was asking for? Somehow, it was different with an actual person.

After waiting for some time without a change in the man's condition, Zumji went home to get a pistol, a pickax, and a shovel. If he was going to do this, it had to be done right and done quickly. A bullet to the head was the best way. But by the time he had returned with the items, the man had stopped moving. Zumji prodded him, and his body gave no response. He was dead.

Zumji looked around for an ideal spot; the side of the road would not do. He saw the mango trees nearby, towering like giants asleep on their feet, and carried the body into their midst. There, in the cool, soft earth, with the great trees and the nearby stream whispering around him, he dug a grave. He dragged the body by its arms to the hole, gently placed it inside, and began to shovel in the earth. Somehow, it seemed right to begin with the feet and work his way up. At the same time, something about the way the dark soil fell on the man's body—onto his skin, into his wound—sat like an uncomfortable mass in the pit of Zumji's stomach, but he had nothing to cover him up with. Zumji shoveled harder, and he was still shoveling when the man woke up with a sharp gasp. Zumji leaped back in fright, dropping the shovel. The man was in anguish again, squirming again. The soil was now up to his chest; his face, neck, and left shoulder were visible. Zumji made the decision then, in those few seconds after the man had woken up. It was barely even a decision—it was a reflex: keep going and end this once and for all. He wanted to be back home, or somewhere else with some measure of comfort, perhaps in Panmun's arms, relishing the way she ran her fingers over his scalp. He wanted to be out of there.

The man's eyes were open when Zumji shoveled loam into them. Zumji concealed the rickshaw in a nearby thicket. As he left the area, he felt something new, something different about himself: the heavy sense of having killed a man. There was something off-kilter about the guilt; it did not sit quite right on his shoulders, perhaps because it was a size too big. He was Zumji. He was a good man. He did not kill people.

He had burned the clothes he was wearing that very day, and in the days to come, he would pace his room, the entire house, sit and stand, sit and stand, grappling with the illogicality of killing a man who was already dead.

Now the sound of splashing liquid filled his ears, and he turned to see the gas pouring over the mouth of his jerrican. By the time he yanked the hose from the barrel and turned around, the man with the hole in his stomach was gone.

Zumji carried the container outside and looked around. Nothing stirred, not even the light. Hoisting the stolen gasoline to his shoulder, he passed through the gate, then looked back: no sign of that man. He took another twenty or so paces before stopping to look back again, this time at the gaping gateway, at the dejected air that surrounded the entire compound. What was he now if not a thief? This was not right.

He simply had to ask. Had to. He concealed his jerrican behind a hedge in the flower bed by the gate.

What if Mister said no? Then he would have to follow through by emptying the blue container back into the barrel, which would put an end to his current plans. He would instead have to leave on foot, holding Panmun's hand and whispering loving words to her. They would walk for days, weeks even, making their way across the sprawling expanse of rocky land broken by fields and woods. How long would they walk before finding a place to stay? Death was not an option. He had made a pact with hope, and hope precluded death.

Up close, he stared at the way the house sat on the ground, at an entire existence, derailed. It was difficult to feel pity for a man like Mister. The front door, frame of metal, body of wood, stood closed. He barely touched it and it gave way, an inch or so, before stopping, obstructed by a weight on the other side. He probably could have pushed it open if he tried, but he went around the house in search of a back door. The flower beds had been dug up in places, yellow-and-white flowers scattered about like confetti at a wedding.

The back door had been completely ripped from its hinges and lay in pieces on the floor. Framed in the doorway was the first dead body: Mister's second son, Wungak. There were several gashes of varying sizes in his head and neck. An eye had ruptured. Going by the blood on the floor, still so lively and red, and the air still untainted by the stench of decay, this man had been killed not more than an hour ago. Zumji had once supplied fifty rabbit pelts to Mister, and Wungak, who was to pay him, slipped over exactly half of the agreed-upon sum. Zumji had cocked his head, and Wungak had cocked his right back, shrugged to say this was the way of the world, and gone back into the house. This very same house.

Zumji tore his eyes from Wungak's body. Every single cupboard, every drawer, anything that looked like a door, had been thrown open, its contents ransacked. Whoever had done this must have been starving.

Zumji ventured into the main living room, where he found the object blocking the door. Another body. This one had no head, only a neck that looked like the stump of a felled tree. Up the stairs, the walls soft with beige and brown, floor soft with woolen carpeting, all were smeared and speckled with blood. The hallway at the top of the stairs led off into several rooms whose doors stood open. Light poured through them and into the corridor. At the end of the hallway, a solitary door, massive with importance, bore the carving of an elephant's head, complete with tusks. Zumji remained at the top of the stairs. What evil thing had done this? What would he find behind that door? He really should get his gasoline and be going, but a stronger force was dragging him into the room, and there was nothing he could do about it.

Zumji opened the elephant door and found Mister lying in a king-size bed. The headboard was a grander version of the elephant carving on the door. And Mister—a solidly built man with a heavy gold ring on his right hand, which rested on the blanket that reached up to his chest. Zumji had seen him only once before, tall and imposing, standing on the balcony when he had come to deliver the rabbit pelts. Mister watched Zumji as he entered the room and stood at the foot of the bed. The Grey had muddied the man's small eyes, causing the whites to look like snatches of plain sky disappearing behind dark clouds. The large room around the bed was intact. Nothing had been violated. Large metal boxes and chests, a huge safe, a cupboard, an ivory-colored chest of drawers, a floor-to-ceiling mirror, an impressive entertainment system, and the light slipping into the tall window, touching the room like a blessing. It bestowed on Mister the glow of a tragic monarch.

"Did you see anybody?" Mister asked. Before Zumji could respond, he added, "Where are those stupid boys? You didn't see anybody?"

Zumji stood there with the answer stuck in his throat. A foul, base smell was rising from under Mister's covers, an ugly counterpoint to the room's tranquil atmosphere.

"I thought I heard noises. But they didn't come up."

24

"Who, sir?"

"The children. You didn't see the children?"

"No, sir."

"Maybe the boys drove them away. Have you ever been frightened?"

Mister was looking at Zumji imploringly. There was a senile edge to his speech: the Grey was somewhere inside his skull, messing with his faculty.

"Yes, sir."

"I heard children screaming, shouting. I think I was afraid," Mister confessed, to no one in particular, to air. "But Nungdima and Wungak must have driven them away." Turning his gaze once more on Zumji, Mister said, "Where are the boys?"

Zumji dragged his eyes away from this man's humiliation, from the ignominy that clung to his skin, to his hands. Face-to-face with Mister, it was impossible not to pity him. Nobody deserved this, no matter what they had done.

"There were two bodies downstairs, but I only recognized one."

"Who?"

"Wungak."

Mister closed his eyes, inhaled deeply, and opened them again. "I could hear their voices. They were screaming. I thought they would come upstairs."

Two days ago, an old man had stumbled aimlessly near Zumji's property, carrying the Grey like a deadweight. He told Zumji he had seen a gang of children—adolescents, teenagers—immune to the Grey, sensing the power vacuum in Pilam and filling it like water. That was all he said, children filling a vacuum like water, before he disappeared into the bushes.

The possibility that what he had seen downstairs might be evidence of the stranger's claim socked Zumji so hard in the gut that he staggered to the window of Mister's bedroom, threw it open, and retched through it—a terrible, empty spasm that shook his entire gut. How could a child be the perpetrator of such carnage?

"Have you ever killed a man?" Mister asked.

Zumji turned back into the room and drew closer, frowning. "What?"

"Have you ever killed somebody before?" Mister turned his head weakly to his right. "I can't reach my pistol." He looked at Zumji. Moved his head again. "That drawer there. I want you to shoot me in the head."

Zumji imagined that if Mister had the strength, he would have raised his hand and placed a finger in the center of his forehead. In entering this house, in an attempt to avoid becoming a thief, Zumji had brought himself face-to-face with a dying man's wish for the second time. The comical nature of the situation stood in front of him, asking him to spare a chuckle, but laughter was a luxury he could not presently afford.

If he walked away right now, would Mister follow him around with the Grey in his eyes the way that nameless man was shadowing him with that gaping wound? Was there some hallowed, inexplicable weight to the demand of a dying man? Had he made the mistake of disregarding it before? He had swept an innocent man and his suffering into the ground, where the ugly spectacle unfolded out of sight, because he, Zumji, did not have the stomach to face it. Zumji wished it were not real, his cowardice, the fact that he had deluded himself into thinking he had done the right thing. So he decided to reverse it all.

He opened the drawer. The revolver was lying there, a shiny, black, rare thing. Crafted to perfection. Fit to shoot a king. Beside the handgun, a single bullet, plated in gold, shaped like an inverted three-dimensional letter *u*. It looked like it had been placed there for a special purpose. Had Mister saved it for himself, for the day when he could not bear the Grey any longer? Zumji loaded the revolver and took a few steps back. He looked directly at the tips of Mister's fingers for the first time: they were mildewed, ashen. The Grey was not just in his eyes; it was in his hands and his body.

"It started yesterday," Mister said with some effort, watching Zumji watch his hands. "It's in other places too. I can't move. I thought I could beat it."

Zumji aimed the weapon at Mister's forehead. His heart was racing. Was he about to help a man, or just kill him?

As though he had heard the question, Mister answered, "God sent you here. My sons refused to do it. But God sent you."

The words were still in Zumji's ears when he fired. The gun exploded and the bullet caught Mister in the forehead, pushing his head into the soft pillow, where it bounced for a moment before going still. Mister had closed his eyes, but between the force of the bullet's impact and the jerking of his head, they sprang open again. The Grey stared out of them.

Zumji fell to his knees, averting his eyes from Mister's body. Something huge and torrential was about to come gushing out of his chest, but he took in a deep breath and held it for several seconds before exhaling. This was it. He needed to get out of Pilam.

3

PANMUN

Panmun clutched the note as though it were an insect she was intent on crushing. It had been a neatly folded piece of square paper when it arrived. Tongrot, who had delivered the message, stood nearby. Panmun had grown fond of the girl after Zumji narrated her story. It had been in one of those moments when they were the only two people in the world and that look had come over Zumji, the look that made his eyes shimmer with passion like a weeping messiah's, the look that made her silently pledge her heart to him again and again. Now the fact that he had felt the need to tell her to stay by the flame tree no less than three times stung so badly that she raised the note and read his ugly hand-writing again through her sunglasses.

There are a few things I need to do before we go. I want us to have everything we need. Just wait by the flame tree. I will come latest by 3. Maybe you can make something for us to carry with us so we can eat on the way, if you find anything. Stay by the tree and don't go anywhere, in case I come earlier.

Please stay by the tree.

Was she an impetuous, restless child who could not keep a simple instruction in her head and had to be reminded repeatedly? And what did he mean by *if you find anything*? Of course she would not be able to find anything. He knew that well enough. After all, he had been the one giving them food since she met him four months ago. It was one of the things that had won her over, the way he seemed to summon what he needed out of thin air, and the way he seemed to keep the Grey at bay without fearing it. When he told her one evening, up on that perch where he had found her, that there was no use in fearing the Grey, she had snuggled deeper into his arms: there would be no safer place.

"Aunty, do you want to send your own letter?" Tongrot asked. "I can take it back."

This made Panmun smile. The walk to Zumji's house was at least a good half hour. It did not matter whether the girl had made this offer in the hope of getting something in return, not in the world of the Grey. If Panmun could, she would have given her a treat as a reward. Zumji's altruism was rubbing off on her.

She caressed the little girl's face and shook her head in response. Tongrot waved goodbye, then walked back up the path that led away from Panmun's house, disappearing in a matter of seconds. Zumji was proceeding with the plan, even though he had not seen her in three days. They were supposed to have met to flesh out the details, identify the items they required, and figure out how to get them. The day before, he had come looking for her, knocking on her door and calling her name, but she had pretended not to hear. Now here was his note, assuming she was still coming, telling her, *three times*, to wait for him by the flame tree. The fact that he had not deserted the plan warmed her up inside. But when she saw Zumji, she would still give him a piece of her mind.

Panmun went back into the house. When Zumji first mentioned the idea of running away three days ago, he had just shown her the rickshaw he had found. She'd had to sit with the idea for a little while and feel its true weight before eventually deciding that she liked it. She had spent the rest of the day trying to contain her energy, then eventually channeling it into worrying about their escape.

"If we take one of the roads through the hills, won't there be a roadblock?" she had asked Zumji.

"There'll be a way."

"Where did you find it?" she said.

"By the side of the road."

"Who was driving it?"

Zumji simply shrugged. Zumji, her man of few words. She had been immersed in a wonderful cloud of joy that day. When she returned home, Panmun stopped in the kitchen doorway and stared at Rit with a focused intensity, feeling as though she were seeing her, actually *seeing* her, for the first time. Rit was by the counter sorting some beans, oblivious to her sister's presence. Panmun almost reached out to hold her hand, tell her how much she loved her, and blurt out the plan, but Zumji had warned her not to tell anyone, so she had to keep the secret locked in her chest.

She went to the living room looking for her pocket mirror and ran into her brother. Everything that had happened in that room remained a blur. All she knew was that if Dunka had not left the room when he did, she would have flown at him with teeth and nails for daring to try to hit her, and she would not have stopped until she had drawn blood— even if he killed her in the process. She still remembered the blast of air that accompanied his hand as it missed her, the fleeting sensation that she was suspended in a dream pool. After he had run away, the fact that her brother had tried to hurt her, together with the news of Nana Ritdirnen's death, became too much to bear. She had fallen back into her seat and simply lain there, letting the sobs out, before going to her room and crying some more. She tried to distract herself by thinking about the planned elopement and whatever false sense of excitement she could squeeze from those thoughts.

31

The next morning, all her pain, excitement, and grief vanished through a trapdoor when she looked in the large mirror and saw the Grey staring back at her. Unlike Dunka's, which began as a speck and grew like ink spreading through water, hers had already covered most of her right eye and all of the left. Even if she stood across the room from the mirror, she could still see the blackness and how it seemed to ooze out of her eyes.

For the rest of that day, Panmun did not leave her room, keeping the door locked. Rit knocked several times and received no answer. Panmun stayed in bed and counted dust motes until the sun fell.

That evening, Rit pounded on the door and spoke loudly. "Panmun, please. Just . . . just tap the door if you're fine," she said, her voice unsteady.

It took all of her, but Panmun managed to make it to the door, where she rapped the wood gently three times before returning to her darkness. She barely heard Rit saying she would leave some food outside the door.

The next day, something entirely unexpected gripped her by the throat and pulled her out of the dark. It dragged her into the weak daylight that drifted in through the paper-thin curtains. It was a monstrous retching that brought nothing up with it. When it subsided, she lay still and stared at the brown paper ceiling, looking for those points of dust—looking in vain, because it was not the right time of day yet. She had watched the color seep out of her vision that first day. She knew the paper ceiling was brown only from memory. Now it was a medium shade of gray. So this was what it was like to see through the Grey.

She ran her tongue over her lips, trying to place the gentle nausea that was coming over her. And then it broadsided her, the only explanation for this sudden heaving, for the fact that her period was more than a week late. She was pregnant. A distinct life was growing inside her, tethered to hers, but a distinct life nonetheless. The awareness sat in her body like a lump of lead, meaningless in the glare of the Grey. She decided to bury it.

How that day went was a mystery, even to her. The day after, she wanted something else, even if it was only a change in banalities. She had forgotten that it was supposed to be the day of her escape from Pilam. She went into the living room and stretched out on the sofa, wearing a pair of sunglasses, which she had salvaged from a box of old things belonging to her father. Rit came over, and Panmun finally agreed to eat something.

"Do you know where Dunka went?" Rit asked while Panmun forced a spoonful of leftover bean porridge into her mouth.

Panmun shook her head without saying anything.

"Why are you wearing those stupid glasses?" Rit said, looking right at her. Panmun stopped eating and put her bowl down. That was all the answer her sister needed. Rit's face crumpled, and she ran out of the room. The sound of her weeping crept up the corridor from the kitchen.

Having been reminded of their plan by the arrival of Zumji's note, Panmun began to get ready. She had always liked colorful things. As she picked out each item, she reminded herself of the specific shade of each color. She threw on a pair of army-green jeans, some dust-brown sandals, and a yellow shirt the same shade as deep-roasted maize. She tied a red scarf over her dreadlocks. If she was going to do this at all, then it had to be on her own terms. She packed clothes into her pink suitcase, stuffed more things into a dark green backpack almost the same color as her jeans. Then she went to say goodbye.

She pushed open the door to their father's room and stood there, taking it in for the last time. Since he moved in, Dunka had done much to impress his identity on the space. The position of the bed had changed, as had the way the curtains were held open for daylight: they were twisted into strips, which he then hung on the window bars. Her father had trusted her alone to clean the room to his liking. As he went out, he would drop the key into her hand like a treat, and by the time he came back, everything would be reset to a crisp, unmarked newness—Panmun had inherited her father's penchant for a cleanliness that had pristine dimensions, with sharp corners and lines to demarcate things properly. Order. However, their bond stretched beyond the borders of cleanliness into a realm where words had become insufficient to communicate meaning. They shared a telepathic link that allowed them to anticipate each other's needs. It worked both ways, in countless renditions, such as her knowing that her father required hot water to bathe in the morning before he had opened his door, or him knowing that his daughter had a crush on a boy in school even before she realized the crush was there. She would hold these premonitions in the silence between her and her father, sometimes acting on them, sometimes simply relishing their existence and letting it roll over her tongue like a sweet. This was why she knew with rock-solid certainty that her father was dead: she felt nothing. And she stored that knowledge deep within herself, in a place where she kept her secrets and those things she wished were not true.

Dunka possessed none of their father's fastidiousness. The room was well on its way to chaos, with a tumble of clothes in a dying chair, sneakers and underwear tossed about, and all the surfaces choking with clutter. Dunka did not deserve this room, but being male and the oldest, he had taken the idea of filling their father's shoes seriously—when it suited him. He was quite content to sit by and watch the rice, beans, and maize their parents had last harvested before the Grey dwindle away, foodstuff that would have been sold at the weekly market in Pishang. The maize was long exhausted, and what was left of the rice and beans was a pittance. What would they have done if she had never met Zumji? The fact that her brother now had the Grey did little to lessen the revulsion she felt toward him, and that was before he had committed the irrevocable act of trying to hit her. They'd had their fights before, but he had never attempted to strike her. Now he had become a lifeless thing to her, unworthy of any kind of emotion, as good as dead.

Panmun went from room to room, saying goodbye with her hands and with her eyes, to the walls, to the falling of light in the living room, to the forever stench of carbon in the kitchen.

She found Rit behind the house sweeping leaves shed by the avocado tree. Panmun would miss the harvest, and already the fruit held the promise of being larger than ever before, but she was glad to know that at least Rit and Panshak would have one more source of sustenance to carry their bodies beyond the reach of starvation, even if just for a short time. She and Rit had not been close before the Grey, but something had flowered between them in the intervening years. When their parents were freshly gone, it had amused Panmun how Dunka and Rit, one utterly negligent and the other incurably self-absorbed, had suddenly tried to put on garbs of responsibility now that there was no one left to rail against their deficiencies. It had been even worse with Dunka, because he only paid lip service to the idea of being responsible—he was gone most of the time. Panmun did not buy this newly acquired sense of duty. In her thinly veiled contempt, she withdrew from them into a world of her own. She had seen through the lens of her father's heart the disdain his son held for him—a man who was less forceful than Dunka wished he had been, a man who seemed incapable of bending reality to his will, as other men appeared to be doing so easily. Now here Dunka was, even more useless and helpless than their father had been, talking about responsibility while Rit tried with her pathetic little body to craft order out of a rapidly compounding chaos. It had made Panmun sick.

With time, as Rit became the de facto mother of the household, Panmun found a bond with her younger sister that surprised her. Rit, all fifteen years of her, fed, fretted, and cared for every one of them, managing to become the single force that held their family together. It was almost as though their dead mother's spirit had risen from her grave and entered Rit's body.

Panshak had been missing for days. And, despite his being dead to her, she could not help wondering where Dunka was. Had he gone off and hurt himself? Had the Grey become so heavy? This was how people vanished and never returned. It was how their father had gone. Panmun felt a sinking in her gut as it occurred to her that she had already seen her brothers for the last time.

Rit turned, saw Panmun, and straightened up, averting her eyes. She had avoided her since she found out about the Grey.

"How are you feeling?" Rit asked.

"I'm fine. I will be fine."

Rit took in Panmun's clothes, the sandals, the scarf. The sunglasses.

"Zumji and I are going to try and leave, Rit. I want you to come with us."

"What about Panshak? And Dunka?"

"When was the last time you saw Panshak? You kept telling him to stay at home, but he refused to listen. Where is he now?"

"They might be alive."

"What if they never come back?"

"You can go, but I'm staying."

"What are you going to do here all by yourself?"

"We're not children anymore. Do what you want to do. I'm staying. If Panshak comes back, I'm going to take care of him."

"You're *fifteen*."

Rit raised her head and leveled her gaze. It was the stare of a woman inside the body of a child, a woman who was waiting for her body to catch up. This woman had taken a stand for the closest thing to a child that she had: her little brother. And she would not budge. Panmun understood what this was. For the first time, the life growing inside her took on meaning. If it had not been there, she might have stayed, waited for her brothers—for Panshak, however long it took for him to come home. But she would not bring her child into a world ruled by the Grey.

36

"Whether they come back or not, I want you to go to Zumji's house; you know where it is. There's a boy there with his sister, his name is Tongzum. Tell him who you are. He will take care of you. I want you to promise you will go."

Rit simply nodded. Panmun knew it was all she would get out of her. Panmun closed the space between them and hugged her sister. When was the last time their bodies had touched like this?

"You know that whether you go or whether you stay, it's all the same. They will kill you out there."

Panmun shut her eyes against this. It had always been there, this suspicion that death was waiting on both ends but in different guises. Still, having a hunch was not the same as knowing.

Rit helped her carry her things but only made it past the door. Panmun knew she was holding back tears and would not cry in front of her. She told her to go back inside. Averting her face, Rit waved a wordless goodbye, went into the house, and closed the door.

Panmun made her way to the flame tree. Her watch said it was a few minutes past three. When she reached the top of the soft slope that led up to the tree, she turned to look at the house she had grown up in one last time. She had never really liked the way the house looked from outside, had never liked the fact that the whole world knew they could not afford to get a new roof, that the best they could do was use rocks and pray against another storm. None of that mattered now.

She walked up to the tree and caressed the large *X* in the smooth bark. She looked around. No one was in sight. After telling her—*three times!*—to wait by the tree, here she was and there was no sign of him. She sucked her teeth with so much passion it startled a twittering bird on a lower branch of the flame tree. Depositing her things on the ground, she sat down, propped herself against the tree, took off her glasses, and closed her eyes. She was trying to breathe, let air into her lungs, stem the rage that was like mighty waters in her ears.

She opened her eyes. Zumji was never late. His entire existence was as measured and reliable as a clock. He knew the rhythms of the sky, when it would get dark, when it would rain. How many times had he taken her back up to that ledge where they had first met? They would be somewhere—at his house, or among a growth of trees where he had laid a trap—and he would look at the sun and say they should go if they wanted to catch the sunset. They were never late, and they would watch the sky like two statues. They did it every day they were together, and on days when she was not with him, she knew he would be up there on that rock, watching the sun die. Sometimes, when she was beside him on the rock, she would watch him instead of the sunset, watch the way the golden light caressed his features and made his moist eyes glisten—how he seemed more than a man in those moments, a god weeping for his creation.

Zumji was never late. If he was not here by three, as promised, it was because something had happened to him.

She knew her Zumji. He was no jilter. Integrity began and ended with him. If ever there was a man who embodied the essence of purity, it had to be him. Which was why she would often question the reality of their relationship, of his love for her. She sometimes did strange, unexpected things when seized by a panicking doubt, like breaking the rhythm of their lovemaking to ask him how much he loved her, or adamantly refusing to give him his flint knife just to see how angry he would get, or accusing him of liking another girl even though Zumji was essentially a hermit and girls her age typically remained indoors nowadays. Stupid things. Cruel things. And his love for her never broke. Unless he had loved her patiently all these months, slowly and meticulously, with the intention of breaking her heart. There was only one way to find out.

As she stood, a strange despondency descended upon her, covering her like a dark, heavy sheet, but it left as quickly as it had come. She looked at her bags. They were what she cherished most. In the light of recent happenings, of recent disappointments, hurts, and losses, she realized that her cherishing of things had been diminishing, and she saw things for what they truly were. *Things.* Now they had no color. She was suddenly overcome by a furious urge to sever all bonds between herself and things. That included people. And she saw with painful clarity the path that was her life, trailing down the length of the day and ending abruptly where the day also ended, where love splintered into a thousand shards of heartbreak.

All that remained for her to do was to get to the bottom of why Zumji had failed to show up. Nothing really mattered beyond that.

4

DUNKA

Dunka emerged on the other side of the tunnel with dirt on the front of his clothes and his dignity in pieces on the ground. He felt like a rat squeezing through a hole half its size. A copse of baobab trees, their branches lush with growth, stood near the barricade. As he cautiously made his way through the trees, he spotted tended fields far ahead where the trees ended. They stretched away toward the first houses of Pishang, their crops blooming in the sun. The simple difference between this side of the barricade and the one he had just left brought him to tears. Before he had caught the Grey, he had always wondered what it was like to have it. The only thing he knew was that it killed you in the end. Nobody talked about what it felt like in the interim.

As the sickness settled inside him, he began to feel it. Like water collecting inside a bucket, drop after drop, at first it felt like nothing. Then he began to sag under its weight. One day, Panmun spat at him. She *spat* at him and walked away. Dunka sat down on the living room sofa and closed his eyes. He was not angry or hurt. He realized that he, in fact, felt nothing. When Rit brought him his meal that evening, there was no warm swell of gratitude and affection in his chest for his sister. Sometimes he felt things, like the occasional burst of heartache when he saw something that reminded him of all they had lost, like Rit standing with the wrapper over her chest trying to look like their mother. Most of the time, there was only a gaping emptiness, and he was getting used to it. Which was why his reaction to Panmun three days ago had surprised him—and why the tears he was now shedding confused him all the more.

Once he was beyond the trees, Dunka put on his sunglasses and looked for Goma Street. He was no stranger to Pishang. In the time before the Grey, he would accompany his parents to sell their grain at the market. Maize, finger millet, guzuk. They moved the sacks in the back of his father's old pickup truck. They would set up their makeshift stalls at the marketplace, and Dunka's mother would sell the grain. While this was going on, his father would use his pickup to ferry buyers' goods between several villages. The sky-blue contraption managed to surpass expectations every week and successfully make multiple round trips. Dunka and Panmun were meant to learn the trade from both parents, and for her part, Panmun stayed with their mother. But Dunka would disappear into Pishang to rendezvous with his friends at a small pond at the foot of a hill, where they swam and leaped off overhanging rocks into the water, shrieking with delight. A woman served a sour brew near the pool, along with peppered pork and goat meat, and they would drink and swim and dry their bodies on the rocks. The side of the hill facing the pond was a sheer cliff face of pure granite. There were special evenings when the sun would splash against the rock face, bathing it, and the water, and the grass, and the occasional grazing cattle in a sheet of pure gold. Each market day, Dunka would look out for it.

Presently, he crept down a footpath that would end in a fork, with one branch leading to the pond and the other to the computer center. Memories of the pond and his friends and the thrilling tang of the heady alcohol were now meaningless to him. Where were his friends now? The people he had known all his life had turned out to be masked strangers, hypocrites who would murder him to save their own necks without any hesitation. He passed them on the road now, the strangers, the hypocrites. A couple of elderly women carrying firewood. A throng of children in uniform, even though it was not yet school closing time. All hypocrites. No one paid him any attention as he went on, past the computer center. He soon turned onto Goma Street.

It was only when he got there that he realized the house number Nana Ritdirnen had given him was useless. None of the houses were numbered. He began to knock at random. The first gate was slammed in his face by a surly older man who told Dunka to take off his sunglasses if he was going to address him. There was no response at the second gate. All he had to go by was the name Nana Ritdirnen had spoken: Matyin. He had just knocked on the fifth gate when a powerful urge to end his life there and then came over him. He lurched forward and placed a hand on the fence to steady himself. He was submerged in a wave of liquid despondency, and his hearing became muffled. He could feel it on his skin, the viscous consistency of it, as though he were trying in vain to move his body through water at normal speed. He was not prepared for the intensity with which it assaulted his senses. After several seconds, his ears regained their clarity and his sight became steady. It had passed. For now.

He looked up and found a diminutive young man staring at him from the doorway. He had sleepy eyes that looked heavy. Despite his pewter vision, Dunka would have recognized those eyes in an explosion of faces. Polu's face had changed, grown leaner, the skin rougher, more pockmarked. He was an acquaintance from before the Grey. They had occasionally met at the drinking spot by the pool, but their interaction had been limited because Polu was older. Polu stared at Dunka languorously, waiting for an explanation.

"I want to see Matyin," Dunka said.

"Does she know you're coming?"

"Yes."

"You called her?" Polu said, blinking.

Dunka did not remember the last time he had seen or used a phone, but he said yes.

"Who are you?"

"Dunka."

Polu disappeared for several minutes. He came back accompanied by a young woman in tight jeans and a tight top. Her skin was dark in certain places, like her elbows and knuckles, and burnished in other places, like her face and her arms.

"You want to see Matyin?"

"Yes."

"What do you want?"

"Her aunt sent me with a message."

The girl looked at Polu, confused for a moment. "From where?"

"Pison."

"Wait here," the girl said and went back inside.

Dunka had known to say Pison because Nana Ritdirnen had told him Matyin was originally from there, a small village on the other side of the hills. He looked up at the sun. It was growing bolder, beating the strength out of him.

Polu reappeared and held the door open for him. Could it really have been that easy? He hesitated for a moment before proceeding into the compound. Under an awning large enough for two cars, Dunka saw only one. Neatly trimmed hedges bordered the house itself. The thin girl held open the front door, and Dunka stepped inside. She led him through a small foyer with marble tiles on the floor. Against one wall stood a mirror, and on another wall hung a life-size painting of a light-skinned woman dressed in a glittering, flowing gown and bedecked in gold. Dunka was surrounded by shiny door handles, shiny surfaces, shiny ornaments that ranged from miniature glass rabbits and ponies to other objects he had never even seen. They stepped into a large living room, where a woman sat waiting on the three-seater. She had extensions on her nails, extensions on her hair. A cloying, sickening perfume clung to her, smothering everything in range. She wore a light gown with long frills that trailed on the floor. She sat very still, watching Dunka with a forceful, penetrating gaze.

"Whose son are you?" Matyin asked.

"My name is Dunka. I need your help, please."

"Where did you say you came from?"

"I'm not from Pison. I'm from Pilam," Dunka said, taking off his sunglasses. "Nana Ritdirnen said you could help me. Your aunt, Nana Ritdirnen from Pilam."

The thin girl let out a small squeal. Matyin grew stiff, like she had just seen a walking corpse. She slowly rose to her feet.

"Nana Ritdirnen?" She was trying to appear normal, but her voice shook.

"She's dead."

Dunka had not had the chance to ask Nana Ritdirnen why she had never mentioned this woman in all the time the Grey had been with them. Perhaps she had saved her as a last resort. He always remembered her words: "Nothing to lose."

Matyin spoke slowly. "You should go back home before people find out you're here."

Dunka sank to his knees. "She said you would help me."

Matyin closed her eyes and said, "Go home, Dunka, before something bad happens." She walked out of the room.

Dunka remained on his knees for several seconds after she had left. He had been right. They were all hypocrites, everybody on this side of the fence. He felt a hand on his shoulder and turned to see Polu.

"Didn't you hear her? Let's go."

Dunka allowed himself to be steered out of the house. Polu shut the pedestrian entrance as soon as Dunka had passed through it. Dunka stood there with his eyes closed. Only then did he realize that his shoulders had been hunched defensively against the fatigue that was clinging to him, trying to pull him to the ground. He sat on one of the concrete blocks lying against the fence. He was so tired that if he closed his eyes, he would fall asleep. Perhaps it was all in order. That debilitating force that had nearly crippled him earlier was a stirring of the Grey. He knew it would increase in both frequency and intensity until the day he could bear it no longer and decided to end it. Maybe this was as good a place as any to end it. He could simply lie here, fall asleep, and let them find him.

Dunka failed to notice the girl at first. She came up the street and passed right in front of him, stopping at the gate. The sound of her knocking made him look up. She was dressed in a school uniform: a white shirt and a skirt that, to Dunka, looked dark gray. She had to be twenty at the oldest, maybe younger. She had dark skin and short-cropped hair. As she stood there waiting, she clutched a few books to her chest. Dunka did not notice that she was beautiful in the way that could make a man's heart forget an entire beat. He did not notice the way her large eyes adorned her face, nor the shape of her lips, nor the way the early afternoon light sculpted the side of her face, accentuating her tapered chin. He did not notice any of it because of the Grey. All he noticed was the terror of recognition in her eyes when she looked at him. He knew she was seeing the Grey in his eyes. The gate was opened, and the girl dragged her gaze away from Dunka and hurried inside.

Dunka forgot about her in an instant. A fresh resolve closed around his heart like a vise. He was not going back to Pilam without an answer to their predicament. He thought he had secretly come here to die under the pretext of finding help, just so he could get one over on Panmun. Now he knew he would not go back and let Rit, Panshak, or even Panmun grow up just so that they could die. And he would not go back just so that he could perish without leaving them with some concrete hope.

He moved his hand and touched the knife attached to his hip. His next thought seemed to be naturally linked to the thought of the knife, as though the two had been born at the same instant. So was the next thought, and the next. By the time they had finished springing into being and arranging themselves into a line of action that was as intricately linked as a chain, the inevitability of the path before him was blinding. His grandfather had given him that hunting knife for this moment.

Calmly, Dunka let his staff fall to the ground and stood. He knocked on the gate. The knife was already in his hand. It had a strip of black cotton wound round the handle so that its grip was soft and full. When the door swung open, he charged through it, seized Polu by his shirt, and raised the weapon to his face. Polu was quaking from head to toe. Without a word, he led Dunka to the front door and knocked with urgency. He knocked again when no one came.

The girl in the school uniform opened the door. She saw the knife at Polu's throat and backed away into the house, too petrified to scream.

"Go and call Aunty," Polu said, trying to keep his voice level.

As they waited inside the foyer, Dunka stole quick glances around the room. There was probably no way out of this for him. Matyin rushed in and gasped.

"Please, please," she said, "I don't have any money."

"I don't want to hurt anybody. I just want something that will protect my family from this," Dunka said, widening his eyes to indicate the Grey.

Matyin opened her mouth to say something, but Polu spoke first. "Aunty, please, just give him what he wants. Please."

Matyin took a deep breath and hurried out of the room. All the ways the situation could go wrong flashed across Dunka's mind. He had not thought this through. Matyin could give him a handful of ashes, and he would have to take her word for it. He had no way of testing whatever she was going to bring him. He had taken it for granted that she would know what to do. And how many other people were in the house at that moment, hidden behind these walls, making calls to the police or the vigilantes? He was alone and exposed. This whole time, despite the direness of his situation, his breathing had stayed the same.

He was as relaxed as he had been that morning while looking for what to wear. Death was twirling around him, and all he felt was a steady, unbroken calm.

The girl in the school uniform returned with something in her hands. It was concealed inside a black plastic bag, but the shape of a bottle was evident. Keeping her distance, she offered the bottle, and Dunka told Polu to collect it. As Dunka slackened his grip on Polu's shirt and reached to take the bag from him, Polu suddenly found his spine. He hurled his body into Dunka, and the two of them crashed into the wall. The knife left Dunka's grip. They wrestled, at first against the wall, then on the shiny floor, like two slippery rodents, twisting and spitting and slithering. Finally, Dunka freed a hand long enough to gather a punch and deliver it to the side of Polu's head, which snapped back into one of the marble tiles with a loud thump. Polu went still.

The girl had picked up the bottle of cure, and she stood there, holding it in two hands. Dunka rose, breathless, while a sudden quiet swaddled them. An entire world began to flower between them as they stared at each other, and if Dunka had not been smothered by the Grey, he might have sensed a fluttering in his stomach. Without a word, the girl tossed the bottle at him and he caught it.

"What's your name?" he asked.

"Arrit."

Slipping the name into his pocket like a souvenir, Dunka nodded his thanks and fled through the open door. The quiet followed him out into the compound, where the world seemed to be holding its breath. He slipped the sunglasses back on. As he moved toward the gate, a car pulled up outside and the driver began to honk impatiently. That was when the Grey kicked him again. He keeled over, and the bottle fell to the ground. His skin felt like a heavy suit that he *needed* to shrug off. And deep inside, he was overwhelmed by the sensation that if he did not kill himself right now, in this instant, he would die from utter misery, which seemed much more unbearable. When it started to lift and the edges of the world began to regain their shape, he tried to stand up.

A crude, heavy object crashed into the back of his head, and he thought to himself that death had finally taken his hand. He had never known how to dance, but this, this was not so bad after all. Growing up, he had hated parties because of the dancing, which also felt like dying. And dying was hard. How wrong he had been. Dying was easy, and so was dancing. The two were the very same thing. He should have danced more.

5

Zumji

There was renewed urgency in Zumji's steps as he walked from Mister's house to where he had stashed the blue jerrican. Back at the rickshaw, he filled the tank, feeding the fuel through a funnel he had made from a plastic bottle sawed in half. He stowed the remaining fuel in the back, along with his sacks, and circled the vehicle once, inspecting it. On the day they had agreed to escape, he had taught himself how to drive it, with Panmun in the back seat squealing in delight each time the rickshaw lurched dangerously off one wheel.

Satisfied with the state of the vehicle, he circumvented Pilam on foot to the other side, where the houses petered out from the center, toward the softer wilderness of wildflowers and rocks and baobab trees, to the flame tree he had carelessly scarred with a cross, an X, to mark it as theirs. Panmun had told him how its red flowers covered the ground in a carpet of scarlet during the rainy season. He looked at her house, roof pinned with rocks and peering out from the gentle dip beyond the gentle rise. He absently fingered their cross in the smooth bark of the tree. They would sometimes lie in the shade of its green leaves and stare at the long pods, wondering how soon it would flower so that they could lie among the petals instead. They had been waiting for it.

Now they were going to miss it. They would have to find some other flame tree out there. She said she would love to sweep up the flowers and scatter them in her room, on her bed, where she could fall asleep to the scent of mint and cloves, and he would say something about the flowers smelling not of mint but nectar, and she would ask him how he knew that, and he would say he had discovered it on his trapping runs, and she would say that all flowers had nectar, so flowers couldn't smell of just nectar because they would all smell the same, and they both knew that flowers never smelled the same. On and on, back and forth, until they agreed that they did not know what the flowers smelled like, but they smelled nice all the same. And they would kiss until they ran out of breath.

Zumji removed his hand from the cross and began to walk toward the house, and then he saw her, a pretty dreadlocked girl of eighteen, slowly rising into view, wearing sunglasses. She was lugging a pink suitcase and a backpack the color of moss. At the sight of her, the fact that he had not seen her in a couple of days gripped his chest so tight he nearly gasped: he had missed her. Turning to take one last look at her home, she missed him by the tree. He hid behind a clump of bushes. He liked to watch her exist in the world, the way she swam through the space around her, the way she *was*. She went up to the tree and touched the very spot he had been caressing barely a minute before, looking around, seeing no one. She released an angry hiss and dropped her backpack and other things to the ground, then also dropped herself to the ground.

With the trunk of the red tree behind her, she took off her glasses and raised her face to the sky, eyes closed. He was close enough to see the dark spot of the birthmark on her chin. Even if she looked in his direction, she would never know he was there—his clothes blended him into the greens and browns of the bushes. He watched her breathe in and out. Red-hot anger was pulsing through her brain at that moment, Zumji was sure of it: he had seen it many times before. This, this closing of the eyes, was a method she had devised to contain her temper, to keep herself from those sudden outbursts in which she burned and attempted to burn everything and everyone else along with her. He had held her close to him at such times, bare skin to bare skin, ember to ice, calming her. He was about to reveal himself, hold her again, laugh a little at her, the way that only she had ever made him laugh. He was about to do this when she opened her eyes, and there was the Grey staring out of them. One eye was already all black, like something had scraped her insides out and she was now empty and hollow. He wondered for a moment if perhaps the distance between them was preventing him from seeing properly. But it was not much of a distance to begin with, and one glance at her face across it was enough to know that something was very wrong.

Time carried on as though nothing were amiss. The birds kept singing from the trees around. From high above them in the clouds came the thick drone of an aircraft, leaving a brilliant white trail in its wake. The unrelenting azure of the sky was so beautiful it was an affront to the moment. Nobody noticed. His Panmun was now carrying the sickness. His heart was splintering, his world unraveling—and nobody noticed.

Zumji wanted to leave. He could not wait for the sinkhole to finish opening inside him while he was still watching her. He had to get away from there, but he could not move, because she would see him. And he could not take seeing her like that. The way she was against that tree, dead before she had died—he could not bear it, the desecration, the extinguishing of an entire world, a world that had come to be his. Now it was his turn to close his eyes. How could she be sick with the Grey when the last time he saw her, just three days ago, her eyes had looked like two sparkling pebbles picked fresh from a river? Something about her there, pinned against the tree, reminded him of the man buried among the mango trees and the ways in which a careless act could circle the world and knock you cold from behind. There had to be a link somehow between the Grey in Panmun's eyes and the ghost following him like a second shadow. One had to have led to the other, even if he could not understand it. Panmun was sick with the Grey, and Zumji was to blame. He should have brought life and joy to her, but he had succeeded only in bringing death. He did not deserve her. She would be better off without him. The only thing left for him to do was what he should have done in the first place. He would do this before discarding himself into what was left of the future that the Grey had succeeded in snatching from him.

Panmun picked up one of the seedpods and rattled it idly. She tossed it aside, stood, and stomped away. He knew she was going to look for him, but she was walking away from him forever without understanding what she was doing.

When she was gone, he returned to the rickshaw and got a shovel and a pickax, the same tools he had used just days prior to commit the evil that now haunted him. He also got an old once-white sheet that had become permanently brown with age. Twenty minutes later, he found the grave right where he had left it. As if it could have moved. Its soft, fresh earth set it apart from the rest of the soil. Zumji touched the ground there, as though feeling for a heartbeat. The dank, dark loam caked between his fingers, and he raised it to his nose and inhaled. The small stream was not twenty yards away, gurgling gently over small rocks and pebbles, a result of the last rain that had fallen weeks ago. He had caught one or two creatures among these trees. A rabbit, a porcupine. Water was a meeting place between man and animal, predator and prey, life and death. This was why he laid his traps beside the water, barely concealed in earth, and watched from a perch in a nearby tree, trigger at the ready. Sometimes, he could wait for hours before the unsuspecting creature came along to lower its snout to the peaceful brook and drink, and his heart would threaten to snap in two at such beauty, which seemed too sacred to be touched by human hands. Still, he would pull the string and set off the trap. Man's ultimate recourse was to survive in spite of beauty—and also because of it.

Marking the perimeter around the grave, Zumji began to dig. If he did not make amends now, he knew the ghost would haunt him until the day he died. He swung as though each stroke were an utterance of penitence, apologizing to the man he had buried alive. It was all an apology—this brushing of the dirt from the dead man's face, this raising him out of the ground, this disregard for the stench clawing at his nose. As Zumji carried the body to the stream and laid it on the bank, as he knifed the clothes off the dead man until he was bare and the wound in his belly was without obstruction, as it dropped into Zumji's mind that the wound had been made by an object with a sharp, thick point, he was thinking of her, wherever she was, looking for him. What would it require of him to go back and perform the small mercy of telling her he could not live to watch her die, giving her the chance to rant and rail him into the ground until she drew blood? What would it take for him to break her heart to her face?

Zumji took off his brown shirt, dipped it in the stream, and squeezed out the excess water. As he brought the wet cloth to the man's small, hairless chest, he looked at his face properly. Who had he been? How far had he come? People were running *away* from the Grey, so why had he come here? What was he fleeing from or, perhaps, running to? Who was he in the middle of becoming before he had stopped being altogether? The rickshaw yielded no trace of information regarding the man's identity. His pockets contained nothing but the same dirt that now filled his mouth and nostrils. Zumji wiped and washed and squeezed and wiped until the man's skin appeared smooth, clean. He was a fair man, his complexion deepened by the sun. He might have been a mechanic, for his fingernails carried the eternal grime that came with fixing machinery. Faint furrows ran like farm ridges along his scalp, his balding pattern exposed by tiny hairs. Dead people were supposed to be still and silent. Seeing the stillness up close, touching the silence with his hands, caused a knowing and a trembling to pass through Zumji's body like a current. How his father would prepare, wearing his best clothes, often a long dark red caftan with the hat that was a size too small, before going out to perform the task of washing the dead in honor of many a friend. How he came home slumped, presumably, by the weight of knowing death too closely, too intimately, without dying himself.

Zumji returned to the small pile of things he had left beside the grave, picked out the sheet he had brought. As he straightened to return to the body, he heard bare feet quietly slapping water and turned to find the man in the middle of the stream, just as Zumji had seen him framed in the doorway of Mister's storehouse. He looked over his shoulder at Zumji, then turned and walked on, down the aisle formed by the great tree trunks. Soon he vanished behind a bush of tall, dry elephant grass where the trees ended.

Zumji wrapped the body and used a piece of rope to secure the sheet under the corpse's feet. He returned the body to the grave. By the time he was done filling the grave with earth, the patch of ground looked no different than it had before he had exhumed the body.

6

PANSHAK

It was a new day, but he felt no different. He had not slept, and he was still upset about the camera. In a way, the camera had become his only friend. And now Goshi had taken it. Panshak lay still on his back, listening to the voices that drifted in through the dormitory windows. His heart had clamped around a righteous anger, and he wanted to go home.

Home. He had refused to go back at first because of the letter, the letter that had led him to the camera. It was after he had attacked Rit and hated himself for it; she probably hated him too. He had carried the letter around with him for a few weeks, reading it multiple times, remembering the man who had written it. He also remembered the silence when he knocked on the recipient's front door and the haunting, gnawing suspicion that the recipient was inside the quiet house, dead. The letter was addressed to a Nenpan, who could have been a man or a woman. When Panshak went to return the letter, the man who had written it was swaying from the tree in front of his house. Panshak had simply looked up, acknowledged the dead body hanging from a branch, and gone away.

After the incident with Rit, he had left the house in a rush, afraid that he might hurt his sister irrevocably, crushed by the possibility that he had done so already. He walked the empty streets for a while. Electrical poles and cables stretched away into hopelessness. He remembered the day the lights went out. He had been watching a cartoon in Nana Ritdirnen's house, since his parents had never bothered to get them a TV. The screen went blank, and the house was suddenly quiet. Somebody threw the usual casual curse at the anonymous person responsible. It was a routine power failure, but unlike all the others before it, it was never reversed. Next thing, the Grey was in Pilam, laying waste.

As he walked, thinking about what he had just done to his sister, Panshak saw a figure in the distance, but it vanished between two buildings before he could make it out. Where had the sand come from? It was in everything, in the culverts, in the soulless windows; it had gotten into his own skin. A faded piece of paper on one of the wooden electrical poles advertised a nameless candidate for governor, bringing to his mind a world with dimensions and order—and the soldiers who had barricaded them in this prison. There was a pothole in the middle of the road with a clump of grass growing inside it, breaching the gaping, tarred lips of the hole and reaching toward the sky. Tires and yellow and black jerricans adorned the streets. Market stalls with wooden walls and stilts and zinc roofs stood empty like eye sockets. The trees, undisturbed by humanity, flourished and shed their leaves with abandon: thickly foliaged mango trees, lime-leafed avocado trees, thick-stemmed baobab trees, all burdened by the same weight, the same perfect sadness. A little girl of about four emerged from a cluster of buildings and then scurried away.

Panshak's legs had carried him to the place the letter had described in gentle, beseeching words. He had read it so many times the words were on a loop in his head:

. . . where the road is rocky. It's the road adjacent to the uncompleted house that Mister started building many years ago. The land is at the end of that road. I don't know where the documents for it are, but I left something for you there inside a mango tree, if you change your mind about taking things from me. When you climb to the first branch, there is a hidden hole covered with some painted wood. If you ever change your mind, it will be there waiting for you.

Panshak climbed the branch and found a silver-colored digital camera in the heart of the tree. It was hidden behind a sheet of dead wood painted to look like part of the tree's bark from afar. The alkaline batteries in it were still in good condition. Panshak instinctively pushed the little button at the top, and it came on with a tiny birdsong squeal. He pressed the "Play" button on the back of the camera, and a picture taken in the gracious glare of morning light appeared. The face of the man who had given him the letter, more wizened than hopeful, but with the eyes of a newborn, eyes so soft and bright that for a moment Panshak failed to notice the Grey in them. A thin, elderly man, smiling. He had pointed the camera at his face and chopped off the lower half of it, clumsily including the background in the process: a yard that contained a small brown car with faded paint and deflated tires. Also visible was a little patch of vegetables, onions and cabbages by the look of it, all dead in the ground. A slash of sunlight fell across the man's face. The next picture had more of the man's face and less of the background. The light in his eyes had not dimmed. There were no other pictures. It was hard to reconcile these images with the man whose body Panshak had found in the tree, the same man who had asked him in halting speech to deliver the letter before saying he had no form of payment to offer. But it *was* the same man. The Grey had settled so deeply in his face that it was practically expressionless. As for the body in the tree, it was just that—another dead body.

When Panshak was younger, he had known death from only a distance. It had looked so terrifying back then, so distressing—a shapeless black mass that seemed like the end of all things. When it finally came close, taking his father and mother within a matter of weeks, he realized that death was just a small thing after all, with dimensions that were in not the scale of an abyss but that of a human being. It was possible to put your arms around death, stare it in the face, and still live.

How had things gone so wrong? When he first arrived at the orphanage—"This is my house. Not an orphanage, my house," Nana Kanke had corrected him—there had been no indication that anything was out of the ordinary. The first thing that seized his attention was the great neem tree that towered above, standing in the center of a little roundabout made with red bricks, its branches extending very close to the building. After that, Nana Kanke took over; she was a tall, sharp woman with rich gray hair tied in a bun—but her gray hair did not mean her eyes could not see across the room and through walls. It did not mean that she could not move as quickly as any of the children who were under her charge. She had been spared by the Grey, and she had the entire place in a firm grip.

Or so it had seemed.

There had been nearly fifty children when Panshak arrived. He went into Nana Kanke's office and was ordered to sit down. She got right into it.

"If you're going to stay in this house, then you will live by my rules. The first rule is that you're either here or you're out there." She pointed at "out there." "Do you understand?"

Panshak nodded. A large brass bell sat on Nana Kanke's desk. It looked like the one the timekeeper in Panshak's old school rang to signal break time or closing time. Before the Grey.

"What did I say?"

"I'm either here or there."

"No, that's not what I said. That means something entirely different. I said you either choose to stay in this house, or you go out—and *stay* out. If you leave this compound for any reason without my permission, I won't let you come back in. Do you understand?"

Panshak nodded again. He could not take his eyes off the bell. It was so large and looked so old, with the image of a large house engraved into the brass. Panshak wanted to ring it.

"You say, 'Yes, Nana.'"

"Yes, Nana."

Nana Kanke followed Panshak's eyes. "That's real brass. My husband brought it back from one of his travels. How old are you?"

"Thirteen."

"Do you have any family?"

He had two dead parents, a brother who had the Grey and never spoke to him, a sister who was more like a ghost gliding through the house, and another sister who carried their home on her small shoulders.

"This place is for children who have nowhere else to go. If you have family members that can take care of you, you shouldn't be taking up the space of another child with genuine need."

"No."

"Are you saying you don't have a family?"

"No, ma'am. I mean, yes."

Nana Kanke looked at him with her piercing eyes. The Grey had become so entrenched in their existence that it was a bit disquieting to see an adult without it.

"Of course, I will have to take your word for it. I know that at least half of you are lying to me when you say you don't have any family left. But since I am a staff of one, I have no way of verifying, and I can't turn you away based on a mere suspicion, can I?"

Panshak sat still, unsure whether it was a question he was supposed to answer. When he was in the same room with her, he felt a constant anxiety that he would say something wrong. This feeling would never let up, even after he had spent a bit more time in her house, so forceful were her conviction and courage.

He learned the first night that, like all rules, Nana Kanke's were not unbreakable. Four boys climbed out the dormitory window, crossed the dark compound, and jumped over the fence. One was going to check on his father, who had the Grey and had become so sick he could barely take care of himself, let alone another person. One was going to see his girlfriend, who could also get away from home only at night. The other two went simply because there was a rule to be broken.

Nana Kanke made some of them responsible for growing vegetables on a portion of the land—things like sweet potatoes, cabbages, and onions. They took turns doing house chores. Both boys and girls cooked, cleaned, and maintained the property. All the food produced on the land was kept in the large pantry attached to the kitchen, and Nana Kanke had the key.

She arranged them by age into classes and assigned different rooms for each class. Where the books would not go around, they shared. They carried out their studies independently.

Each weekday morning, they would have an assembly in the large living area downstairs, and Nana Kanke would speak to them on a range of issues.

"Some of you have been with me for nearly two years, as long as the Grey has been with us," she might say. "Some of you only a few days." She would sweep the room of boys and girls with her gaze and let her eyes settle on someone like Panshak. "The reason this place is a haven from the evil out there"—and she would point at "out there"—"the only reason this place runs as smoothly and efficiently as it does is because each of you plays his or her part, each of you takes responsibility, each of you respects order."

Pacing the room as she spoke, she would say, "I don't know why I don't have the Grey. I don't know how long before I get it. You are all growing up so fast"—a small, rare gleam of pride would cover her face, which would then be doused by something darker—"but we mustn't deceive ourselves. Some of you will catch the sickness before long, and it is of the utmost importance that we do not lose our heads. I strongly believe the exercises I have devised can help us in our vigil against it, whether sick or not. As I keep telling you, the Grey isn't a disease of the body, but of the spirit. We must keep our spirits alive."

She called the exercises "sensory drills," and for the most part, the children could make neither heads nor tails of them, enduring them merely because it was either that or get kicked out of the house. Nana Kanke said that there was a strong connection between the spirit of a person and the tangible world around them. She said what happened around you affected how you felt inside. Each of your five senses, she explained, was a window to the world. And if the world was rife, brimming, bursting with beauty, then such beauty could be experienced only through your senses. Beauty was not a matter of the eyes alone—every good thing was beauty.

None of it made sense, of course. They would all sit there, bored to within an inch of their lives, while the sun dragged itself across the sky. They sat and waited for the practical exercises that were sure to follow, determined to endure to the very end.

An exercise would go something like this:

Goshi brings in a tray bearing thin slices of avocado.

"One slice each, please," Nana Kanke instructs.

When everyone is settled, an avocado slice suspended patiently between forefinger and thumb, Nana Kanke says, "To appreciate the true, inherent beauty of an avocado, we must experience it without any embellishment. In this case, without salt. Now close your eyes and put the avocado in your mouth. Chew slowly—I said slowly."

It was the first "seeing drill," though, that made Panshak feel like he was beginning to make sense of it all. It was like he had been looking at the world through a veil this whole time.

"I want you to imagine that the sky is a tree and the stars are its fruits."

A moment of silence. Panshak's mind sat there heavily in the silence, too lazy to move or imagine.

"I want you to reach out and pluck a star. Just one star."

Another silence. Panshak opened his eyes a fraction and stole a glance. In the open night, the children were reaching up toward the moonlit sky and closing their fingers around thin air. Stars were visible high above, far beyond the fingers of the great neem tree that extended from its branches. He shut his eyes again.

"Is everyone holding a star?"

The murmuring that followed was confused and uncertain. Nana Kanke asked again, more firmly. An unconvincing *yes* rose and fell across the cool grass.

"I want you to bite it."

After stealing another glance to make sure nobody was looking at him, he brought his empty hand to his lips and took a bite out of the thin air. He chewed the piece of air slowly.

"What does it taste like?" Nana Kanke asked.

"Pear."

"Guava."

"Mango."

"Orange."

It did not taste like anything at all to Panshak.

"Hang the fruit back on the tree and open your eyes."

Panshak opened his eyes. The sky nearly fell into his head as his mind teetered on its hinges. It seemed to him that the firmament had become magnified, and it was now covered in a special coating that made him headily aware that he was looking at more than just sky. He looked around. The air throbbed as though it were alive. The neem tree looked like it might stoop low at any second and speak to him. The boys and girls around him stirred on the dusty, dead grass, imbued with a fresh energy that had not been there before. In the last few seconds, they seemed to have acquired an invisible aura, a higher form of being that made them hallowed. The grass, the trees, the rocks, the two dead cars parked in the driveway, the world itself—everything had suddenly come alive. If only he could freeze an image of *everything* and carry it around with him forever. After that, he began to take the camera with him everywhere he went.

For the most part, living under Nana Kanke's rule was an idyllic experience. Panshak began to follow some of the boys over the fence. They would wait until afternoon, during their napping hour, when Nana Kanke also napped. Those were the times he visited home, to see how his sisters were doing, to sustain the impression that he was still a Runner (he suspected they would feel betrayed if they learned he was staying at Nana Kanke's), and to bring a little food stolen from the pantry. He would have gladly continued in this poached happiness if Goshi had not gotten into trouble in the first place.

Panshak met Goshi before the end of his first day in Nana Kanke's house. Older than all the boys, he seemed unmatched to his world. He looked very awkward, with large features on a skinny body. Looking at him, Panshak could not decide whether he was looking at a boy or a man. It was difficult to guess his age. But what Panshak found most disorienting was that he had the Grey in his eyes. His appeared as specks of black, making his eyes look like two mottled pools in his head, but he seemed fine otherwise. Nobody could explain Goshi's presence in Nana Kanke's house, or in her life. It was generally presumed among the children that he had been living with her even before her husband, a wealthy farmer, had died from the Grey.

Naturally, theories abounded as to the exact nature of the relationship between Nana Kanke and Goshi. Someone said he was her nephew who had come under her care when he was little. Another said he was her secret son. Someone else said he was her grandson. Whatever the case, Goshi was the closest thing to a staff that Nana Kanke had, and she relied on him to help her keep the children under control. Panshak learned on that first day that Goshi's strange appearance belied a subtle intelligence that drew respect, and a bit of fear. He had a way with Nana Kanke that no one else managed. He could banter with her, and he knew her soft buttons, so that she would simply smile and shake her head with a vexed fondness.

Most of the other boys also feared Goshi. He made them do his own chores and threatened to report them to Nana Kanke if they refused. Afraid that they might be kicked out, they always gave in. He knew where the spare key to the pantry was kept, and he would sometimes reward those he favored for their compliance, which always became loyalty in the end. This was how Panshak was able to get extra grain to take back home from time to time. Only those who were in favor with Goshi could scale the wall and go on their escapades, because he would turn a blind eye. In this and so many other ways, Goshi wielded his influence and helped Nana Kanke run the house.

Goshi was in love with Yitmwa, a pretty sixteen-year-old girl who had come to the house not long before Panshak's arrival. This was apparent to anyone who cared to notice. He stopped her in the hallways and tried to speak to her. Sometimes he would send one of the younger boys to give her a garden egg or a sweet potato wrapped discreetly in a black plastic bag. Yitmwa never gave in to his advances, so the gifts were always returned untouched. The boys joked about this when Goshi was not in the room. The fact that he could not have the girl he wanted diminished his power in their eyes, but only in secret. Nobody dared to openly mock him. He remained, after all, Nana Kanke's lieutenant.

This was why it stunned the entire house when Nana Kanke threw Goshi out. The children had gathered out front, under the great neem tree. She carried his suitcase to the white gate herself, unlocked the gate, and hurled the suitcase out. She dragged Goshi out with her two hands, surprising them all with her strength. He begged as she locked the gate and walked away. The whisper was that he had tried to rape one of the girls, though no one could say who at first. As Nana Kanke passed the watching children to enter the house, Panshak saw that she was crying.

By evening, everybody knew that Goshi had forced himself on Yitmwa. Her screams had drawn Nana Kanke to the pantry, where he had her pinned to the floor, her clothes ripped. Yitmwa spent less time among the rest of the children after that day, eating her meals in Nana Kanke's office.

Two days later, everything changed forever.

"Wake up! Wake up!"

It was barely first light when the voice reached Panshak in the dorm, where he had been asleep with the other boys. Slowly, they sat up one by one and rubbed the sleep from their eyes. The voice drew nearer, growing louder. Fingers of yellow light from a lantern crept down the hallway and into the room. Then Goshi followed.

The boys were too startled and too sleepy to say anything. Goshi flashed a smile at them.

"Come and see," he said, before turning away from the room.

The boys scrambled after him.

Panshak followed at a distance, his camera clutched tightly in one fist. Curious as he was, he also did not want to get too close. Whatever they were about to see could not be good.

By the time Panshak arrived at Nana Kanke's bedroom, there was barely any space left to stand. He had to strain to see over the heads of the other children. Nana Kanke was spread-eagled on her bed, her four limbs tied to the four corners. The sight of her subdued and helpless seemed to Panshak completely against her nature—it was like seeing an elephant treated like a goat, or carrying boiling-hot water inside a glass bowl. Nana Kanke had always seemed too dignified to be treated like this. She did not look disturbed by the fact that she had been strapped down like a bull, or by the presence of the children. She watched Goshi with a cool expression, as though interested in what he would do next.

Goshi paced the crowded room, trying to contain his energy. He twirled a stick with a large, rounded end that was as long as his arm.

"It's time for a change," he began, like one of the politicians Panshak remembered watching on TV before the Grey came. "Do you like doing chores all the time?"

The response was weak, barely two or three voices. Goshi kept going all the same, agitated and locked in the orbit of his own madness. A lump had formed in Panshak's throat.

"Do you like living under stupid rules?"

"No."

"Do you like staying in this stupid house all the time?"

"No!"

The lump grew bigger as more children joined the chorusing.

"Do you like doing stupid sensory drills?"

"No!"

With each question, Goshi seemed to draw closer and closer to the heart of the matter for the children, eliciting a stronger response each time. Panshak kept his eyes on Nana Kanke's face. When he walked into her office that first day, she had been waiting, waiting for the next random child to enter her life; she had watched him cross the room toward her desk, making him conscious of the placement of his feet and the way his arms swung at his sides. She had that same watchful expression now as she scanned the scene. At the end of the interview, after she had interrogated and harangued him, her watchful expression had given way to a smile that washed away his anxiety and left in its place a perfectly balanced sense of gratitude. There and then, he had wanted to shore up all the loyalty he could muster from his being and place it at her feet in deference.

Now the lump in his throat had stolen his tongue. He felt culpable for the betrayal that was unfurling before his eyes.

"Do you want to be free to do what you want, to eat what you want?"

"Yes!"

Lowering his voice, Goshi turned to Nana Kanke.

"You have heard, Nana. The majority has spoken, the children want their freedom. I'm going to ask you a simple question. Just once." Goshi raised a single finger. "It is left for you to decide what happens next."

Nana Kanke was smiling at Goshi, a knowing, mocking, patient smile.

"Are you going to let the children have their freedom?"

"This is my house, not a voting chamber. If you don't like my rules, you can all get out."

"I hereby sentence you to death, Nana," Goshi said.

He raised the stick and brought the rounded end down. He had to do it only once to kill her. It happened so fast that nobody said anything. Panshak's mouth fell open. Some of the girls began to cry.

"Ritji, Tongzum, Podar, take her outside and bury her in the garden."

As the three boys obeyed, Panshak stared at the blood on the soft blue sheets. It looked like little red roses blossoming against a pale sky.

Things changed only a little at first after Nana Kanke's death. The classes and the sensory drills stopped, but the chores continued. Goshi told them all to stay in the house so they could be together, like a big happy family. The more they were in number, the better they could take care of each other. He would be the father; Yitmwa would be the mother. Nobody challenged him.

The next day, a few of the children left and did not return. When Goshi discovered that Yitmwa had been among them, he went into a bloody rage and smashed his stick into Ritji's arm. The crunch of bone filled the dormitory.

"Where were you when it was happening?" he shouted.

He warned that if anyone ran away again, he would track the person down and kill him and anyone he loved. Most of them believed that he would do it.

He took over Nana Kanke's room. He ransacked her things and those of her husband, emerging with a few clothes, which he shared among the boys. He also found an impressive hunting rifle, which had no bullets, and a black top hat, which he began to wear at all times. It became like his crown. One day, he used a bell to gather everybody in the front yard. When Panshak arrived, he recognized it as the bell that had been in Nana Kanke's office. Goshi raised the bell and explained that he would use it from now on to summon them, and he was the only one allowed to ring it.

"When you hear it, stop everything and come here." Changing topics, he asked, "Why do you think the sickness doesn't affect children?"

Nobody said anything.

"Because children are the future. Children are supposed to run things."

"If you're a child, why do you have it?"

It was a girl who spoke. She was one of the oldest girls, about sixteen or seventeen, and had also been with Nana Kanke for a long time. Her face was set hard against Goshi's madness. Goshi clubbed her with the butt of his rifle until her face was bloody. Some of the other girls took her inside the house.

"We are supposed to run things," he shouted at the top of his voice. "We can take over this place. We can even go outside Pilam, when we're stronger and older."

Panshak knew everyone was thinking it: How long would that take? Wouldn't they all be adults by then, which would mean it was too late? But nobody dared say it.

Panshak secretly missed the seeing drills. He had already started taking pictures of things, wishing to see them the way he had seen the sky and the grass that first night. He took a picture of the common room on the ground floor, noting the dour manner in which the large space and the furniture and bookshelves and reading chairs and toys sat. He took a picture of the dormitory, capturing a blast of sunlight that came through the window and hit the rows of beds at an angle. He took pictures of plants, insects, clouds (those did not go so well), some of the children. Sometimes, he felt like he was on the verge of glimpsing something more, something magical, but the moment would slip away, and he would leave disappointed, having seen only a dead insect or a blade of grass.

Nana Kanke's grave was a rectangular patch of disturbed earth on the lawn. Panshak scoured the grounds until he found a flat concrete slab that was large enough to serve as a headstone. He spent some time trying to chisel her name into the slab—just as he had done with the rock Dunka had placed on their mother's grave—but he made little progress because he did not have the right tools. He gave up and erected the headstone without a name. It would have to do. He was trying to find the right angle from which to take a picture of the grave, with its new headstone, when Goshi arrived, catching him unawares.

"Where did you get that?" Goshi said. He was seeing the camera for the first time.

"My father gave it to me." Panshak was lying on his stomach in the grass. He turned the camera off and slipped it into his pocket as he stood up.

Goshi looked at the grave. "It was harder than I thought it would be."

Panshak scrunched his brow in confusion, but he said nothing.

"The way things should be. She refused to see it." Goshi's mottled stare was unsettling. There was no telling what might provoke him. It was like facing a wild animal. "She treated me like a child, like I was crazy. Do I look like I'm crazy?"

"No."

"I didn't like it at first when she was letting people in. But after, I realized it was a good thing. It was like she was building an army of children, but she didn't see it. I told her, 'They are very powerful, Nana, you have to respect them.' But she wouldn't listen. Now look at her."

Panshak looked at the grave again.

"People think we don't know anything. But did you know that in the Bible, there was a king who was just a small boy? And he ended up being one of the best kings they ever had."

Goshi stood next to the headstone, placed one hand on it, the other on his hip.

"Take a picture of me," he said.

Without meaning to, Panshak became Goshi's personal photographer. There was not much else to do anyway. Over the next few weeks, they continued to have conversations, one-sided discussions in which Goshi seemed to be speaking as much to himself as to Panshak: "We are the first children to not be raised by any adults. We can do anything we want."

Panshak liked that there was enough to eat, that Goshi did not hoard the food: "You can eat anything you want, any time. Food is not a problem."

Soon the chores ended, and the days came and went in idleness: "Everybody can decide what to do with their time. Except when I ring the bell. Then you must come."

Eventually, it was boredom that drove them out of the gates and into Pilam, with Goshi at their head. The children began to feel Goshi's passion for the things he was saying. Some even believed in him. After a few days of drifting like lost cattle, their enthusiasm was spent. There was nothing for them to do out there. One day, they had strayed past the last houses of Pilam and were in the middle of deciding to turn back when they heard something approaching on the road. When it appeared, it was a yellow-and-green thing, so incongruous that someone swore out loud. It was an auto-rickshaw. The driver parked it on the side of the road and came down. The man waved at them. Nobody waved back.

He was a middle-aged man with a bald spot on his head. They stood there watching him approach. Panshak's heart was screaming, banging on its cage, because something bad was about to happen. He knew it as instinctively as the body knows pain.

The man reached where they stood.

"Do wundung," he said in greeting.

Goshi, in his beguiling manner, shook the man's hand. They walked back to the rickshaw side by side as the man explained that he was looking for someone. The other boys followed.

"Where are you coming from?" Goshi asked, inspecting the vehicle. From where he stood, Panshak could see balls of cabbage and sacks of potatoes stacked in the back seat.

"From Pitong," the man said. "I'm looking for a woman, my brother's wife. Her name is Yilamka. Maybe you have seen her."

The man took out a small photograph from his pocket and gave it to Goshi. Goshi barely looked at the picture before putting it in his pocket. Everything after that unfolded in a smooth, quick sequence that seemed as inevitable as the falling of water. Goshi extended a hand, and Podar handed him the homemade spear he was holding. Goshi ran it through the man as if he were a pig. The man remained standing, staring down at the point where the stick had impaled him, staring at Goshi's face, staring at the faces around him—he even looked at Panshak. Goshi pulled the stick out. The man crumpled in stages, to his knees, to his side, until he had reached the end of his crumpling.

"Panshak," Goshi yelled.

Panshak knew what he was going to say before he said it.

"Take a picture."

Panshak looked stupidly from Goshi to the man. There was a gap in the logic of the situation, and he was trying to bridge it.

Goshi tapped Panshak's cheek with a palm. "Are you high? I said take the picture."

Panshak raised his camera and took the picture. That evening, without even thinking about what he was doing, he deleted it from his camera.

Everything came tumbling down after that. Days later, one of the boys said they should go to Mister's house, that he had been a rich man. By then, most of them were carrying around crudely made weapons of various kinds. They arrived at Mister's house and knocked on the front door. When no one answered, they went around to the back door. One of Mister's sons opened the door, saw the armed children, and shut it in their faces. Podar hacked the door to pieces, and they went right into the kitchen. Mister's son had a rifle aimed at them, but for some reason, he did not fire. Panshak, watching from a distance, realized it was empty. Everybody else seemed to realize it at the same time, because the children all charged at him. Panshak remained outside while the noises of screaming and dying drifted out to him through the door.

Goshi called Panshak in and there were two dead bodies, one in the kitchen and the other in the living room just inside the front door. Goshi led him to the second body. It had been decapitated, and one of the boys—his name might have been Chishak or something close—was holding the head in two hands.

"This thing is heavy," the boy said.

"Take a picture," Goshi said, indicating the scene. His eyes seemed detached from all reason.

Panshak ran outside and vomited his breakfast. Goshi looked like he was going to attack Panshak next, but the laughter saved him. The boys were laughing at him, and Goshi relaxed and joined them in teasing him.

They spent that day wandering around Pilam with no direction and no purpose. Goshi was unraveling. He kept changing his mind as to which way they should go, or what they should do. In this manner, they drifted once more to the outskirts of Pilam. The sun's rays were beginning to collect in concentrated puddles of amber. Suddenly, the shrill roar of an approaching vehicle broke through the quiet. The sound was coming from around a nearby bend. Goshi had never looked so happy. He silently motioned for them to arrange themselves across the width of the road, blocking the way. They waited.

"Make sure you get some good pictures," Goshi said to Panshak, slinging his hunting rifle over his neck.

Panshak poised the camera at the ready. His hands were sweating.

It was the same yellow-and-green rickshaw, rounding the corner and stopping. Its engine coughed gently. Panshak felt something trying to rise through his throat. It was going to happen all over again.

The boys began to move toward the rickshaw. The driver, as though sensing the danger, launched the vehicle forward. It all became a blur. Goshi tried to swing his rifle at the vehicle; everybody attacked. Once the rickshaw got past their human barricade, however, they scampered after it. Panshak, relieved that this driver was putting up a fight, ran after it. He raised his camera in celebration of the possibility of escape for this person, whoever they may be. Podar was in front of him, leaping onto the side of the racing rickshaw and wielding a metal rod.

"Take the picture, take it, take it . . ." Goshi yelled from behind Panshak.

The weight of the boys was slowing the vehicle down, and Panshak managed to draw level with it and raise his camera. He could see the legs of the person in the back, but Podar was blocking him.

"I said take the picture!"

The driver swerved right and left, shaking the boys off like drops of water. Panshak was about to take the picture when he saw something that made him stop dead in his tracks.

Goshi picked up rocks and hurled them at the back of the vehicle, all in vain. Another second passed and the rickshaw was gone.

As Panshak collected his senses, Goshi turned and erupted. "Did you get any pictures?"

Panshak barely heard him. Who had he just seen in the back of that rickshaw?

Goshi seized his shirt and nearly lifted him off his feet. "Are you listening to me?" he shouted, so close to Panshak that spittle flecked his face. "I'm going to mess you up. Give me the camera."

Goshi snatched it out of his grip and tried to go through the pictures. He could not make sense of it. He threw the camera on the ground and walked away without another word. The boys followed.

Panshak picked up the camera, checked to see that it was still working, and followed the boys home, the whole time trying not to think of what would happen when night came and he was trapped in the same house with Goshi.

7

PANMUN

Her legs carried her to the first place where she hoped to find him. The front door was locked. She went around the house to the backyard, where he slaughtered and skinned his game. The slab of concrete, permanently tinged with the crimson of blood; the long branch of a smooth dead tree from which he suspended larger animals for skinning; the spit where he roasted or singed hair off hide; the empty room where he stored his traps and hunting tools. An ancient motorcycle stood defiantly against a far wall, its tires deflated and useless—Zumji's father's motorcycle. The door to one of the grain silos was open, and the chattering of maize against metal was coming from inside.

She waited.

A few seconds passed, and a boy of about thirteen wearing only a pair of shorts climbed out. There was a bowl of maize in his hand. He nearly dropped it when he saw Panmun.

"Good afternoon, Aunty," he said.

He seemed small for his age, as were most kids these days. The whites of his eyes were inflamed, like he had been crying.

"Tongzum, where is Zumji?"

"I haven't seen him."

"Where is your sister?"

"She's at home . . ."

"How is your father?"

Tongzum paused and looked at the ground. "He died this morning. He drank rat poison in the kitchen."

The effort to hold himself together, his voice, his body, the bowl of maize, was as broad and plain as a mountain. Panmun felt it in her throat and swallowed. She had just told herself she had to stop caring, but she could not help it as she went to Tongzum and hugged him. He remained still for a second, and then pulled away.

"I have to take this, so my sister can eat something."

Panmun nodded. She watched as he locked up and left.

The next place was the coppice, where Zumji had taken her to show her the carefully concealed rickshaw. She had stared at it that day, the paint bright yellow and bright green, like sunlight and grass, like a field of golden wildflowers. How could something so ordinary have become so wondrous? That was when he had declared, with the flair of an adventurer poet, that they should run away and start a new life somewhere else. The rickshaw would carry them wherever they wanted to go, and if they were without the sickness, nobody would fear them or want to harm them. They could get a pastor somewhere to marry them; Zumji could bring along his trapping tools and make a living off the ground, buy a plot of land and build a nice clean house for them to live in. That was supposed to be the future.

She found the rickshaw among the bushes. There were things in it she had not seen the last time: sacks containing food, a jerrican of gas, Zumji's tools. These things could mean he was dead. Or he had been delayed and was still planning to come for her. Zumji once explained the strategy he used in laying his traps. He said patience was the most important thing—learning to wait. It could take hours or days, but as long as a creature was alive, it would come. As long as Zumji was alive, he would return to the rickshaw. The question was, how long would she have to wait?

A nearby cashew tree beckoned to her. Its branches almost touched the ground in a bow. She sat and leaned against the tree trunk in the same manner in which she had sat against the flame tree. Enclosed within the cool olive sanctuary, she watched the rickshaw and waited. Rotted cashews from the year before surrounded her and the tree, scentless, while newborn ones hung in what should have been a kaleidoscope of reds, purples, and greens. Instead, to her eyes, they simply appeared dreary and dark. Sunlight filtered through the leaves and bounced against fruit and foliage; the tactile quality of the light filled Panmun with the sense that she might be inside a dream. Should she have told Zumji about the pregnancy? And about the Grey? If he was truly betraying her, could his betrayal be a just righting of the scales? Were they even now? Did she have enough moral ground to feel let down?

Before she knew it, she was dreaming in full color.

About a child, a boy, born to her in the dead of morning while the earth is splattered with rain. Before he can speak, the boy is able to communicate with her in the language of portents and premonitions. Then she realizes that the boy, her son, is also her father. She gives him her father's name—Yilwe. But when she looks into Yilwe's eyes, she finds the Grey in them, roiling and churning, a thunderstorm being born. He becomes a squall of a man, carrying the Grey with him like a second soul, a man shadowed by destruction but never swallowed by it. Everything that her father wished and failed to be, the boy becomes. Greatness fills his grasp with the potency of possibility, where infinite worlds lie in parallel, waiting, and he discovers and explores each completely in the span of a single lifetime. Yilwe, her son, shares a striking resemblance with Panshak, her brother, whom she had not seen in days. But the two shall never meet, because Yilwe will be born in a place far away, a place she will run to in her attempt to flee the Grey. A man's back is visible as it appears to shimmer in and out of definition: the back of his head like a smudge of black ink, the line of his shoulders as straight as the line where the ground meets the sky. Before the image can become permanent, it is pierced by an arrow. It vanishes and she is alone with Yilwe, braving the world, seeking joy and, in the very end, finding peace.

The roar of an engine snapped her eyes open. Framed by the foliage of the cashew tree from twenty feet, Zumji was arranging things in the rickshaw, which was growling with life. He was shirtless as he secured his cargo, tying a rope over the sacks and containers to keep them from shifting. He came over to her side of the vehicle, turning his bare back to Panmun. Her heart began to race. If only she had something—a gun, a bow and arrow, a knife—to plunge into the scheming bastard's back. She saw a rock, snatched it up, leaped to her feet.

Panmun took a few steps forward and raised the rock. Zumji turned around and saw her. She was trembling. Zumji just stared at her with burdened eyes. Where was his shirt? And was that water on his skin?

"You told me to wait," Panmun said, holding her voice steady. "You said you would come. You told me to wait by the tree. Three times. You wrote it: wait by the tree."

"I'm sorry, Pan," he began.

"I waited."

"Panmun . . ."

"Why didn't you come?"

"Panmun, I'm sorry."

"Stop saying sorry. Why didn't you come?"

"I had to do something."

"You said you would come. And you always do what you say you will. Why didn't you come today?"

"Something happened," he said. "Something happened, and I had to do something about it."

"Were you going to leave me?"

Panmun was crying now, and hating herself for it. How could she be crying because of a lying, scheming, shameless hypocrite? She was better than this.

Zumji let out a sigh, as though the question were a pair of hands that removed a load he had been carrying all this time. "I thought I could, but I made a mistake. I'm sorry."

"You can't just do something wrong and say sorry and expect that everything will be fine. It's not fair." Panmun slammed the rock into the ground.

Zumji rummaged through a wooden toolbox at the back of the rickshaw, produced a knife. He took off the goatskin sheath, and the iron blade sang in the light. He offered it to her without a word. Panmun took it. She had seen this knife in action, knew the way it sliced clean through flesh, tendon, and bone as he dressed his animals. She looked at his bare chest, his dark skin. What was she going to do? If sorry was not enough, what would quench the thirst of her fury?

This was ridiculous, and she was being silly. He had made his point, and she despised him even more for it. His grounded reasoning, his annoying common sense. She threw the knife on the ground and went back to the shade of the cashew tree, where she sat down. He followed her.

"I'm still angry," she said as he lowered himself beside her.

"I know."

"You know how these things make me feel."

"I'm sorry."

"Stop saying that and just shut up, please."

"I will never leave you. I thought I could, but now I know I was wrong."

"You don't know what you're saying," she said.

She raised her sunglasses and turned her face toward him. Zumji did not flinch when he saw the Grey. He touched her chin instead.

"I will never leave you, Panmun. I swear on my mother's grave."

She ran her gaze over his face. The only other time he had ever spoken of his mother was to say that he had never known her, because she had left the world as he was coming into it. He told her how he wished he had met her, gotten to know her, loved her; Panmun should be grateful because she had known her mother *and* father.

"My father went to look for our uncle and never came back. I never even saw his body," Panmun had said, competitively.

"Did he have the Grey?" Zumji had asked.

"Yes."

"My father left before the Grey even came. He also went out one night and didn't come back."

Zumji had said it calmly, but it put the matter to rest. His grief had crannies and contours that she could not comprehend. On a scale, it would outweigh hers without question. Yet they had something in common: fathers who had vanished and left behind questions. This was one of the things that endeared her to him, because it felt like a bond through which they could begin to try and understand each other. This shared fact of missing fathers became so precious to her that she locked it in the secret place with her other private treasures.

Now he was swearing by his mother's grave to never leave her. She held his face in both hands and kissed him.

There was no time to waste. Panmun jumped into the back of the rickshaw, and they were on their way. She looked at the sky. The sun, filtered silver by the Grey, was already sinking. The roar of the rickshaw filled her ears. She watched Zumji drive, the way his shoulders responded to the curves in the road, strong shoulders that could break the world for her, shoulders that existed solely for her and the child in her womb. When would be a good time to tell him? She closed her eyes against the wind. He had seen the Grey and acted like it was nothing: she knew then she would lay down her life for him if it came to it. And they had to figure out what to do. Otherwise, what was the point of running away when the thing they were running away from was already in her, clinging to her? She could almost hear his answer: "We will win in the end. If the Grey is a living thing, I will find a way to kill it."

Zumji followed the bumpy road into a pass between two large hills. The one to the west threw its shadows across the miniature valley, bathing the stretch in the soft grays of dusk. He slowed down, then gradually came to a stop.

"What's wrong?" Panmun asked, leaning forward and looking through the windshield.

"It's them," Zumji said. He did not explain, but if she had ever heard fear in his voice, this was it.

A group of children blocked the road. All boys, adolescents and teenagers, armed with an array of crude weaponry. Metal spikes, grotesque flails, machetes, cutlasses, axes, sharp sticks, sickles, rocks. The tallest one among them carried a hunting rifle, slung casually over his shoulder. He was dressed in a top hat and a long black jacket that reached down to his knees, and he stood at the front of the little rabble of twenty or more children. He began to strut toward the vehicle, and the children followed. As he approached, his appearance became more defined. He was a man-child trapped in the tussle between adolescence and adulthood, with grown-up facial features that sat awkwardly on his elongated but childlike frame: his face was a medley of thin lips, tiny eyes tucked deep in their sockets, and a strong nose. His eyes were glazed over, as though there were no one inside, as though there were only his body, moving of its own accord. Whoever this person was, he was insane, and he had all the children tethered to his will.

Suddenly, Zumji shifted the vehicle into drive and charged forward, and the small army before them responded. It was like throwing a burning match into a keg of gas. The man-child clubbed the windshield with his rifle, and cracks spread across the glass. The side of the rickshaw collided with him, knocking him off the road. The children raced along with the vehicle and began to leap onto it. Panmun saw disembodied hands reaching toward her, grabbing desperately. Zumji struggled to maintain control without slowing down. Ravenous children clung to the sides, screaming like drunk devils. A voice was shouting something indiscernible in the madness. A hand blindly swung an ax and narrowly missed Zumji's head, but the blade continued along its path, straight toward Panmun. She blocked it and wrenched the weapon from the surprisingly feeble grip. A large rock crashed into the windshield and shattered the glass. A boy jumped on the front of the vehicle and reached through the gaping window with a stick sharpened to a deadly point, aiming for Zumji's chest. Zumji grabbed the spear and pulled the boy toward him. Releasing the controls for the briefest moment, he punched the child so hard he slipped and fell on the road. Panmun let out a squeal of horror as the rickshaw rolled over him unsteadily.

The path before them was now clear. Most of the children, unable to hold on to the racing vehicle, had fallen off, but they still chased it. They began to pelt the back of the rickshaw with rocks, and the deafening crashes made Panmun shut her eyes and ears. Children were sweet and silly and annoying. They did not attack people with deadly weapons. Something was wrong, terribly, terribly wrong. Terribly terribly terribly terribly . . .

"Panmun, it's okay. It's okay."

She opened her eyes. She was on the ground beside the rickshaw. Zumji was holding her.

"It's okay. It's going to be okay. Stop crying."

"Where are we? What happened?"

Zumji looked at her. "You nearly fell out. You were crying and screaming."

Panmun touched her face. It was wet. She looked up. They were parked beside a deserted roadblock. The makeshift military shelter beside the road was empty and overgrown with weeds. A pile of great rocks had once blocked the entire width of the road, but a small gap had been made to allow room to pass. Few things larger than a human being could go through, and a rickshaw happened to be one of them.

The gap seemed to have been made specifically for the vehicle. They got back in and drove through it. Panmun felt like they were passing through a portal between two worlds.

As they went along, she remained still. She could not remember anything of the last few minutes. Not what she had felt, heard, or done. Was this something the Grey did? She thought about Dunka. He had wished for them to talk the other day, before she had thrown words at him, words chosen to hurt him. Why had she not given that conversation a chance? They could have said so many things to each other. Maybe kind things, good things. She could have asked him to describe what the Grey felt like. It was the one connection they might have shared, and it would have been something.

The road inclined along the side of a mountain and turned into a ridge. As they climbed, everything fell away like a curtain opening, and Panmun saw the world. It was there below her, stretching on and on to the point where the sky began. Zumji stopped the vehicle. As though controlled by a single impulse, they came down from the rickshaw. Panmun took three steps until she was standing on the tip of the ledge. The sun was already being swallowed by the earth. In the depths below, where grassland and baobab trees and boulders and houses in the distance melted into a patchwork of grays, the Grey continued its silent siege. She could even see Pishang in the distance.

She turned to find Zumji watching the giant sunset in tears. Panmun wiped his face with her fingers.

"Those children," he said huskily. "I saw what they have done. But it wasn't their fault. It made them do it."

"I don't understand what you mean."

"What if Panshak was among them?" he said.

Panmun shook her head. "Panshak doesn't kill people."

"And when was the last time anybody saw him?"

Panmun received the truth of his words with two hands. From a place deep in her being, perhaps deeper than the secret place where she stored her private treasures, a place she did not even know existed, a memory escaped. It was so disturbing she had locked it away without knowing she had experienced it, without knowing she had locked it away.

A fuzzy image of a boy chasing the rickshaw along with the other wild children, raising something up, maybe a weapon. Maybe he's looking for striking room. But his comrades are in his way, so he contents himself with running beside the waylaid vehicle. Panmun reaches to push a hand that's groping madly toward her and she locks eyes with the boy, who recognizes her and stops dead. Before Panmun can render the image into meaning, the boy falls out of sight as the rickshaw rumbles along.

Panmun squeezed the memory back into the deep place and locked it again. She was not prepared to consider the possibility that the boy was her brother. She would attend to it later.

"I'm pregnant."

Zumji looked at her with a long, wordless expression of love. He pulled her into his arms and held her there, and then something in his chest erupted like a monsoon, and he began to sob. Panmun closed her eyes and existed in the arms of her crying man, who was also in her arms. She had never loved him more.

Panmun saw the moment—this present moment, and each present moment after that. She saw it for what it was: the truest thing she would ever know. The past was in the middle of being forgotten, and the future was hidden behind a wall of mystery. But the present, this ever-living present, was what was true, because it was now. Panmun's now was a happiness that rose above the landscape of her childhood as corrupted by the Grey, a happiness engendered and preserved by the man she loved, weeping in her arms; by a child of her own making, growing in her womb; and also by the fading light of the sun as it was shed in silvery sheets across the endless world that stretched away behind her. There was no color in her eyes, but she still felt like she had conquered the world, like every good thing was hers.

And, for now, that was all that mattered.

8

RIT

Rit cried and cried, but sleep never came that night. It was her first time in the house alone, all by herself in the dark. If her siblings had been gone for a night, perhaps for a sleepover, to be back the next morning, that might have made it easier to bear. But her two brothers were missing, and her sister had abandoned them. When would she ever see them again? It was like looking into a well so deep it was impossible to see the bottom.

She tried to go through her daily routine in the morning. Make her bed—it had been her mother's bed, and her mother's room—clean the house, sweep the backyard, and put on the fire to heat the bathing water. The process of starting a fire—the clacking and sparking and hoping for the tinder to catch the flame—wore her out, but she did it all the same, every day, for as long as was necessary. She had just finished pouring the water from a bucket into the pot perched over the fire when the last of her strength caved in. She could not continue with this charade any longer. The futility of everything was too heavy. She was alone in the world.

Rit sat on the low stool and stared into the fire. She began to sense something else: relief. She had become unburdened of the mixed sense of duty and guilt that had taken root in her and refused to let go after they had buried her mother. She went now and stood by her grave, tucked in a corner of the backyard. It was nothing more than a square of unmarked ground. Dunka had brought a large rock and laid it at the head of the grave: it looked like a bed with its pillow neatly in place. It was Panshak who had carved the letters into the rock, spelling their mother's name, not her given name but the name they, her children, called her by: *NANA*.

Rit's memories of her mother were not quiet memories; they mostly had the gravelly sound of her mother's voice, filling her head, accusing her, and comparing her to her sister. Her mother accused her when she went on long solitary walks, got lost, and found her way home again, buoyed by the joy of adventure; she accused her when forcing her to pay attention in the kitchen to how to correctly make a pot of puk fori so that it wasn't too sour; she accused her when she came home from school with a report card that said, "There is room for improvement." And then her mother had gone and died. They had removed all the potential poisons from the house—pesticides, bleaches—yet they had no idea where she had found the rat poison she had used. At first, Rit had expected to finally be free of her nagging, but to the contrary, she found herself questioning every action, wondering what her mother might say about this or that. Death had bestowed on her the supremacy of being right.

Now Rit could lie in bed all day, or stay out all night, or burn the house down. It would not make a difference to anybody what she did anymore. She no longer had the strength to hope for her brothers' return. The Grey had finally made Dunka go off and kill himself some-where, she was sure of it. But what about Panshak?

What about him? He was too young to have the Grey, and too stubborn and stupid to realize that she cared about him, which was why she had done what she did. He had probably tried to cross the boundary fence and gotten himself killed. Stupid, silly boy. Now she sounded like her mother. Was she really like her mother? People said she was, but that could not be true. Not when her mother had been the single most disagreeable person she had ever known.

As the morning progressed, Rit began to think she might grow accustomed to this feeling of loneliness. She managed to take a bath using the finger-size piece of soap that remained of the bar that Panshak had brought home several weeks earlier; he had refused to say where he got it, but she suspected it may have been a small shop somewhere that had been overlooked during the looting that accompanied the early days of the Grey. After the bath, she lay down and tried to go back to sleep, but her mind kept returning to the day Panshak had left. How long had it been now? Two weeks? Three?

Panshak had fancied himself a Runner. Thirteen years old and he was already concerned about his inability to contribute to the family home. He had to learn to be a man. That was what he said when Rit asked him where he went. He had secured employment to ferry letters back and forth across Pilam in exchange for food, which he would deposit on the kitchen counter with a gleam of pride in his eyes. That had been nearly four months ago. He occasionally came by the house when he was on an errand. He liked to preen his image in the eyes of his siblings, show them what a responsible young man he was. He would wave the object of his errand, invariably a handwritten letter, in Rit's face. He would ask if she wanted to read it. She always said no, that it was wrong to amuse oneself with other people's miseries, the sort of thing her mother would have said.

Three months later, he was still spending chunks of time away from home, occasionally stopping by with a folded note. By then, everybody knew that the Running network had ground to a halt because the village head's daughter had hanged herself from an electric pole in front of her house.

The last time Rit saw Panshak, he had stood in the kitchen and brandished another folded piece of paper at her. It was late evening, and the dying light had turned blue, painting the windows and the reflections on the walls with its sad hues. Panmun was out with her new boyfriend, Zumji; Dunka was somewhere around.

"Are you sure you don't want to read?" he said with a mischievous grin.

Rit was going to ignore him at first. Looking back now, she wished she had just said yes. Instead, she said, "There's nothing in it. So stop pretending."

"I'm not pretending."

Rit took a step forward so she could stare him down, but the difference between their heights was barely an inch. "You think we're idiots? You think we don't know?"

"Don't know what?"

"Your boss is dead."

Panshak held her gaze stubbornly. It was impossible to know what he was thinking.

"The Runners have stopped working. So where have you been going this whole time?"

"Don't call me a liar, Rit."

"You're lying. I said it. People are disappearing all over the place, you go away for days and nobody knows where you are."

"I'm not afraid of you."

"I'm trying to make sure this house stays together. I cook and clean every day just so that Nana and—"

"Nobody asked you to do that. Just because Nana is dead, you think you can order me around?"

"I'm your big sister."

"You're just two years older than me. Even Panmun doesn't do that."

Rit had tears in her eyes when she turned away. "Nobody cares about this family anymore." She pulled herself together and turned to face him again. "Where do you go when you're not here?"

"I'm not a child."

"Answer me, Panshak."

"No."

Rit grasped the front of his shirt. "I said answer me."

"No!" Panshak shoved her, but she held on. "Let me go!"

"Answer me!"

They jostled each other around the kitchen, spinning and spinning. Panshak struggled to free the grip on his shirt. Rit clung on stubbornly. They bumped into things. Panshak bit her hand. Rit slapped him so hard it resounded throughout the room. Panshak went wild, launched his entire weight at her. He clobbered her. He shook her. Finally, he threw her on the floor. She was no match for his strength. She wanted to get up, but the look in his eyes warned her. And then he was gone, leaving behind the dark silence of the evening.

The following morning, Dunka asked for Panshak and she said she did not know where he was. She never mentioned the previous night's incident. Never mentioned that he might have run away, all because of her. Eventually, they grew used to his absence.

Rit shut her eyes against this ugly memory. She should have said yes, she would love to read his stupid letter. She should have asked him whether he was hungry. Her brother was gone, probably dead, and she was the one responsible.

This time, she managed to cry herself into a long, dreamless sleep. When she woke up, she could not remember which room of the house she had fallen asleep in. The light through the window seemed young and pure. She found her way outside. There was still dew melting on the grass that grew in patches around the backyard, dew dripping from the roof. It slowly came back to her. She had fallen asleep in their father's old room, Dunka's room, trying to mourn him, but had ended up thinking about Panshak. She had slept all day yesterday and all night. And she was hungry.

In the pantry, she found precisely three beans. She looked in the other containers. The maize Zumji had brought them was also gone. For the first time in her life, starvation was staring Rit full in the face. After the Grey, finding food had become difficult, but they'd had their parents' reserves of grain, which lasted a year. They managed to get by on mangoes and guavas when they were in season, and this was a welcome stopgap, allowing them to stretch their reserves. They could not put off going through everything forever, but by the time they were considering what they'd do when the rice finally ran out, Zumji had entered their lives, bringing bounty. It was not much, but in the time of the Grey, anything seemed like a lot.

Rit could not say how she came to find herself literally counting beans, how the situation had crept up on her. She entered the pantry nearly every day. She took responsibility for rationing the food. She thought she had been paying attention. She went to her room, sat on the bed, and stared at the wall. She had heard the stories of people who had starved to death inside their houses and remembered thinking that it could never happen to her. She had always had a subconscious sense of being somehow special—not better, but special. She felt that everything happening around her was going to happen *around* her, but not *to* her. She had never seriously considered the possibility of dying.

Rit lay on her side and curled her little body around the hunger that had begun to worry her insides. Perhaps she could squeeze it into a thing so small it would just disappear. She was not unused to hunger. Rationing food would sometimes require them going hungry until evening, and she, as well as everyone else, would have to endure it. But there had always been an end in sight, a break from the relentless gnawing in their bellies. And she had never been alone.

Time stretched beyond recognition, but sleep did not come. Time. It was the true enemy, wasn't it? Standing between her and everything else. Between her and a little food. Between her and death. Eventually it would move aside and she would be in death's embrace, but before then, it would torture her. She could not stand it any longer. She threw on a frayed boubou without thinking, slipped on her worn, holey flip-flops, and left the house.

She climbed the slight slope that led away from their house and stopped by the flame tree, recognizing her sister's things. She stared at the backpack and pink suitcase blankly for a moment, then continued on her way. It did not take her too long to arrive at Zumji's property. The short pathway that led up to the house had cacti growing on either side and was wide enough to let a car through. She had never been beyond this point; crossing it, she half expected something to happen. The stillness around the house was like an endless, dreary note, precise and unnerving. The front door was shut. Rit went around the house, studying it from a distance, its creeping vines and thatch roofing. The backyard looked more like a museum than anything else. She saw strange constructions of metal and wood, a pile of iron implements that seemed dangerous and myste-rious, a log of wood that had blackened with age and served as a bench, and a dead tree with a smooth, worn bark that still stood as though it were alive. It had a lone branch draped with suspended lengths of string. A collection of small mud structures stood in a cluster, with little doors that looked like windows. The grain silos.

Rit looked for shade. She went among the cluster of silos and sat under the thatched eave that extended from one of the roofs. The shadow was narrow, and it grew even narrower as the sun moved across the sky. What was she doing here? Perhaps she was simply waiting for something—anything—to occur. As though in response to this thought, something did.

A boy about her age appeared, wearing shorts and a dirty brown shirt. His shoes were tired leather sandals that were so worn they barely made any sound as he walked. He was carrying a large metal bowl and dragging an old chair behind him. He fetched a set of keys from the thatched roof of one of the silos, opened a tiny door. He had to stand on the chair to be able to climb through it. Rit stood up. She could not see into the dark space, but she heard the unmistakable sound of grain being fetched. When he came out, he saw her.

"Who are you?" he demanded. An unfriendly, guarded look leaped into his eyes. He placed the bowl on the ground and locked the door. Rit stared at the bowl—it contained golden grains of maize. The boy was about to return the keys to their original hiding place, but he looked at Rit and pocketed them instead. Picking up his bowl, he fixed her with a venomous stare.

"Are you Tongzum?" Rit said.

"Answer my question first."

"I'm Rit. You may not know me . . ."

Tongzum clearly did not have time for this. He walked away. Rit remained where she was, stunned. This was what she had become: a pariah, a beggar to be shunned, ignored, walked away from. Tears came gushing forth from a place she did not know. She hid her face while her chest heaved and heaved with a pain that was intent on crushing her.

9

ARRIT

Polu was acting up again. His food sat on the floor of the storeroom that was across from the gate, where he was now sleeping since he had been asked to vacate his room for the prisoner. He picked up the plastic plate of yam pottage, spat into it, and slid it across the cement floor toward Arrit's feet. Arrit stared at the food. She had spent two hours of her morning making it. She had nicked extra dried fish and some cauliflower from under Bimorit's watchful eye. Now it had spittle on it, white spittle, like a rabid dog's froth.

Arrit clicked her tongue, picked up the plate, and left the room as Polu threw his arm over a sack of maize. He knew that if any food was left over, she would be forced to eat it. The rascal. Uncle Yilshak would stand over her and make sure she had cleared the last bit of food.

"You never had three square meals in your father's house, so why are you wasting food?" he would ask. She could not explain that it was not her food but Polu's. She was not allowed to explain because it was talking back. Talking back invariably earned her, at the very least, a slap.

This time, she was prepared. In the kitchen, she pulled out Uncle Yilshak's plate—a blue ceramic dish with gold twirls across its face—and upturned what should have been Polu's meal into it. Now it was Uncle Yilshak's, saliva and all.

If anybody had caught a whiff of the fact that she had been speaking to him on the sly, it would have reached Uncle Yilshak's ears. And then he would have come for her. When he came for her, he did not curl his hands into fists. There was no rush to his movements. He beat her lazily, as if it were a task he was obliged to carry out, as if it were all her fault. What made each episode truly frightening was that he eventually reached for the least cumbersome object at hand to aid him in the task. Depending on where they were located at the time, he had used a mopstick, a large beer bottle, a phone charging cable, the leg of the ironing room table that he ripped clean from the body, and the sharp heel of his wife's shoe.

Arrit's scars outlined a good number of the beatings she had received since coming to live with Uncle Yilshak and his wife, Aunty Pagak (who most people called Matyin—medicine woman), seven years ago. A small gash at the back of her head, mercifully dressed by hair, she obtained when Uncle Yilshak slammed her into the edge made by two walls. One of her large upper front teeth was chipped, so that it looked like something a mouse had nibbled on, but it was revealed only when she smiled. Her scars were all like that, small secrets tucked away.

Whatever had possessed her to speak to the prisoner? The prisoner. It was such an odd thing to think, let alone say. Uncle Yilshak had forbidden anyone in the house from mentioning it to outsiders. For the last two days, when she went to school, she could not brag about the fact that she had met someone with the sickness from Pilam face-to-face, that they had him locked up in the guardroom, which had been Polu's room. And Polu, who had nothing better to do with his irritation, targeted it at her, the weakest member of the household.

She did not have any friends to brag to, anyway.

Uncle Yilshak's intentions for the prisoner remained unclear. Why had he not turned him over to the vigilante men? They would have dealt with him permanently. Arrit remembered how he had been crossing the compound with the bottle of cure when something had knocked him to the ground and immobilized him. Uncle Yilshak's car pulled up outside the gate. Bimorit materialized in front of Arrit and began to scream at the top of her lungs.

"Wat! Wat!" Thief! Thief!

Uncle Yilshak had appeared then with a lug wrench. He struck the prisoner as he was trying to get up. In the ensuing ruckus, Arrit noticed something on the ground. It was the dagger the prisoner had used to threaten them. It had a strip of black material around the handle. While Polu and Uncle Yilshak heaved the unconscious body across the compound and into Polu's room, Arrit slipped the knife into her waistband, hiding the handle under her shirt. The blade felt like a cool balm against her hot skin, but it threatened to bite; one wrong move and it would have dug right into her flesh. Later, after the thief had been locked in the guardroom and Aunty Pagak's nerves had been sufficiently calmed, Arrit stole away to the room she shared with Bimorit, Uncle Yilshak's niece. In the small corner that was all she had to herself in the world, she raised the lid of the black metal trunk containing all her belongings, slid the knife under some clothes, and left the room.

That evening, Arrit delivered the prisoner his first meal through the small window at the top of the wall. Uncle Yilshak had instructed her to feed him once a day. She left the bowl of food on the interior part of the windowsill. Before she left for school the next day, she looked into the room: the food had been untouched; the mun and puk kom tori, made with dried baobab leaves, was cold and hard. This annoyed Arrit because it meant she would be responsible for making it disappear.

"I won't bring you any food again until you eat this," she had said into the dark room before leaving for school. When she got back, the bowl on the windowsill was empty. She served him dinner and went to bed.

The next morning, she tried to gaze into the room, but it was too dark inside.

She barely paid any attention to her lessons that day. Her mind was back home with the stranger. When he had raised his sunglasses to look at her on that first day, she had felt like she had been seen, her presence in this world acknowledged for the first time. That was why she had given away her name without pause when he asked for it. Why some part of her had hoped he could get away clean.

"Arritmwa, are you with us?" Miss Rotdel, the literature teacher, said.

Arrit's heartbeat snagged against the moment as she realized she was about to endure yet another humiliation.

"Stand here, in front. Good. Repeat the last three sentences I said."

Arrit's spirit left her body and moved aside to observe the scene. There she was, taller than her own teacher, with the body of a fully grown woman, in that ridiculous uniform, standing in front of a class of fourteen-year-olds. Of course she could not remember what Miss Rotdel had been saying. She did not know what *irony* meant, and she could not list a single figure of speech.

Arrit was often the target of ridicule. At the same time, she knew that most male teachers looked at her with more than a passing interest. They seemed to enjoy observing her. She knew what they wanted, what they would do if she let them have their way. Their stares reminded her of the way Uncle Yilshak began to look at her after her body had morphed and expanded in certain places, but *his* stare was devoid of even an artificial fondness. He had been watching her without seeing her, doing things with his eyes when she was in front of him that she instinctively felt he should not be doing. She had felt this even before she knew what a man could do. By the time her teachers were ogling her, she had understood that sometimes a man did not need permission.

"Be careful," Bimorit said when Arrit told her about the stares that followed her in school, in a rare moment of openness between them.

She scanned Arrit's body when she said it. Arrit thought it was out of pity, but she did not pursue the matter with more questions, because Bimorit's kindness was a switch that flicked on and off without warning. Only later did it occur to her that if Bimorit could have killed her and inhabited her body, she would have done so without a second thought.

Arrit had been living with Uncle Yilshak and his wife for five years when they began to hear of a strange sickness that was affecting people in nearby Pilam. For her, it began with frightened murmurs from her teachers. A parent of one of the students who lived in Pilam had mysteriously died. The rumor, whose source remained cloaked in mystery, was that this woman's eyes had turned black overnight. The boy had been in a different class, so Arrit never got to hear any firsthand accounts, but the details would float through windows and seep through walls, passed on from teacher to student to parent: the woman had become inexplicably bedridden, though there was no medical explanation for this; the woman had grown restless and unresponsive in turn; the woman had crawled out of bed and drawn a butcher's knife across her abdomen. In a matter of weeks, other students from Pilam also stopped coming to school, and each case of termination of attendance was accompanied by news of another sick parent.

"How the general mood changed from curiosity to fear is something for the history books," Mr. Pogak, the history teacher, said sotto voce before changing the subject to the topic of the day. Teachers across the country had been forbidden by the government from bringing up the matter of the sickness in Pilam, let alone discussing it.

While the people of Pishang were still trying to wrap their minds around what was happening to their neighbors, Arrit went to church one Sunday and the preacher opened to a Bible passage where leprosy had begun to spread between the Israelites.

"It is simple," Pastor Gogol said. "They have sinned. Our neighbors, the people of Pilam," he said, pointing west, "have sinned against God, and now God is judging them."

He threatened, begged, cajoled, and appealed to them to stay away from sin. Any sickness that plagued adults and spared children could only have its genesis in sin, because God did not hold children responsible for their own actions until they had matured. Sin. Sin. It had to be sin.

Similar messages were heard all over Pishang and across the land. People stopped visiting their friends in Pilam, sick or not. They stopped welcoming their friends from Pilam, sick or not. When the people of Pilam who were yet to contract the sickness packed up and tried to leave with their families, the people of Pishang refused to let them through. What if they were carrying the sickness and infected innocent, helpless people? What if they would pass the judgment that was hanging over their heads to other communities? Guilt had become a communicable disease. The military came and mowed down insistent trespassers with their guns. The village head of Pishang met with the local chiefs and, in consultation with all the other villages that surrounded Pilam, raised barricades to obstruct passage. They formed vigilante groups and had them patrol the boundaries. Arrit began to hear about clashes at the boundary, about desperate men and women with the black evil in their eyes trying to cross over by force and being killed on the spot. Soon, reports of crowds trying to escape their judgment died down. Eventually, Arrit heard about only the occasional theft, because the people of Pilam had lost their ability to farm as a result of the curse. She heard about the babies who were left at the barricade, abandoned by their parents to the elements or the mercy of their neighbors, rather than to the sickness.

If Arrit had been paying closer attention in class, when she was asked to explain irony, she might have said that irony was the way Pastor Gogol's admonishments to stay away from sin had failed to catch on. She might have said irony was Uncle Yilshak coming home with a prostitute, sometimes two, when Aunty Pagak was away on a trip. Or their neighbor, Napar the carpenter, borrowing money from several people and hiding in Uncle Yilshak's compound while his wife explained to the angry creditors on the other side of the fence that her husband had traveled out of town on a long assignment but promised to send the money soon.

She might have described irony as the way their lives carried on, undergirded by an unbroken peace, while the adults around her lied and stole and cheated each other, and the strange sickness continued to ravage the village across the way because its people had sinned.

After school, Arrit returned home and stole another glance into the prisoner's room. Still she saw nothing. The sun never touched the place. She went to her room and tried to do her homework. The house had grown quiet in recent months. Aunty Pagak had not been receiving as many clients because she was pregnant. After the incident with the stranger from Pilam, she and Uncle Yilshak had decided it was best not to see anyone until she'd had the baby.

Despite all her years of living in Uncle Yilshak's house, Arrit could not place a finger on what it was exactly that Aunty Pagak did. Some people called her a witch. Others called her a healer. Arrit had once heard somebody refer to her as an *alchemist*—she did not know what that meant. One of the rooms served as her "kitchen," where she housed her burners and stoves and pots and mixing utensils, her roots and herbs and the strange ingredients that she procured from unheard-of places. Often, an acrid smell would permeate the house, and they would all know Aunty Pagak was at it again.

A year ago, Mr. Walshak, the math teacher, had called Arrit into his office. It was not the first time a teacher was summoning her so. The first time it happened, when she was fourteen, the teacher in question, Mr. Cen, had pulled the curtains and locked the door. When he turned to face Arrit, she began to cry, and he let her out at once. Mr. Walshak, however, did not close the curtains or anything like that.

"Sit down."

Arrit sat. Mr. Walshak raised himself onto his desk so that he was looking down at Arrit, almost vertically.

"You're a very beautiful girl. Do you know that?"

Arrit shook her head.

"I know, it's good to be modest. How is your aunty?"

"She's fine, sir."

"How is her business?"

"Fine."

He was smiling, almost kindly, but his gaze left an uncomfortable crawling sensation on the nape of her neck.

"What do you think of it?" Mr. Walshak asked.

Arrit looked at him with a scrunched-up brow.

"What do you think of your aunty's business? Is what she does legal or illegal?"

Arrit had never thought of it in those terms. "She helps people."

"What kind of people?"

"Sick people."

"But is it just sick people she helps?"

"No."

"Has she ever given you any of the things she makes?"

"No."

"So you've never tasted it."

"No, sir."

Mr. Walshak fell silent, and Arrit looked away.

"How old are you?"

"Eighteen."

"Eighteen," he repeated. Finally, he said, "So you've never considered that your aunty might be making drugs?"

Arrit looked at him again. She shook her head. She had begun to suspect early on during her time in the house that Aunty Pagak's cures were a sham. It seemed plain to Arrit in the casual way she mixed substances and herbs, as though she were making it up as she went along.

But people came sad and left hopeful. They came with hunched shoulders and left with a spring in their step. How could she argue with that? She had never considered the possibility that there might be anything illicit about her wares. After Mr. Walshak dismissed her, Arrit went home and asked Bimorit.

"Does Matyin sell drugs?"

"Where did you hear that?"

"One of my teachers was saying something."

"I'm sure it was a woman who is jealous of Matyin's success."

"It was a man."

"Men don't like it when a woman is more successful than them."

That was all Bimorit had to say about the matter. Arrit never asked again. If Uncle Yilshak heard that she was asking such questions, she knew what would follow. In the months that had elapsed since, she had done her best not to let even a toe slip out of line. She was doing rather well, considering that she had not received a beating in over a year. Some part of her was determined to sustain this streak, but she knew, truly knew, that she could never. Her uncle would find something, a pretext, a made-up reason, just so he could lay his hands on her. She knew this as naturally as she knew how to breathe. What she did not know was what she was going to do if he came for her again.

10

PANSHAK

By evening, Goshi's temper had not improved. The girls made dinner, and Panshak joined the line for his food. Goshi came up and pulled him away.

"What's the use of eating when you can't keep your food down? You just end up wasting it." Goshi shoved him toward the staircase. "Go and bring the camera. I'm waiting."

Panshak went upstairs to the dormitory. He was so hungry he thought his stomach would cave in. He removed the camera from under his pillow, took it downstairs, and handed it to Goshi. The whole room was silent.

"I'm going to seize your camera," Goshi said. "And tomorrow, if I'm still angry, I'm going to beat the shit out of you. Then I'm going to kill you. Do you understand?"

Panshak nodded. Goshi slammed him into the wall. The back of Panshak's head stung.

"Say, 'Yes, Nde Goshi.'"

Panshak's tongue felt heavy, like it would not move at all no matter how much he tried. Goshi hit his cheek so hard the sound rang like a cymbal. It was like being doused with icy water.

"Yes, Nde Goshi."

"Now make yourself disappear from here."

Goshi tossed Panshak across the floor. Panshak got up and went back upstairs, where he sat on his bed and raised a hand to his cheek. The sting of the slap reverberated through his head. He lay down and closed his eyes against red-hot tears. Something was gathering in his chest. As hunger ravaged him, he remembered his family. He did not sleep. Rather, he navigated the night through thoughts of Panmun and Rit and Dunka. More than anything, he just wanted to see them again. By morning, the thing in his chest had resolved into a serene wrath. He knew what he had to do to be free.

He got up from the bed and went downstairs. It was a clear, beautiful day. Most of the children would be outside playing. He did not have to look hard for the bell. It was on the dining table. He carried it out to the driveway, where the two cars sat, squashed by time and neglect.

Panshak stood in the middle of the front yard and rang the bell. The sound went across the compound and into the house, brought back children. It also found Goshi. He stepped out of the house and stood by the cars, watching him. Panshak knew this was death he was playing with, but he did not care. There was death within him too.

"I want my camera."

"Is that why you woke me up?" Goshi seemed tame, tethered to the ground.

"Fight me," Panshak said calmly.

Goshi's response was to turn and go back into the house. Panshak knew what would follow, and if he was not ready by the time Goshi returned . . . well, he was not ready. He had been a bit too quick, a bit too careless. What could he use to defend himself? He cast about. Some old tires piled up beside the garage. Too heavy. The neem tree. Maybe a branch from the tree? But they were all too big. Goshi came back out, passing the long stick with the rounded end from one hand to the other and back again. The tethered look he'd had in his eyes merely a minute before was gone. He wanted blood.

The sight of the raving Goshi made Panshak reconsider the tree. Without a plan or a weapon, he ran to it and began to climb as quickly as he could manage. He got out of reach just as Goshi swung a deadly blow where his leg had been a second before. The head of the stick tore chunks of wood from the bark of the tree. Being in the tree made it feel even bigger, with its branches extending high above the house. The tree would be his weapon.

Panshak had found plenty of occasions for tree climbing when he was growing up, so he moved fast. He looked down to see Goshi coming after him, with the stick tucked into the waistband of his trousers. The older boy was just as sure-footed. When Panshak reached the top, he discovered that something had changed since the last time he had climbed a tree, because his vision tilted horribly for a moment. He hugged the trunk and watched helplessly as Goshi came closer, breathing loudly, hungrily, maniacally. There was only one branch sticking out from where Panshak clung, and it was not much of a branch. But it was his only option.

Ignoring the fact that he was nearly fifty feet off the ground, he stepped out onto the branch. Panshak saw his life dangle before him, but he steadied himself and made his way toward the tapering end of the limb. He soon ran out of branch—there was nowhere else to go.

Panshak turned and waited for Goshi to climb up. He curled his fists into tight balls. Goshi arrived at the branch, faced Panshak, and withdrew his weapon. The limb sank, bouncing tentatively under their collective burden. Goshi began to edge forward. He licked the corners of his mouth. He truly looked unhinged. Panshak had been cornered by something that was not human.

Goshi swung hard—very hard—at Panshak's head. Panshak ducked, feeling the rush of air. Seized by a momentary flash of insanity himself, he found the nerve to throw himself against the branch, hug it as tightly as he could, and bounce it up and down. Goshi, who was still steadying himself from his first swipe, was not prepared for it. He lost his balance, teetered for one endless second on one leg, released a hair-raising scream, and fell from the limb. There were no branches to break his fall, and his body plummeted right to the ground. A deafening thud. A gigantic exhalation. Silence.

Panshak climbed down quickly, almost slipping. By the time he reached the ground, Goshi was attempting to stand. Both his arms stuck out at such odd angles that Panshak almost felt the pain on his behalf. He groaned like a wounded animal—and yet, some inexplicable rage was driving him, pushing him to his feet. Panshak found the stick, the one Goshi had used to kill Nana Kanke. A window had opened somewhere in his consciousness, and he had climbed through to a place where he was not himself any longer. Panshak took aim at Goshi's bloody head and brought the shiny, rounded end of the stick down, closing his eyes as it made contact. For the rest of his life, Panshak would never forget that the sound of a hard piece of wood striking a human skull was almost the same as the sound of a machete biting into a coconut.

Panshak finally took note of the faces that had crowded around him and the body on the ground. Boys. Girls. They all looked so helpless with their drawn, haggard faces. The Grey had done this. Were they waiting for him to say something, to give direction, a meaning to their lives? He did not want to say anything. He wanted to lie down.

He exited the circle, and the children parted to let him through. He went upstairs to Nana Kanke's room, looking for his camera. The sheets on the bed, once a gentle blue, were now so dark with grime that the room stank. Nana Kanke would be turning over in her grave, but Panshak had no strength to try to make it right. When he lifted the camera from the bedside table, he saw the photograph that the rickshaw driver had given to Goshi. Panshak raised it and saw a young woman's face. He remembered her name: Yilamka. Who had she been? What had she wanted? Did any of it even matter anymore? He put the photograph down and took the camera with him to his bed, where he lay down and clutched it to his chest. He wanted to sleep and forget the strange thing that was in the center of him right then, like dirty oil swirling inside water, like a tightness in the part of himself that was not flesh.

Panshak closed his eyes. Images of Goshi's blood and body and madness went on flashing behind his eyelids, like grotesque revelations. Crying might have made him feel better, but no tears came.

11

RIT

Rit waited for her tears to subside, then followed the insolent boy in the direction of the house. He was standing by the back door, which now stood open. A tiny girl Rit assumed to be about eight sat on the steps, playing with her dirty toes. Tongzum squeezed past her into the kitchen. Rit watched the little girl from a distance. She was oblivious to everything around her, singing to herself a soft melody that was as frail as she was. Tongzum returned with a grinding stone and set it on the steps next to the girl. He sat and began to crush the maize one handful at a time.

Rit's stomach rumbled rudely as she said, "You shouldn't do it like that."

Tongzum and the little girl looked up at the same time.

"There'll be . . . other things . . . dirt. If you do it like that."

Tongzum continued grinding the maize resolutely. The girl leaned in and whispered into his ear. He stopped.

"My sister says you look like somebody we know."

"Panmun," Rit said simply, hoping that would be enough in proving her identity.

"What's your name?" the little girl asked.

"Rit. What's yours?"

"Tong—"

Tongzum placed a hand over the girl's mouth. "What do you want?"

What did she want? Rit looked at the ground. Was it so difficult to admit that she was hungry? Would it really saw off a part of her dignity if she asked for help? Certainly not from this boy. She did not like his haughtiness, and the way he looked at her—

"We can't give you any food."

"I don't want your stupid food," Rit snapped.

"Well, what do you want?" Tongzum said. There now seemed to be a shimmer of amusement in his eyes. He was enjoying this, the little rat.

"I'm looking for my brother."

"He isn't here."

Rit was trembling. How dare he? Just because Zumji had left him his house and some food, he felt he could speak to her as though she had come to beg. She touched her face and realized the tears had come back. The whole time, Tongzum had not taken his eyes off her. She stormed off, not thinking clearly. Anything, including a lonely, hungry night back in their house, was better than this humiliation. She was so lost in her rage she did not hear the footsteps behind her; she only felt little fingers touching hers, and she jumped. She realized it was the little girl. Embarrassed by the fact that she was crying again, she wiped her tears away.

"My brother made you cry, I'm sorry. He doesn't know how to cook. All he keeps making is plain mun, nothing else. He doesn't even know how to make it properly. It always has lumps in it. I'm tired of eating mun without puk. Can you make something else?"

"It depends on what you have."

"Some things in the store. I can show you."

"What did you say your name was?"

"Tongrot."

Tongrot turned, and Rit followed her back the way they came. Tongzum was still there, hunched over the grinding stone. Tongrot marched up to him and stretched out her hand. "Give me the key."

"So that she can go in and take whatever she wants?" Tongzum said, without looking at his sister.

"She's going to cook something different for us. I don't like your cooking."

Tongzum sat up and glared at his sister. "If you don't like my cooking, cook for yourself."

"I have a better idea. Aunty Panmun's sister will cook something delicious for us."

Tongzum glared at Rit over his sister's shoulder. "You don't even know what brought her here," he said.

"She's here and she can cook. Why are you acting as if Uncle Zumji didn't tell us that we should share with Aunty Panmun's brothers and sister?"

Rit's eyes flew up and met his. So.

Tongzum did not bother to hide his displeasure as he stood up and dug his hands into his pocket for the key. He led the way to the silos.

"She can cook for you. I don't want to eat anything she touches," he said without turning.

He opened the door and stood watching as Rit climbed in and looked over the provisions. She had to squint against the darkness to see. A couple of bags of maize. Beans. Sorghum. Groundnuts. Where had Zumji gotten all this? She had always been curious about the source of his supplies, how he was able to have enough for himself and extra to give out.

Rit reached for the groundnuts. They were in a large metal basin. She wanted to run her fingers through them, feel the coarseness of the shells, hear the way they clicked against each other.

"Don't touch it. You can only use the maize or the beans," Tongzum said. He was looking through the small opening, monitoring her every move.

"Why don't you cook the beans?" Rit asked.

"He doesn't like beans," Tongrot said.

"Do you like beans?"

"Yes."

"Me too."

Rit was bending to get some beans when the idea hit her. She turned to Tongzum. "I saw some bitter leaf growing near the fence. Why don't I make some puk and we can eat the mun with it? But on one condition."

Tongzum said nothing.

"I will also make the mun," Rit said.

Tongzum folded his arms. "I said I'm not eating your food."

Rit shrugged, fetched some maize. She was going to have to teach this boy a lesson. Stupid boy. Daft boy. As if she were his mate. She would have to set some rules, put him in his place. By the time she was done, the keys to the store would be in her possession and anything he wanted would have to pass under the spotlight of her approval.

"How old are you?" Rit asked Tongrot when Tongzum went to fetch water from the well.

"I'm going to be eleven next month. I want to celebrate my birthday, I wish I had a cake."

"What about your brother?"

"He's just fourteen, but he likes to behave as if he's an old man."

So there was a whole year between them. By the time she was done with him, he would be calling her Aunty. Stupid boy.

"What about you?" Tongrot asked.

"Twenty."

"But you don't look like you're twenty."

"Everybody looks smaller than their real age. Like you, you don't look like you're ten, do you?"

Tongrot looked at Rit thoughtfully, as if this were only just becoming clear to her. Rit smiled. She liked her. When all this was over, she would make her take a good hot bath. She could just imagine what her mother would say at the sight of the girl's filthy feet.

"And by the way," Rit said, "your brother didn't make me cry. I just had something in my eyes."

Rit made sure she did everything within watching distance of Tongzum, who was busy preparing his mun. First, she used a large tray to winnow the maize. As she tossed the yellow grains into the air and watched the chaff blow away, she stole a glance at Tongzum. He had paused to watch. Good. She knew she was showing off, that she did not have to throw the maize that high.

While Tongrot ground the maize, Rit went to pluck some bitter leaf and washed it. There was no oil, so she would have to improvise.

"There's some mwir-pet," Tongrot said, her eyes going wide with glee. She ran into the house before Rit could say anything and returned with a large bottle. Rit's heart swelled with joy at the sight of the black pear oil.

Tongzum yelled, "Tongrot, take that back! Uncle Zumji said we shouldn't waste it!"

"We're not wasting it, we're using it," Tongrot shot back.

"We'll only use a little," Rit said with a sweet smile. Tongzum turned away, scowling.

Rit set up a new fireplace and found a pot. On rare occasions, the flame would start on her first attempt, which was what happened now. She made the puk first. She asked for salt, and like a little fairy who made wishes come true, Tongrot ran into the house and returned with salt. When the puk was ready, Rit made the mun. As she stirred the gradually thickening paste, she found it hard to believe that she was about to have an actual meal. A full meal. The golden mun looked so creamy that she dipped a finger into it and brought it to her mouth, relishing the smoothness. She looked up and met Tongzum's gaze. He was eating his mun plain, moving his mouth as if he were swallowing clumps of mud. Rit dished the mun for Tongrot and herself, then the puk. Tongrot dived right in.

"Will you stay with us?" she said, swallowing a hot mouthful.

"You have to eat slowly, Tongrot," Rit said, fighting back a chuckle. She ignored the question and picked up her plate. She put it back down, got a small bowl, and spooned some of the puk into it. As she carried the bowl toward Tongzum, he saw her and froze, eyeing her as though she were approaching with a knife in her hand. Rit offered the bowl to him.

"I said I'm not eating your food."

Rit observed the small metal plate in his hand, the hard, dry mun that looked like it had been left out for a week. She noticed the strain in his face, his clenched jaw, his eyes that now refused to look at her, eyes that were beginning to swim in a strange mist. She was not enjoying this as much as she had thought she would.

"If you change your mind . . ." she said gently, placing the bowl of puk beside him. She did not look his way for the rest of the meal.

When she took the first mouthful, she closed her eyes at the raw pleasure of it. She had never put anything in her mouth that tasted this good. In another time, under different circumstances, she might have turned her nose up at such a meal had her mother placed it in front of her. She might have complained to Panmun that it was the blandest thing she had ever tasted. She might have chosen to go hungry that night. She would have never known, even in a hundred years of living, that a night like tonight was even possible.

Tongrot cleared her plate and asked for more. By the time they were done eating, most of the sun was gone. They began washing up. Tongrot retrieved Tongzum's dishes: there was no puk left in the bowl.

"Is your name just Rit or is it a short form?" Tongrot asked.

"Ritdirnen. But nobody calls me that anymore. Only my mother did."

Rit remembered Nana Ritdirnen then. How she had found her dead in the white chair. Her parents had named her after the now-deceased neighbor. It was the greatest honor they could give her after she had delivered Rit in the bed of their father's pickup, when the vehicle had failed to start and all the phones had died because there had been no power. Rit preferred not to dwell too much on the fact that she had been born in the back of a truck, but it struck her how normal their new reality was becoming: the lack of phones, the lack of electricity. Now even Nana Ritdirnen and her doting, sometimes annoying, presence were no more.

"Where is she?"

Rit looked up at Tongrot. "Who?"

"Your mother?"

"Dead."

"Our father died two days ago. He took rat poison." Everything about Tongrot slowed down as she spoke—her energy, her voice. She paused. "The thing that made him do it. It makes people kill themselves."

"Yes," Rit said, thinking about the rat poison her mother had also used.

"If it makes you want to kill yourself, but you find a way not to kill yourself, then you won't die."

Rit looked at the little girl beside her who was too small for her age. Her hair, copper brown and extra soft from malnutrition, should have been an affront to the eyes and to reason, but it had become such a normal thing. She was stooped over a basin of water, where she rinsed the dishes Rit passed to her. She swirled a bowl through the clear water, running her little hand over it to make sure it was properly rinsed. After she had placed it on the tray among the other clean dishes, she looked up and met Rit's eyes, clearly oblivious to the import of the words she had just spoken.

Tongrot did not want to have a bath. Rit had to threaten that she would leave and never come back and they would all go back to eating plain mun. Grudgingly, she brought a bucket, and Rit poured the hot water.

"Do you have any soap?" Rit asked.

Tongrot shook her head. "I don't remember the last time I saw soap."

Tongrot carried the bucket of hot water to the outdoor bathing area. Her little head appeared just over the low wall as she took off her clothes and began to bathe. Rit turned to find Tongzum sitting on the back steps. She could not make out his eyes in the twilight, but she knew he was looking at her. He stood up and went inside.

After her bath, Tongrot showed Rit around Zumji's house. Tongzum had lit a candle, and they carried it around from room to room. The house had one bedroom, a bare living room that had a couple of worn-out sofas, and an indoor kitchen that was all but empty. The walls, once painted a deep blue, were faded and scratched and dirty. A corner of the ceiling in the living room had caved in partially, making the room look like it was a little out of tilt. The bedroom had one large bed and a thin mattress on the floor. A dirty browned mosquito net hung over the bed from the ceiling. Tongrot said that Zumji had told them he and his father used to sleep in the room together, before his father disappeared.

It was dark and there was nothing to do, so they turned in early. Rit stood in the living room, unsure of where she should sleep. Tongzum passed by with the candle after he had shut the back door.

"You and Tongrot can sleep on the bed, I'll use the mattress." He did not wait for her reply. She followed him into the bedroom.

Later, after Tongzum had turned off the light and Tongrot was sleeping soundly beside her, Rit was still wide awake. Her senses were primed. She was acutely aware of the fact that a strange boy whom she had never met before today was merely inches away from her, sharing this darkness with her. The faraway barking of a dog floated over the silence without disturbing it. She turned in search of a more comfortable position that might help her fall asleep.

"The puk was nice."

Rit knew he had carried those words around in his throat all evening. She also understood it was his way of saying thank you.

"I heard your father died. I'm sorry."

There was a long pause. Rit was afraid she might have said something wrong. Maybe she should not have brought it up at all.

Tongzum said, "I found his body in the kitchen. I did not want Tongrot to see it, so I told her to come here and get something for me. I made her use the front door. Then I buried him behind the house. I don't think the hole was deep enough."

Tongzum was not speaking to her; he was just speaking. If he could see her, would he say what he was saying?

"Tongrot came back; I took her to the grave. I told her what happened. She didn't even cry. She just said the Grey made him do it. That was all she said." Tongzum sniffed loudly. "Uncle Zumji told us you have two brothers. Where are they?"

The question took her unawares. He *was* speaking to her.

"I don't know." She wanted to say something more, something different, but she simply said again, "I don't know."

"Are they older than you?"

"Dunka is older. Panshak is thirteen." She took a breath before continuing. "Panshak left because of me. I drove him away. All he wanted was for me to read his letter, and I drove him away. If anything has happened to him, it's because of me."

She was lashing herself with the words, but she had not earned the right to cry for him. She could cry for the others. But not Panshak. The darkness was making it so easy to say things, things that she would never have said in daylight, or even known that they were there to be said at all. And now she could not stop herself.

"After Panmun left, I was alone. I felt like I was the one who was lost, and nobody could find me. I wanted to be found."

"Our mother was still alive when Zumji found us," Tongzum said. "Tongrot saw him on the street one day and followed him here. He gave her food. He was nice to us. He wanted us to treat him like a big brother. He taught me how to use his traps. He showed me the things he was growing. If he hadn't found us, I think we would have starved to death."

"What were you doing before you met him?"

"My mother and father were both sick. They couldn't take care of us. So I took Tongrot to Nana Kanke's house. Do you know it?"

"It's on the other side of Pilam."

"It was nice at first. I used to go and see how my parents were doing. But strange things began to happen in the house. I didn't like it. We ran away and came back home."

"What kind of strange things?"

Tongzum was quiet for a moment before he replied. "I don't want to talk about it."

Rit heard him turning in the dark. The conversation had ended. She did not know when she had crossed over from wakefulness to sleep, but it seemed like only a few minutes had passed when she felt someone shaking her gently, waking her up.

She opened her eyes. Soft, gray light was coming in through the window. Tongzum stood in front of her.

"I want to show you something," he said.

Tongrot was still sound asleep as they left the room. Rit followed him outside and around the house. There was a chill in the air; the world was drenched in dew. They walked toward a part of the cactus fence that, curiously, had an opening in it that had been concealed by a creeper. The unsuspecting eye would never have noticed it. The leaves of the creeper hung in the doorway like a curtain, and Tongzum moved them aside and passed through. Drops of moisture leaped onto Rit's hair, then her neck. Groggy as she was, it made her feel deliciously alive.

They were in a small clearing about the size of a large room. Rit froze at the sight before her. There were rows and rows of different kinds of vegetables. Tomato vines, tethered to horizontal slats, crept up their stilts. A whole row of cabbages grew next to carrots and lettuce. There were chili peppers and bell peppers, eggplants and squashes.

"Did Zumji do this?" Rit said.

"He said it took him a very long time to get it right. They kept dying at first, but he didn't give up. He said it would work this time. He said we could harvest them in a few weeks. He said don't keep it for yourselves alone, he said always share. And don't let the plants die. I water them every day."

Tongzum turned and looked at Rit. "If we work as a team, I think we can survive. You can cook, I'll hunt and farm. Uncle Zumji even said we could start an animal farm. I'll try."

Tongzum had run out of words, so he smiled awkwardly. The morning light was in his dark, lovely eyes, which were lively with ideas. And passion. Whoever this boy was, Rit knew, she could not have asked for a better companion to brave the uncertain future with. The vegetable garden lying in the arms of the morning, whose light blessed each plant, each leaf, with a blissful halo—it was all a kind of tonic for her heart. She did not know about the future or the past. Did not care. This sight had to be the most beautiful thing she had ever seen.

Tongzum was turning to go when he suddenly stopped. "I think I can help you find your brother."

He led her through Pilam, like the keeper of a lost city, guiding her and showing her secret passages she had never suspected could exist. They would emerge on the other side of the village, and she would find him at last in the belly of a great house, her lost brother, his chest rising and falling. She would see his face, like a waning moon that had made peace with the fact of its dying. She would see his body and the ways it had bent to accommodate the blows of the world. Her heart would shatter against the gossamer of his suffering. And then she would wake him up.

12

ARRIT

Arrit picked out the plastic bowl she usually served the prisoner's meals in. She was about to dish out the food when she paused. Instead, she selected the best plate in the house, Uncle Yilshak's plate, the same one she had just washed, the blue one with the gold twirls that danced across it like spirals of sunlight. She felt compelled by some unknown force to see the prisoner eating off this plate. The idea, and the fact that she would be responsible for it, made her feel powerful and free. Something had happened in the last two days that took her flat understanding of the world and folded it into shapes she had never considered. Otherwise, she would never have said a word to the prisoner, let alone served him like this.

As she carried the prisoner's food to him, Arrit had the hunch that something was about to be upturned if she did not desist. She had been pushing her luck for two days now. She had to stop this nonsense; she had to stop fraternizing with the enemy. She reached the window and passed the plate through it. She opened her mouth to speak quietly. A hand crept out of the darkness and held her, and she released the plate and drew back. There was the crackle of china breaking. He had been standing beside the window.

"I'm sorry I scared you," he said.

Arrit glanced around. Uncle Yilshak still had not returned. Polu had gone out.

"Don't touch me again."

"I'm sorry."

"You broke it."

The clink of ceramic pieces being picked apart came through the window. He placed the broken shards on the windowsill, where she could see them. There were other plates in the set, so it would not be immediately obvious that one was missing. Still, it was bound to come out in the end: Uncle Yilshak sometimes hosted guests for dinner, and he liked these plates for such purposes—unless he bought a new set and forgot about these, which was unlikely to happen since these were barely a month old.

She had some time.

Arrit found a plastic bag and moved the broken pieces into it. Throwing them in the dustbin was not an option. Uncle Yilshak sometimes inspected the trash before it was taken out to ensure that food was not being wasted in his house. She would have to hide the broken plate until the next day and dispose of it on her way to school. She was moving from the window when he spoke.

"Arrit."

Arrit stopped. It was the first time he had used her name in the two days he had been here. He said it softly, as though it too would break if he spoke any louder. Her name on the lips of a stranger. Why did it sound so familiar? She realized she did not know his name. They called him a prisoner, a thief. For all the fear they harbored for the people behind the barricade, this young man seemed . . . normal. In fact, but for the black marks in his eyes, he seemed like any other person. And he must have had a name.

"What's your name?"

"Dunka. My name is Dunka. I have two sisters named Panmun and Ritdirnen, and a brother named Panshak. I have to go back to them."

Arrit stood on the tips of her toes and tried to peer inside the room, but all she saw was the curve of his shoulder where he stood against the wall.

"Panshak. Panmun, Ritdirnen, Panshak. They're waiting for me."

The names were coming out of his mouth in a dazed chant, somewhat slurred, like the words of someone on the precipice of sleep. He was speaking to himself.

"Dunka," Arrit said into the darkness. "Dunka."

He kept on muttering.

Arrit hid the pieces of the broken plate under her mattress. She tried to forget about Dunka and his mumblings. Did the sickness also make you lose your mind? If he truly had family, would they be looking for him now? Had he promised to bring back a cure for them? That was what he had asked Aunty Pagak for. Uncle Yilshak had picked up the bottle she had given Dunka from the ground that day, and Arrit remembered seeing it on the counter in Aunty Pagak's cooking room. The day after, she overheard Aunty Pagak confessing to her husband that it was useless, that she had mixed neem leaves with some baobab powder. Dunka had come all this way for nothing.

Later that evening, she served Uncle Yilshak dinner as he sat with Aunty Pagak in the living room and watched the news. There had been a time when Pilam had been the constant headline. Analysts and scientists and health officials came on to postulate and proffer solutions. Ministers and priests debated the nature of a sickness that seemed to affect the soul itself. Now Pilam, its inhabitants, and the mysterious sickness had become a black hole in the consciousness of the nation.

As Arrit cleared the dinner plates, Uncle Yilshak told his wife he had contacted a scientist in a foreign country, who was interested in conducting extensive tests on a living subject.

"What kind of tests?" Aunty Pagak asked.

125

"All kinds. They may even cut him open and take out vital organs, to see."

"Won't that kill him?"

"If they get what they want in the end . . ." he said, shrugging. "They're willing to pay a lot of money."

Uncle Yilshak explained that the scientist was planning to travel to Pishang and rent a small house, since taking the prisoner out of the country would not be possible.

"How soon will he be here?"

"Next week," Uncle Yilshak said without taking his eyes off the screen.

After she had cleaned the kitchen and gone to bed, Arrit lay awake. Bimorit snored across the room. Hours went by, and try as she might, Arrit could not fall asleep.

She got out of bed and picked up the flashlight Bimorit kept at her bedside. She let herself out through the kitchen door. There had been a power cut, so the compound was unusually dark, which was so much the better. She navigated her way to the guardroom by memory and stood next to the window, black against the darkness of the night. Turning on the flashlight, she directed its beam into the room and received the fright of her life. The prisoner—Dunka—sat on the floor with a long shard of china from Uncle Yilshak's plate. He was working its sharp end into his flesh, digging a hole in his arm. His blood was already staining the floor.

Arrit tore her eyes away, back into the night. She stood there with her heart in her throat. He was killing himself. She had to think of something. She scurried over to the storeroom, where Polu was fast asleep. Once inside the room, she turned on the flashlight and looked around for the house keys. They were on the mattress next to Polu's head, and they jangled softly as she picked them up. Polu was a notoriously deep sleeper—she could have dropped them on his head and he would have been none the wiser.

She opened the door to the guardroom and paused. This was madness. He had a sharp object. He could overpower her, kill her. But he'd had the chance to hurt her two days ago, and all he had done was ask for her name. Emboldened by this, Arrit moved into the room. Dunka took no notice of her as she squatted next to him. Carefully, she reached for the broken ceramic piece. He let her take it out of his hand without a fuss. His forearm bled freely, a steady flow of dark blood from a jagged wound. Arrit closed her eyes and resisted the nausea that attempted to grip her.

Back inside the house, she selected from her trunk a clean white blouse. Aunty Pagak had an entire first aid kit in her bathroom, but it would have been reckless to try to get it. She fetched some water and a bread knife, and when she had placed the things on the floor next to Dunka, she closed the door from inside. Cutting the shirt into several strips, she washed the wound, cleaned out as much of the blood as she could, and then bandaged it with the strips. She made a tourniquet with another strip and tied it around his forearm. Dunka was quiet, still. When she finished, the terror that was creeping up from her belly and into her chest told her to leave, but she ignored it.

For the first time in two days, she took a proper look at him. The way his clothes sagged on his lean frame told her they had once been a perfect fit. His eyes were closed, and he was breathing gently.

"Why did you do that?" Arrit said.

Dunka opened his eyes, looked at her, looked away. His gaze unsettled her, as it had done the first day. The shadow in his eyes was its own presence. It was a void, threatening to rise and swallow her.

"Everybody does it in the end," Dunka said.

"What is it like there? On the other side?"

"There is nothing on the other side. Only ghosts. Isn't that what you want to believe?"

Dunka looked at her again, and again she felt the ground shifting beneath her consciousness. She did not know what she believed, or what she wanted to believe.

"Is it true that the sickness doesn't affect children?"

"I used to be a child."

She fell silent. She began to get up. With some effort, and she noticed this in the cranking of his head, Dunka moved the silence aside.

"Why are you helping me?"

Arrit considered the question and realized it was a mirror. When she saw him sitting by the gate that day as she returned from school, he had seemed defeated, trampled on. After he came in and brandished his knife, where others saw a dangerous armed thief, she saw a frustrated, helpless person who required only a little kindness. She saw herself. Everybody looked down on her because they thought she was provincial, even though it had been seven long years since she had come to Pishang. Because she was slow in comprehending lessons and older than almost everyone in her class, even those who should have been her equals despised her. Her teachers tolerated her at best, and those who demonstrated any goodwill toward her seemed to expect something in return, something she did not wish to give. How many times had she been told that she was beautiful? She knew it was a lie. The people who said it had motives she could not trust, and the people who should have loved her never said it. So it could not be true. This was why she was helping him, why she had served his dinner on that stupid plate.

"I don't know."

"If you want to help me, let me go home."

"I can't. My uncle will kill me."

"I've heard the way he shouts at you."

After her father died, Uncle Yilshak had shown up at their doorstep in need of help in his house, someone he could put through school in return. Before her mother bundled her up and handed her over to him, all within the space of an hour, she explained in vague terms that he

128

was a relative and would take good care of her. Barely a year had passed when Arrit heard that her mother had died from a sudden illness.

"If he was really your uncle, he would never hurt you."

Arrit did not know why Dunka said that, but he had touched a nerve. She turned off the flashlight to hide the tears that were forming, then wiped them away.

She stood and left the guardroom, locking the door behind her. She was halfway to the storeroom, where Polu was still sleeping, when she stopped dead. She was literally holding the keys to another person's freedom. A helpless person. She knew what they were planning to do to him. His family would never know what had become of him. For once in her life, she had the power to do something meaningful. This was about more than dishing food on a plate, more than skulking about and committing small, useless acts of defiance behind Uncle Yilshak's back. This was about a real life. She had real power. How could she just walk away from it?

Arrit unlocked the door to the guardroom again and held it open. "You have to promise."

"What?"

"That you won't ever kill yourself. Promise and I will let you go."

A long, tired sigh came out of the darkness. "I promise."

"Come quickly," she said. "Hurry up."

Dunka followed her to the gate. He walked unsteadily. She unbolted the pedestrian door and stood there, waiting for him to pass through. He turned to her. It was too dark to see his face.

"There is a baobab tree not far from the barricade," Dunka said quietly. "If you walk in a straight line from that tree toward the sunset, you will find a flame tree with a cross marked into it. If you ever have to leave here, wait for me there. I will find you."

Arrit smiled. He could not see it, but she smiled anyway.

Dunka turned and staggered into the night. Arrit locked the door to the guardroom and returned the keys. She did not know how, but she had to find a way to pin this on Polu. She crept back to the room, replaced Bimorit's flashlight, and climbed into bed. Her heartbeat resounded throughout her body. She realized that Bimorit, the eternal snorer, had not been snoring when she entered the room. There was a sudden movement, and the beam of the flashlight fell on her face.

"Where have you been?" Bimorit was standing over her.

"My stomach was upset," Arrit said simply.

Bimorit left the light on her face for a moment longer, then turned and left the room. Arrit tried to rein in her breathing. Her bladder suddenly felt full. And she could smell it—pain. She knew the smell of pain well. She could even summon it at will. It would rise as a cloying sensation from the pit of her stomach, make its way up her throat, and enter her nostrils. And it was always accompanied by the stink of her uncle's sweat. She had been found out. There was no point in staying here any longer and pretending. When Bimorit entered the room again, Arrit shut her eyes against what she knew was coming, willing it to disappear and waiting for it to reach her at the same time. Five minutes or an hour, she could not say how long she stayed like that, but in the end, all that reached her was the sound of Bimorit snoring once again. The grunting sound had never been more precious to her.

It took a while for her panic to subside, and even then, she could not sleep. She finally decided on her plan as the first rays of the sun began to creep into the room like a herald. She would remain in bed, pretend to be sick, and stay home all day. That might throw them off her track. But then, she decided, it would seem too convenient and suspect. She would have to maintain her daily routine and act like everything was normal.

She got up and did her morning chores. As she swept the compound, she stole a glance at the guardroom. Nobody really bothered about the prisoner. Where could he possibly go? If she could just make it out of the house before questions were asked, then she would really stand a chance at getting away with it.

Arrit had a quick breakfast standing in the kitchen.

"Why are you eating so early?" Bimorit asked.

"We have a test. I have to go early to study with my classmates before the teacher comes."

Arrit had finished dressing up and was buckling her school sandals when Bimorit appeared in the doorway.

"Uncle is calling you."

Arrit's throat instantly dried up, yet she did not miss a beat as she stood and followed Bimorit to the living room. She had to appear oblivious. Uncle Yilshak was in his pajamas, his slight belly protruding through the gap between the shirt and waistband. Polu was standing there with an air of irritation about him. They all turned to look at her. No words were spoken, no questions were asked, but her legs began to quiver. The questions buzzed about Uncle Yilshak's eyes like a swarm of angry flies, and her trembling body answered them. The stink of his sweat clambered up her nose, and Arrit knew that something was going to change forever in the next few seconds. As Uncle Yilshak threw himself and all his rage at her, as she bounded for her room, time slowed and she remembered the most memorable and most secret of her scars, a perfect wedge in the small of her back, the way it was formed three years ago as he lifted her clean off her feet and slammed her naked body into the wall, pain distilled to its purest form, entering her back through the protruding nail and scattering inside her body. She remembered the blood that seemed to pour from every orifice and how he had pinned her to the wall and threatened to kill her with his bare hands if she told anyone, the blood she had been forced to clean up afterward—all of it hers, and therefore her fault—before Aunty Pagak returned from her trip. Only after she burst into the room and flung herself at her metal trunk, which she threw open and searched with desperate fingers while her uncle grabbed her legs, attempting to smother her with the fullness of his rage; only after this, and after Dunka's knife was in her hand, did she realize that the killing was going to be done by her. Turning around, slippery as a catfish, she brought the blade through the starched pajamas and into her uncle's side. She felt the metal sink in without resistance. Her uncle's body shuddered in shock, before going still on the floor. She did not know where the strength came from to turn him onto his back so that she was now the one on top as all the blood, this time his, spoiled the floor. Raising the knife high above his chest, she brought it down with firm resolve, and his breast swallowed the blade whole. She did not pause to survey the damage, did not spare a single backward glance at the dying body of the man who had never truly been her uncle, nor at Bimorit, whose screams Arrit had somehow muted in her head, the same Bimorit who had borne witness and kept silent for three years.

A petrified Polu stepped aside as Arrit ran past him. And she ran: through gaps in walls and gaps in fences, gaps between trees and crops, through the gap opening up inside her chest as the implication of killing a man welled up like a maelstrom and filled it. Through the gaps of wanting that had soaked her days.

She ran.

II

BURYING THE DEAD

13

ZUMJI

By the time they reached the top of the mountain, it was too dark to keep going. The headlights of the rickshaw had been smashed in the ambush. Zumji parked the rickshaw behind a boulder off the road, where they spent the night. He cleared the back seat of their cargo and Panmun stretched out across it, and then he curled up on the ground on the only blanket left. The air on the mountain was cooler, and he was grateful for the heat that persisted in waves from the surrounding lowland. He barely slept.

In the morning, he inspected the vehicle, surveying the damage. A good swath of the plastic hood had been ripped away, partially exposing the metal ribs that were like curved beams in the roof of the rickshaw. There were dents in the back. The side mirrors were missing. The windshield was nothing but a gaping hole. At least none of it would stop the rickshaw from taking them to where they needed to go. Zumji still did not understand what had happened back there, why the children had attacked them. He sensed there was a link between the original owner of the rickshaw and those children—how else could one explain the wound in the man's belly? But he would never understand why they had done it. And he had no wish to.

They had a quick breakfast of groundnuts and honey, with Panmun doing most of the eating—she needed it more than he did. They drove throughout the day across the mountain, pausing for breaks to stretch and relieve themselves. He had never come this way before. The road was rough and treacherous without cease, but forward movement was all they had. He pushed the rickshaw on, but gently, mindful of her in the back seat, mindful of the things she carried in her, one precious without question, the other a thing of death. Life and death. She carried life and death. A part of him felt that if they got far away from Pilam as quickly as possible, the Grey might decide to leave her alone. The unexpected, alarming joy of knowing he was going to be a father was tainted by the knowledge that this other thing was there, twisting like a serpent, and he hated the Grey all the more for it.

As the day began to unwind, the wind carried fwep fwan butom, the scent of the promise of rain, earthy and fresh, across the starved fields, through the gaping windshield, and into his nostrils. Everything else faded a notch, from the rumble of the rickshaw's engine to the sight of the valley bathed in the shadow of the mountain that they were descending. Even his awareness of her presence behind him and the things she carried receded into the background as the scent took over his senses. He closed his eyes briefly and took it in.

When he opened them again, the rooftops of Pigika, the next village, were visible in the valley below. The sun was beginning to set on the other side of the mountain, creating the shadow that bore down on Pigika. The shadow reminded him of the sickness. It seemed monstrous and unrelenting and unassailable. He glanced around at Panmun: she had fallen asleep, leaning against the cargo that filled half of the back seat. A certain shell of fragility had formed over her in his eyes since he learned that she was pregnant, and when his attention was taken away from her, it was quick to return, like whiplash, for fear that something may have cracked the shell. When they were on level ground, Zumji pulled over next to a very large rock that was not far from the road.

Looking at the sky, he estimated that it would be dark in less than two hours. They needed a place to spend at least a night so he could scope out the village. He was not comfortable going into Pigika without some kind of assurance that they would be safe.

Panmun had woken up. She rubbed her eyes and looked around. When her gaze landed on Zumji, who was watching her, they smiled softly at each other. No matter how many times he looked at her, he would never get used to the way the Grey hovered over her eyes, a shadow quietly eating her up. He could not believe that just the day before, he had thought he could leave her, that he could live without her. What a fool he had been. A fool and a coward.

"Where are we?" she said.

"Near Pigika."

"Is that the place you mentioned?"

Zumji nodded. He pointed at the rock. "I'm going to find a place we can sleep. Wait here."

"I'm coming too."

Panmun looked resolute, her face straight and matter-of-fact. Zumji was afraid she would overexert herself on the climb, but the alternative was leaving her here by herself, unattended. He knew the better choice. He also knew there was no point arguing with her.

They entered the bushes, stepping over dead grass and shrubs and little rocks. Zumji could still smell it. His fwep fwan butom, earth and water, mixed together for the first time, a harbinger of each rainy season. It was pleasure and torment at the same time because he wanted it to rain—needed it—but the sky did not hold the same promise as the air. It had rained somewhere far off, most likely to the east, the direction they were going in, hence the smell. Pigika lay between them and that place. Though he could not say where this place was, it became, to his mind, their destination. The place where the rain was. If there were a way to bypass Pigika altogether, he would have.

He made a path along the edge of the great rock where it rose out of the ground, circumventing it and climbing higher as the ground rose. He looked back periodically to ensure that Panmun was keeping up. It would be easy to lose one's footing and tumble down the slope. He finally came to a gap where another large rock rose overhead to meet the first one, creating a partially enclosed cavern. It was not perfect, but it would have to do. Zumji inspected the space, checking for scorpions or snake nests. He told Panmun to wait there and went back to the rickshaw to get their things.

The rickshaw was too exposed where he had parked it, but there was not much plant cover around. He pushed it farther in from the road, then draped a large sheet of tarpaulin over it. The covering had a faded brown color that would make it blend into the surroundings more easily. Someone coming along the road would have to look hard in that direction to know something was there.

Carrying their blankets, a candle, some cured pork, his pistol, and a large gourd of water, he made his way back to the cave. It was already twilight by the time he reached it. Panmun, who was curled up on the ground, sat up and watched him arrange their things around the space. He lit the candle and prepared their bed, and they sat against the wall, leaning against each other and drawing warmth from each other and basking in each other's silence. He cut the pork into pieces with his knife, and they ate quietly.

When she was asleep and his heart pulsed with gratitude that she had not asked him about where they were headed, he stood by the cave opening and looked out toward Pigika, marked in the darkness by just a few house lights. He was banking on the size of the village, hoping that its smallness would make their passage through it easier. There were no stars, because deep clouds rising in the eastern sky had blocked them from view. Zumji could still smell it, his fwep fwan butom. It was beginning to look like rain, and Zumji could feel the cool breeze. He snuggled up next to her, ensured she was properly covered, and closed his eyes.

When he woke up, he knew he had overslept. Panmun was standing by the entrance, silhouetted against the day. He kissed her without a word, then looked out at Pigika in the distance under the clear sky. The fwep fwan butom had vanished. Heat from the sun bounced against the landscape and on them as they stood at the mouth of the cave.

"I'm going to scout the village," he said. "We have to make sure it's safe."

He looked at her. "How are you feeling?"

"I'm fine."

She smiled and he saw through it, right down to her worry. But he did not know the thing that was worrying her, if it was not the Grey.

"Are you worried about the sickness?"

Panmun shook her head.

"Is it the baby?"

She looked at him, then shook her head again. "I said I'm fine."

"You're not fine."

She made an exasperated sound with her tongue and went inside the cave. She sat down and drank some water. Zumji knew to leave her alone for now. Hopefully, by the time he was back, her mood would have improved. He tucked the pistol and his paring knife into his waistband, pulled on an old leather shirt, and told her he would see her later.

He decided to check on the rickshaw first to be sure it was safe. When he followed the bend around the rock and the rickshaw came into view below him, he saw a man standing beside it, looking inside. The tarpaulin cover was lying on the ground. Zumji retreated and ducked, then peered around the side of the rock. The man was pulling things out of the vehicle and arranging them on the ground. He was dressed like a hunter, with a sleeveless jacket made of animal hide that hung open on his body, revealing a sturdy chest and long, toned arms. There was a long musket slung over his shoulder. When he was done, he inspected the haul on the ground. Zumji recognized his sacks: one with the animal pelts, one with his watermelons, and the other two with the guzuk and beans. They were still linked in pairs with the thick ropes he had used two days before to carry them. That was all the food they had. He watched helplessly as the man placed the yoke over his neck and hoisted the sacks away.

Zumji's first instinct was to get Panmun and leave. But if they had no food, they would be at the mercy of a hostile world that would kill them the first chance it got. Their survival out there depended on them being self-sufficient. Zumji allowed the man a head start of a couple of minutes before following. He crossed the road and entered the bushes on the other side. Moving silent and unseen was no difficult thing for him, and it helped that the man carried a heavy load that caused him to lumber through the bush, making him easy to track.

The man looked over his shoulder every now and then, and Zumji would duck out of sight or lie on the ground. They were heading gradually in the direction of Pigika. The man would stop at intervals, inspecting hidden traps on the ground or in trees. He picked up a couple of dead rabbits along the way. This stranger was Zumji's fellow woodsman, a colleague, a kinsman of nature and trade. They should be allies, not adversaries.

After some time, they came to a small clearing that looked like a sort of camp. There was what appeared to be a fireplace with a couple of large, blackened pots. A bloodied patch of ground, which Zumji assumed to be a slaughtering and quartering area, was off to one side under a mango tree. There was also a small hut made from sticks, out of which another man emerged. This man was younger, about Zumji's age, and shirtless. He collected the rabbits, and they spoke in low voices. Zumji could not make out their words, but he knew they were speaking about the sacks, which now sat on the ground, waiting to be inspected.

They looked at the pelts first and ran their hands across the different furs. After they had gone through everything, they took the sacks

140

inside the hut. When they reemerged, the younger man was wearing a red shirt. They closed the door to the hut and ventured off into the bushes, each of them clutching his musket with one arm and swinging a cutlass idly in his free hand.

Zumji waited until they had disappeared from view and the sounds of their footfalls had faded into the trees. He opened the door of the hut. It was larger than it looked from outside. His sacks were on the ground against one wall, and there were other things in the hut. Stacks of firewood. A bed of reeds. Pieces of clothing hanging from a nail. Peering through the tiny window to make sure no one was coming, he inspected the room, having no intention of taking anything that was not his—until he saw the large bottle hidden between the bed and the wall. The liquid inside looked like water, but he knew it was not. The bottle was halfway empty. Zumji picked it up, unscrewed it, and took a whiff. Gin. He and his father would drink from the same bottle late into the night while they sat outside and smoked meat and talked about everything except his mother. Even alcohol did not have the power to make his father forget himself and speak about his dead wife. Zumji relished the faint citrus scent, then screwed the bottle shut and returned it to its spot beside the bed. It was tempting, but he was no thief.

He hoisted the sacks and left the hut, hurrying along but planting his feet lightly, quietly, on the dead grass. He had gone a small distance when the first shot rang. He dropped the sacks and threw himself behind the closest tree. There was another shot, and then another. He pulled out his pistol. It was a revolver that had been sold to his father by the itinerant blacksmith, Munkiwe, who used to come to Pilam once a month, shortly before his father's disappearance. All its bullets were intact, because it had never been fired. Zumji primed the weapon and looked around the side of the tree. The younger man was running toward him with his cutlass raised. He was already so close, moving silently, as though carried by air. Zumji raised the pistol and shot him clean in the chest when he was only ten feet away. His body and the cutlass he carried and the hunting musket that was still slung against his body crashed to a halt at Zumji's feet.

Zumji stood over the body and looked at the dead man's face. He was about to look around for the second man when there was another shot close by. He felt the impact in his abdomen, a sharp pain that made him double over. When he raised his head, the second man was also charging forward with his cutlass. He threw it while he was still yards away. Zumji barely stepped out of the path of the spinning blade. It spiraled past and thudded into the ground nearby. The man was still coming, this time with a knife in hand. Zumji raised his revolver, aimed at a man's head for the second time in as many days, and shot. The faces of Mister and the ghost that had been following him swam before his eyes.

When the man was still, Zumji turned him over with his foot and looked at his face. He had felt nothing when he killed the first man; he felt nothing now. Their faces and the glare of their dead eyes and the bullet hole in the cheek of the older man and the still-warm bodies that had been pulsing with life and malevolence mere seconds before registered no meaning to him. He felt nothing but a sense of rightness with the two dead men at his feet, men who had stolen his lifeblood and had been about to steal his life. He could not bring himself to imagine what they might have done to Panmun. He felt around the puncture in his stomach. The pain had subsided some, and when he looked at the wound, it did not seem too serious. He felt rather fine. When he tried to carry the sacks, he found he could manage.

He crossed the dirt road, placed the sacks back inside the rickshaw, and rushed to the cave. There was no time to lose. Things were going wrong because they had wasted time when they should have powered through Pigika, consequences be damned. The farther they were from Pilam, the better things would be. Panmun was asleep, curled into a ball. Before he woke her up, he looked at his shirt and realized blood had soaked right through it. She must not see it, must not know that he was wounded. He tore his stained shirt into strips, tied one strip over the wound to stem the bleeding, and pulled on another shirt over it. As he was finishing, Panmun stirred awake.

"You're back," she said groggily.

"We have to go."

"Is it safe?"

"Yes," he said.

They carried their things back to the rickshaw and loaded up. As they pulled into the road, Zumji felt a sharp pain from his wound. The possibility that it would get worse in time occurred to him, and then precipitated his next thought. He glanced at the fuel gauge and decided the idea was worth pursuing, even if only for a few minutes. He pulled over and turned the engine off. He looked at Panmun.

"Come to the front," he said.

Panmun frowned. "Why?"

"Just come and sit here. I want to teach you how to drive."

"Why?"

Zumji felt a prick of impatience. He had forgotten how stubborn she could be.

"Do you trust me?" he said.

"Zumji, I'm not a child. If you want me to do something, you have to explain why. Why do I have to learn how to drive if you can already drive?"

Zumji swallowed his irritation and said slowly, "If anything happens to me, I want you to be able to keep going."

Panmun held his gaze in the silence that stretched until it was too thin, until it almost snapped, the Grey heavy in her eyes. He tried his best to seem normal, to seem like he did not have a bullet that was lodged in his waist and going deeper with each move he made.

"Nothing is going to happen to you," she said at last.

"You have to trust me, Pan. Please."

Panmun stepped out of the back, and Zumji moved aside for her to sit. It still amazed him that, based only on his prior experience with riding his father's old motorcycle, he had figured out how to drive this thing. He showed her the controls, the levers, the buttons, the gears. Panmun watched without a word while Zumji prayed it was making sense to her, because there was no time. They had to be on the other side of Pigika by nightfall. Someone was bound to find the dead men soon. He wanted to have a good distance between them and this place by then.

"Do you understand?" he said.

Panmun blinked. "I think so."

"Can you start it the way I showed you?"

Panmun pressed the ignition. When the rickshaw was growling, Zumji told her to put it in gear and drive. Panmun squeezed the throttle and the rickshaw roared, but it did not move.

"You didn't release the clutch," Zumji said.

Panmun tried again. The rickshaw jerked forward and stopped suddenly. A few more attempts and they started moving slowly along the road.

"Remember to steer it," Zumji said as they came dangerously close to the bushes.

Panmun turned the steering head left and right, using her shoulders, her whole body, as she negotiated the bends.

"Go faster," Zumji said.

The rickshaw screamed as Panmun pushed it forward.

"You have to change gears."

She kept going. The sound of the engine did not let up.

"Have you changed your gear?"

Panmun did not respond. Her eyes were fixed on the road ahead.

"Panmun, you have to change the gear."

"How do I do it?" Her voice was slightly high pitched, as though she were holding her breath.

"Use the clutch."

She tried.

"You have to hold it down."

The vehicle was going faster, screaming louder.

"No, no, not like that . . ."

Panmun released the controls, and the rickshaw slowed down and stopped. She buried her face in her hands.

"I want to go home."

Zumji put an arm around her shoulder and tried to hold her, but she shrugged him off and came down from the rickshaw. She stood in the road and looked at him. The Grey was staring at him too, mixing with her tears and her anger, shimmering in the afternoon sun.

"Let's go back to Pilam."

"We can't."

"I want to go back."

"I said we can't. We have to keep going."

Zumji's blood was beginning to boil. Did she understand what she was asking? Had she chosen to forget what it had cost to get out in the first place? She was not in her right mind. Maybe it had something to do with the pregnancy. And the Grey. They were messing with her emotions, making her erratic. Now he had a bullet in his gut, and she wanted them to go back to hell.

"Get in, Panmun," he said quietly.

He got in, started the engine, and stared at the empty road ahead leading to Pigika, to their future, to the place where the rain was. His fwep fwan butom—his promise of rain that had sat in his nose and reached up into his brain like a mighty cooling salve—was gone, all trace of it erased. He refused to look at her. Why was she choosing to betray him? They had dreamed up a future together that was free of the Grey. They had escaped when nobody else had managed to. They were going to have a child. And she wanted them to go back.

Panmun climbed in, and Zumji kicked the rickshaw into gear and sped off. He glanced down at the spot where his shirt concealed the bullet wound—a little blood was beginning to stain it from underneath. The pain was getting worse. He drove on, and neither of them said a word to each other. Buildings sprang up around them, and just like that, they were in Pigika. Zumji had expected it to be more difficult. He thought there might be a wall or barrier of some sort, like the one at Pishang. There were people going about their day, living their lives. The village was small enough that he was sure it was the same straight road that ran from one end to the other, like a spine. All he had to do was stay on it and get through without drawing attention.

But people were noticing. They were stopping in the middle of their business and staring. A man who was bent over the open engine of his car straightened up and watched them. A girl of about ten who was walking along the road with a small basket of tomatoes on her head stopped and watched them. Eyes were popping up everywhere, watching them. Only then did the state of the rickshaw dawn on Zumji as something that screamed for attention. He glanced around at Panmun. She had pulled on her sunglasses and sat looking out at the village as though it were the most boring thing she had ever seen.

A tiny gas station appeared on the right. It had a small shack and only one pump: a dirty, rusted cuboid that looked like it was about to keel over any moment from exhaustion. They were running out of fuel. Zumji had already used up the gasoline he got from Mister's warehouse. If there was gasoline to be got here and they passed it, they would risk becoming stranded. Making a split-second decision, Zumji pulled into the lot and stopped beside the pump. He could make out faded digits in the pump gauge, arranged in rows of four. A couple of digits were lopsided, and there was an empty space between them that looked like a missing tooth. A bare-chested teenager came out from the shack. He stared at the rickshaw uncertainly for a moment.

"Do you have gas?" Zumji asked.

The boy nodded. He pulled out the pump nozzle and began to fill up the rickshaw. While the machine hummed and coughed up fuel, he stared at Zumji, stared at the rickshaw.

Zumji tried to think of what he would do next. He had no money to pay for the gas. He was also feeling slightly faint, and his legs felt heavier, like they were thinking of giving way under him. He wiped his forehead and placed a hand against the rickshaw to support himself.

"Where are you coming from?" the boy said.

"Are you normally this nosy?"

The boy smiled, his face alive with mischief—but his eyes did not smile along. "This vehicle was here a few days ago. But someone else was driving it."

Zumji stared back at him, determined not to give away any sign of his growing distress. The boy's eyes traveled down to his waist, and Zumji followed them. Blood was now plain on his shirt.

"You're from Pilam, aren't you?" the boy said.

It was an accusation. He pulled the nozzle out and stepped away from Zumji and the vehicle. The fear coming off him was palpable, as pungent as the gas fumes. As a reflex, Zumji reached behind him for the revolver that was tucked into his waistband and pulled it out. The boy saw the weapon, turned, and ran off down the street.

Zumji suddenly felt tired of killing and death and all the things that it dragged along in its wake. And shame like he had never known—it covered him, made him feel dirty and queasier than he already was. He had just pulled a gun on a child, and hatred was rushing like a rapid through his body, filling his veins with an intoxicating promise of violence. He looked at Panmun, ensuring that the front of his shirt was not turned toward her so that she would not see the blood. She was watching him, clearly waiting to see what he would do next. Was this what he was becoming? Was this the price of escaping Pilam, what it would cost to stay one step ahead of a world that would never understand them? A world that would always hate them?

Zumji noticed that the boy was leading a group of men toward them. They were armed with long things, sharp things, burning things. The boy pointed. Zumji returned his weapon and got back into the rickshaw. He tried to start it, but it only sputtered and stopped. He tried again, glancing around at the approaching men. They were hurrying forward with their cutlasses and flames. Someone had hoisted a tire on one shoulder. The group was growing, billowing into a mob. Panmun kept looking over her shoulder at them. Her chest rose and fell rapidly; she was hyperventilating.

The rickshaw finally coughed to life, and Zumji made the engine scream. He turned it out of the lot and in the opposite direction, toward the mountain and Pilam and away from the mob and the place where the rain was. Someone threw his cutlass, and it clanged loudly on the exposed ribs of the rickshaw's roof and bounced off. Panmun squealed. The voices were shouting and cursing behind them, but they fell gradually away. Panmun was crying now without pause, gulping great amounts of air.

She had been right, and he should have listened to her. Their place was in Pilam. The world would never accept them. He had insisted on having his way, bringing her so close to death in the process. For that, he would never come close to forgiving himself.

When Pigika had fallen behind and there were no longer houses, only bushes and dried fields and rocks reaching away, Zumji parked and turned around. He held Panmun until her cries had subsided and she was calm once again. She wiped her face with the backs of her hands.

"I'm sorry," Zumji said.

Panmun nodded. They kissed long and hard. Her tears were salty on his lips when they parted.

As he drove, his strength ebbed away. His vision went from clear to fuzzy to clear. The pain in his abdomen was getting worse, getting harder to ignore, but he did not stop and the rickshaw did not falter from its path. He thought about his mother and the life she had lived and the death she had died as she brought him into the world and how his living, breathing body was the only proof that remained of those two things ever happening.

14

RIT

The children had pointed her in the direction of Panshak's room, saying very little with their lips but too much with their eyes. Something had happened, and Panshak had been smack in the center of it. When she woke him up, he sat up and looked at her. When she put her arms around his neck, he did not hug her back.

He asked to go home. Not "home" like the place where the people who loved him were, no, nothing like that. She was sure he meant the house their father had built. The house with the roof that would float away if you removed the rocks. The house with the many empty rooms because all the people who should have filled them were gone. That was where they took him.

On the way, Panshak kept talking. He ignored Tongzum but pointed out random things along the way to Rit, commenting on how nice or odd they looked. He asked Rit if she remembered when they had been chased by Baba Gopi's dogs after they tried to steal his mangoes. Rit watched her brother as he laughed at the memory, a part of her holding back because she was not convinced. Yes, Panshak was usually like this, talkative and playful, but she could not reconcile this energy with the boy she had found asleep on that strange bed, in that strange house.

When they got home, Rit went inside with Panshak while Tongzum waited outside. Returning to the house felt to her like she was walking backward, regressing, growing smaller and younger. Inside his room, Panshak curled up on the bed and stared at her through wide eyes. He fell quiet again and suddenly seemed tired, as though he had just become sedated.

"Are you going with him?" he said.

"You can come too. There's food there."

"I'm staying here."

That same wave of annoyance she had felt the last time they were together surged in her. But her memory of what had happened in the kitchen that day was still fresh. She said, "I'll bring some food later."

He seemed to have gone back to sleep before she left the room. She shut the door behind her and was glad to be out of the house. She made dinner and brought it back to him, escorted by Tongrot. He was still asleep. After putting the food down, she shook him awake. It took some effort, but he finally sat up and ate. Tongrot stood by the door and watched silently. There was so much Rit wanted to ask him, this boy who seemed to have grown old in a matter of weeks. What had he seen? What had he done? He finished his meal and lay back down. When Rit told him she would come back in the morning, he barely acknowledged it.

"Is he sick?" Tongrot asked on the way home.

"I don't know," Rit said. But for the fact that his eyes were as clear as clean water, she might have concluded that the Grey had gotten him.

She woke up early the next morning and began to pound groundnut in the kitchen. Her mother would have been proud of her for getting up so early in the morning to begin housework. The groundnut grew softer as she worked, a bit more compliant. Soon, she would be able to pour it into a pot of boiling water without it leaving lumps everywhere. It was her first attempt at making groundnut puk since she moved to this house. It was going to be perfect—she was not a child anymore who could not even make a decent pot of puk. Up, down, up, down the pestle went. As she brought it up again, she heard shuffling feet and looked at the door. Her dead older brother was standing there in the doorway, looking at her. The pestle struck the lip of the mortar and tipped it over, spilling pulverized groundnut on the floor. It slipped from her fingers and rolled away with a clang. The ghost of her brother stepped into the room and said her name. Still, she did not move. He came up to her. His eyes were dark with the Grey. A dirty bandage was wrapped around his forearm. When he touched her face, she realized she was crying because his hand came away glistening. He took her in his arms, hiding her face in his clothes. The smell of sweat and grime that permeated his clothes filled her with a pure molten joy. It seemed like all she had to do was blink or cough and the vision would dissipate. But it was true: she was receiving another brother of hers back from the dead. She buried her face deeper into his body, ignoring the stink that rolled off him, holding him tightly while they stood on the carpet of groundnut powder, lest he slip away again, this time failing to return.

Before she followed Dunka home, she looked in the bedroom. Tongrot and Tongzum were still sleeping. It had been only two nights, but the three of them had become a single unit in her mind. She and Tongrot still shared the bed, while Tongzum slept on the floor. Last night, as they were turning in, Rit had been about to point out that the bed was big enough for the three of them, but something held her back. She could not say what it was. She simply knew that it was not the sort of thing she should say to a boy. Her mother certainly would not have approved.

She walked behind Dunka, watching him closely. She had to be sure that he was the same person. And he did seem unchanged, talking only when he had to, unlike Panshak, who could not bear a moment of silence. Whoever that person was that she had fed last night, it had not been her little brother, never mind his efforts to seem like he was fine.

They found the impostor already awake, sitting quietly on the bed. He watched them through Panshak's eyes. When they asked how he was doing, he responded with Panshak's voice, smiling. He was at it again, trying to seem fine when Rit just knew something had changed. She sat beside him while Dunka stood in the middle of the room. He looked like he had a few things to say. Rit had no memory of being in the same room with all her siblings like this—well, nearly all of them.

Dunka began. "We should stay together from now on. Don't leave the house alone."

Rit frowned at the words. Could it be that this was another impostor pretending to be Dunka? To start with, her older brother had never cared what any of them did, or where they went. They had barely seen him around the house since their parents' deaths months ago. Now here he was, summoning rules out of thin air, belting out instructions, when they had all found a way of getting by in his absences.

"We thought you were dead." The words escaped her before she realized it. Her voice was shaking with restrained rage. She looked at Panshak. They were both watching her, waiting for her to say what was on her mind. She corrected herself: "I thought you were dead. Or don't you think you owe us an explanation?"

There was a tenderness in Dunka's eyes. Mixed with the Grey, it made it difficult for her to blame him. She resented him for it. He took his time telling them how he had crossed the barricade and gotten caught. He had pauses in which he seemed to consider the right words to use before saying them. When he told them about how he had been locked in a dark room for two nights, Rit's body shook from the effort of keeping herself together. He seemed so small, reduced, her older brother. There had been a time when he carried himself with a swagger and confidence that had made even her discover a little reverence for him. He had been so sure of himself. Her eyes fell once again upon the bandage around his arm. She felt no need to ask what had caused it—it seemed such a normal part of the scenery. Wounds, dead bodies, and gaunt houses had lost their power to surprise. This was their life now, this blood, dirt, and hunger.

"Where's Panmun?" Dunka said without warning. Fear climbed into his eyes as he waited for an answer. When Panshak looked at her, Rit realized that they both knew the answer. But Panshak did not say anything. It seemed that if he had his way, he would never utter another word again.

"She left with Zumji," Rit said, wiping away her tears.

"Who told you that?" Dunka said.

"She did."

Dunka was quiet for a moment. "We have to stay together," he said, and went out of the room.

Rit sat with her eyes on the floor. The question she had buried under her tongue since they brought Panshak back from that house was still there. She moved it around her mouth, unsure whether it was a good moment to ask it. He had reclined on his back and was staring at the ceiling.

"What happened, Panshak?"

He looked at her, met her eyes.

"Where?" he said.

"Back at that house."

His gaze did not falter, but Rit was no fool. She could see his throat undulating as he swallowed. He shifted his jaw from side to side and took his eyes away.

"I saw the body by the tree." This was treacherous ground she was treading, that much she knew. Because he could turn on her. "Did you . . ."

She could not complete the question, but she could not get that image out of her head either. Not the twisted limbs, or the bloodied head, caved in like a rotten watermelon, or the stick with the bloody, rounded end. The fact that her little brother had something to do with it. Her brother, who had manhandled her once upon a time and tossed her on the kitchen floor as if she were a doll. Where had all that strength—all that rage—come from? None of it seemed native to his skinny body or his gentle spirit. Would she ever truly forget that?

Her questions did not end there. What were they all becoming? She had not considered her life beyond any present moment, her life as an object that could be a receptacle for so much meaning. What would it amount to? Where was it leading? A dagger of sunlight reached across the room, cleaving it in two. Maybe it was best to not ask so many questions. She might not like the answers. She got up and left the room.

Dunka was in the backyard, his head bent under the bonnet of their father's pickup truck. When she approached, she saw that he was looking helplessly at the vehicle's grungy entrails. He turned to her.

"Ritdirnen, we have to stay together. This is your home."

"You all left. I stayed here and you all left. I was in this house by myself."

She bit down hard on the diatribe that was so ready to erupt from her chest. Dunka was still freshly returned from death. Harsh words might send him back or make him disappear. She would have said that this house had stopped being her home the morning she woke up and it was empty. That home was not the place where you starved to death, alone. Simply put, home, to her, had become the place where there was not just food, but also people. They did not even have to be people you loved—they just had to be people. Perhaps because she knew firsthand that hunger and loneliness, experienced together, formed the worst kind of misery.

"I'll bring food later," Rit said as she walked away.

Back at Zumji's house, Tongrot was playing outside. She ran up to Rit as she approached.

"We were worried," she said.

"I went home," Rit said. "Where's Tongzum?"

"He went to check his traps."

They looked in the garden and watered it. Rit checked the watermelons. Tongzum had said they could harvest them soon, in a matter of days. The last time she had bitten into the red flesh of a watermelon was . . . she had no memory of it. She remembered the body by the tree and the caved-in head and decided not to think any more about watermelons. After the garden, they cooked the day's meal. She and Tongzum had agreed that until they were certain they could grow their food from scratch without any difficulties, they would restrict themselves to only one meal a day.

When the meal was ready, Rit took some back to her parents' house. Dunka was in their father's room. Or his room. She had to stop thinking in past terms. This was now her brothers' house. And this room, with its big bed and table and books and all kinds of junk, was now Dunka's room. She placed the bowls of food, stacked like the floors of a building, on the table. Dunka watched her. He was sitting on the edge of the bed. The small crease in his brow told her he had something heavy on his mind.

When she was by the door, she said, "Will you give Panshak his food? I don't want to wake him up."

"She's here," Dunka said.

"Who?"

"The girl who helped me escape."

"Where?"

"She's sleeping in Panmun's room."

"Why is she here?"

"She was by the flame tree. I think she had to come here because of me. Because she got into trouble."

Rit stood there, frowning. There was plenty about the world she did not know, but she understood this much: nobody on the other side of that barricade cared about them. If one of them had crossed to come and live here, there had to be some deep-seated motive that was not obvious to them. No one in their right mind would choose a life like this.

Back at Zumji's house, as they ate dinner in the twilight in their customary place outside the kitchen, Tongrot did most of the talking. She mostly spoke about how her father used to bring her sweets every time he went out, before the Grey had come. She asked Rit and Tongzum if they remembered what sweets and biscuits tasted like. Rit said yes, but Tongzum did not answer. He and this new Panshak were alike in that way. However, she had sensed in the two days since she had begun to live there that Tongzum may have been born that way. Which was why she did not worry too much when he was a bit unresponsive.

"Can you describe it?" Tongrot said.

"What's the sweetest thing you remember tasting?" Rit said.

Tongrot thought for a moment. "The honey."

Tongzum had brought home some honeycomb yesterday, along with a few stings on his face.

"That's exactly how it tastes, but it feels harder in your mouth," Rit said. Of course, she did not remember how sweets tasted. She remembered none of those things, like biscuits, bubble gum, and sweet juices that you sucked from a pouch through a tiny straw. She remembered them as things that had existed before, and she remembered what they looked like, but she did not remember what they were like in her mouth.

When the conversation dwindled in the gathering dusk, Rit said, "I have a question." She did not know why she announced it like that. Even Tongzum looked up.

"What would you do if you met someone from the other side of the fence?"

Tongrot said, "I'll beat them so hard they'll never come back here again," and Rit smiled.

But when Tongzum said, "I'd kill them," she knew he was not talking tough. He was leaning forward with his elbows on his knees, with his shoulders rounded and his back hunched. Many years ago, when their lives were still normal lives, filled with normal things, Rit had watched a wildlife documentary about lions. A lion had scattered a group of lionesses who had made a kill—she did not remember what animal it was. The lion ate his fill. When he was done, he did not get up. He remained there, crouched over the carcass, panting hard with blood around his mouth. At that precise moment, of all the things Tongzum could have reminded Rit of, it was the lion that came to her mind.

Later, when Tongrot was asleep beside her, Rit spoke into the darkness of the room. Tongzum was a difficult sleeper, stirring at the smallest sounds. She knew he stayed awake deep into the night because she would wake up sometimes to the sounds of someone sniffing and crying as silently as one is able to cry. When she spoke in the dark, she knew he was listening.

"Do you want me to stay here or go back home?"

There was only quiet, but she knew an answer was coming as surely as she knew that if she called down an empty corridor, her voice would echo back.

"So your other brother is back?"

"Dunka. Yes."

"You want to leave?"

Rit swallowed hard before saying, "I don't mind staying here."

"Do whatever you want to do."

Of course she would do whatever she wanted. She did not need his permission. She was only checking. But what was she checking for? An excuse to leave? Or to stay? Did she even know what she wanted? In her head, the conversation was not over. She had more to ask, to say. More to check for, even if she did not know what she was checking for. And she had to make use of this darkness, and of Tongrot's slumber—the privacy and convenience that both afforded her. When she closed her eyes and opened them, however, it was morning and Tongzum's bed was empty.

He was outside, sorting through the traps at the skinning station. They clanked and clinked as he picked them out, inspecting them. He was still getting accustomed to them. In the last three days, he had not caught anything.

"What does that one do?" she said, taking him by surprise.

He was holding a long wire that had been twisted around itself. He looked at the object uncertainly for a moment. "It's a snare," he said at last.

"How many traps have you laid so far?"

"About three. I'll add more today."

"Did he teach you how to use them?"

"They're simple to use. Nobody has to teach me anything."

The edge in his voice told her to cease with the questions and leave him be. She went back into the kitchen, thinking that she should make something special today, considering that they had a guest. Maybe the beans? But she would wait until she met this girl first. If she was agreeable enough, Rit would make the best beans that anyone in Pilam had ever eaten since the Grey came—even if Tongzum did not like beans. This was not a time for turning one's nose up at a meal. It would be her way of saying thank you to someone who had saved her brother's life. But she had to get to the bottom of why she had done it first—and why she was here.

15

ARRIT

She did not know how she found the flame tree at sunset, nor how long she had been lying at its foot before he found her. She may have fallen asleep once or twice. She remembered neither walking nor being carried to the house. Her memories of what happened between the house she had fled from and the house she had fled to were entwined in strips of blackness. But she remembered the blood on her body, encrusted into a second layer of skin. When he brought her bathing water, Dunka explained that there was no soap. She used only her hands and water to scrub and scrub. Even now, a whole day later, she still felt like she had blood in the corners of her body, corners she did not know how to reach.

Now she lay on the bed and thought that her new room was too big. Not just in the physical sense, but also in its significance. The brown paper ceiling was not like the pristine whiteness in Uncle Yilshak's house when she looked up in the bedrooms or the living room. Even in the corner she had slept in, that whiteness had greeted her every time she woke up. But it had never been hers. This brown paper, however, held up by a lattice of crisscrossing twine, it was all hers. At least that was what he had told her after he brought her in here.

"This used to be my sister's room. It is now yours."

Even Uncle Yilshak did not have a room to himself; he had to share it with his wife. Then she remembered that she had killed him.

She swung her feet off the bed and sat up. She was in another girl's bed, wearing another girl's clothes. Her own clothes, the school uniform she had put on yesterday morning, had been taken away by Dunka to be washed. When she stood up, the blue nightgown she was wearing rose to her knees. And it felt tight around her chest. She searched through the same suitcase Dunka had fished the nightgown from until she found an old wrapper she could tie over the nightgown.

She stepped into the corridor. The cement floor was cold against her toes. She padded to the kitchen, marking each door with her mind as she passed. Nothing moved in the entire house. In all her life, she had never encountered a silence as absolute as this. It was as solid as any wall. She went outside. A far-off bird trilled happily. Its notes climbed up and cascaded back down repeatedly. Every now and then, it would go quiet, then start again. Arrit looked around. She had probably passed by here yesterday, oblivious. She was seeing the things in the backyard for the first time. The avocado tree that stood by the road like a sentinel. Three blackened rocks arranged in a triangle, with a residue of white ashes in the middle. A sky-blue pickup truck with deflated tires. A lonely gray rock that had *NANA* etched into it in large, uneven letters—the soil in front of it seemed different from the rest; it had to be a grave. The pickup and the grave were tucked away in a corner, easy to miss. A slight breeze blew across the backyard, stirring the leaves and some clothes on a drying line. Arrit raised her face to the sky and took a deep breath. When she looked again, she realized that the clothes on the line were her uniform. A plain white shirt and a dark green skirt, dancing in the breeze. The shirt had splotches of a light brownish outline. Dunka had clearly done his best to wash the blood out. She snatched them off the line without thinking and tossed them into the first suitable container she saw, a large metal bucket resting beside the kitchen door. Inside the house, she began to open drawer after drawer. Most were empty. This kitchen did not even look like a place where food was cooked. She realized then that her last meal had been the tea and bread she had wolfed down yesterday morning, before getting ready for school. And where was Dunka? She turned toward the corridor and stopped dead. The boy who was standing there looked like an apparition. He was so thin that he might have been from a different world. His stillness, his sunken eyes, filled her with dread. She searched for the sickness in them, but all she saw was yellow. The hair on his head had a faint brownish appearance.

"You're from Pishang," the boy said.

"Yes," she said. "Are you . . . Panshak?"

The boy nodded. "What were you looking for?"

"Matches."

"No matches. But my sister can start a fire without them."

"Panmun?"

"Rit."

"Is she inside?"

"She's in the other house." Panshak pointed.

"Where's Dunka?"

"He went to the other house. He said you were still sleeping."

"I woke up."

Panshak nodded politely, then turned to go away.

"Where's the other house?"

He pointed again in the same direction, through the wall, to a place outside that she had never been to. Something about his manner and his appearance made this place seem imaginary.

"Are you hungry?" Panshak said.

Arrit shook her head.

"Dunka went to bring food. For when you get hungry. I'm going to my room. Bye."

She waited until he had gone through one of the doors that opened onto the corridor before returning to the room. The image of the boy still stood in front of her, even when she closed her eyes. Ignoring the insistent, digging pain of hunger in her stomach, she lay on the bed and tried to sleep some more. But who was she trying to deceive? She had slept right through the night. She did not know what time it was, so it was possible she had also slept through most of the day. Her eyes kept darting to the door, but the handle did not turn, and Dunka did not appear with a plate of food.

How would she get rid of that uniform if there were no matches? She had to find fire. It was not enough to throw it away. It had to burn. She remembered the day she went to get it from the tailor. When she tried it on, it had been nearly a size too large. Over the years, she had grown into it, wearing it every day, washing it only when she had to because it was the only one and she had to make it last. One day, it had suddenly become a bit too small, but she went on wearing it because she had asked Aunty Pagak for a new one and had been ignored.

The stupid school uniform had to burn.

There was a noise at the door and she looked up. Dunka stood there carrying an orange plastic bowl. He approached and gently placed it on the edge of the bed. There was a large metal plate covering the food inside. The rim of the metal plate overlapped the mouth of the bowl, resting on it like a hat. Arrit did not know what to say, so she smiled.

"You're awake."

She raised herself from her lying position and leaned against the headboard. It felt strange being close to him, like she was beside an unknowable entity. She knew he was human, humane, incapable of hurting her. But every time he looked at her with those eyes, she was reminded that there was something inside him that even he did not understand, something that had the power to kill him if it desired to do so. When he came close, she felt the automatic urge to make a small space between them, just a small space, enough to keep that dark, swirling thing in his eyes at bay. Whether he had sensed that she had pulled away from him just then, she could not say. His eyes were profoundly illegible.

"How's your arm?" she said, looking at the strips of dressing her hands had fashioned just two nights ago. "It's dirty. You need to change it."

Dunka looked at the bandage and shrugged.

"What are you going to do?" she said. It occurred to her that she should have asked herself that first.

"I want to look for my sister."

"Rit?"

"Panmun. She left with Zumji."

"Who's that?"

"Some guy, her friend. You should eat your food before it gets cold."

There was no use in continuing to pretend she was not hungry. She took the cover off the bowl. It was hot and full of mun and a pale brown puddle that had a few leaves swimming in it. Groundnut puk? Difficult to say. Dunka went to the door.

"I'll let you eat."

Once the door closed, she ate mindlessly, not bothering to chew. Everything she put in her mouth was tasteless, but her throat still rose eagerly to receive the moist white lumps. She slurped on the puk running down her fingers and toward her wrists, licking as fast and far as her tongue could manage. She got some of it on her clothes, but she did not stop to clean or slow down. After she had sucked the last of the puk and licked the bowl clean, getting her nose wet in the process, she could taste the far-off creaminess of groundnut, fading away too quickly. She licked what remained on her lips and inspected her hand. She had not even remembered to wash it. She licked it too until there was not a drop of puk left on it. Her belch reached across the room and bounced off the wall and ceiling. She closed her eyes without meaning to fall asleep.

When she woke up, it was dark. Her first instinct was to grab Bimorit's flashlight, but then she remembered where she was, who she had become. The darkness was so thick she was afraid she might crash into it. With arms outstretched, she found the door. In the corridor, she edged along the wall in the direction of the kitchen. The door that led outside stood wide open, framing the night air blessed by starlight. When she reached the doorway, she stopped and took half a step back.

In the open night stood the black shape of a man. He wore a pair of light-colored shorts that seemed to float in the sea of black. She could not tell what he was doing, but it did not seem like he was doing anything. He was just standing there, with his back to her. Something white was wrapped around his arm. When he turned toward her, she panicked and ran back in the direction of her room. Her bare toe kicked the raised concrete in the threshold of the doorway that connected the kitchen and the corridor. She squealed in pain. Then she heard footsteps outside. She found the door and closed it gently behind her, taking care to release the handle slowly so that the spring latch did not snap into place. She lay on the bed and shut her eyes. The door opened. It creaked as it swung, while what she imagined to be the black shape with the light shorts stood there, breathing into the room. She could feel him staring at her. The door closed with a gentle click, and she still refused to open her eyes. What if he was standing in the room, right next to the bed? What if he was leaning over her at that very moment? She kept still, waiting to be touched, groped, forced, hurt. But nothing happened.

She knew she was being silly, so why had she run? Was it because some part of her believed that it was possible for a person to be one thing when there was light and something else in darkness, especially if that person carried a strange, sinister sickness inside them?

At last she allowed herself the mercy of opening her eyes. The darkness was still there, but there were no light-colored shorts floating in front of her, no black figure of a man she knew to be Dunka but who still terrified her because she could not see his face. She touched her right big toe where she had stubbed it. Now that she had stopped hearing the pounding of her own heart, the pain attacked her, fresh as if it had just sprung into being. Her fingers came away moist and sticky. She needed no lessons in the matters of blood. She knew the power of blood, could never forget its ugliness. How it could gush out of a man like a tap left open until he was drained and empty. How sly and slippery it could be under your bare feet, attempting to trip you. How it could smell faintly like water with too much chlorine in it. How seeing too much of it would make it a terror, even if it only came from a tiny cut. For the first time, she was grateful for the darkness. With that gratitude held desperately to her chest, she finally fell asleep.

In the morning, the brown paper ceiling had turned ashen, colorless. The blue nightgown too. And the unpainted plastered walls. And the bed. Everything she was seeing was the wrong color. She looked at her hands. Her heart picked up its pace, and cold terror drenched her as she understood that this was the Grey. No one had told her this before. She did not know that its victims became blind to color, but it made sense that this was how it should be, the way it made sense that if you took a knife and punctured a living person's stomach and blood came out, the person would die. She sat there and stared at the way sunlight pooled on the floor like a puddle of melted silver, thinking again about the contrast between what her life was and what it had been two days ago. Laughter rose from deep within her, shaking her body as she let it out. She had run away from one terror into the arms of another. A week ago, this new terror had seemed like a death sentence. But here she was, entwined in its embrace, knowing its touch, and finding the irony funny enough to laugh at.

16

PANSHAK

Panshak was drawn by the sounds coming from the kitchen. He crept down the corridor to the kitchen door and saw the girl. She was pulling drawers open and slamming them shut. He gritted his teeth at the sight of this stranger from the other side raking through their home. Who did she think she was? As he stepped into the kitchen, she turned around. She went as still as a rock when she saw him. He felt that if he did not say anything, they might remain that way for the rest of time, staring at each other across the kitchen.

When he was back in his room, after she had told him she was looking for matches, he remembered what *he* had been looking for. He went to the next room and found a chair he could stand on. The room had a big bed and several boxes that contained their mother's clothes. Once their mother's room, it had become Rit's room. Now it belonged to nobody. His room had always been his, but before that it had also been his and Dunka's. Then their father's room had become Dunka's room. And Panmun's room, which had once belonged to Panmun and Rit, now belonged to the new girl. Dunka had told him her name— Arrit. Dunka explained that she was in trouble because she had helped him. But what kind of trouble would force her to leave the comfort of the other side for this hell that was their lives?

He brought the chair back to his room, stood on it, and reached for the corner of the paper ceiling. The chair swayed and creaked beneath him. As he tore the paper through the lattice of twine, he had to take his hand out of one square and slip it into the next to continue. He counted five squares, made an angle in the paper, and tore horizontally. Soon he had the paper spread on the bed, a large rectangular surface that he could write on. It was about the size of the window. The gap he had left in the ceiling yawned darkly, allowing a continuous wave of heat from the zinc above to flood the room.

He used the piece of charcoal he had taken from the bottom of the coal pot to draw his own grid, black lines that crawled first down the length of the paper, and then across. It reminded him of Nana Kanke and the schoolwork she used to make them do, the order she had tried to impose on the chaos around them. Those days felt like a long time ago. He completed the grid and wrote out the days of the week, with each day occupying the top of a column. Rit came in, and after he had explained about the calendar, she touched the first square.

"Is that today?"

"What's today?"

"I don't know."

Panshak could not remember the last time he had thought concretely about the day or the month. It came to him, as softly as the breaking of day, that the thing his calendar was supposed to save them from had already happened. They had forgotten time. If anyone could have kept track of time without faltering, it would have been Nana Kanke. As far as he knew, even she had marked time not by the days but by the hours. But what if she had kept a diary or a notebook with the days labeled?

He looked up to find Rit watching him intently. Was she going to start interrogating him again? What would it take to show her he was fine and did not need anyone's pity? What had happened back there beside that tree had happened; he had done what needed to be done. He had forgotten all about it until she had reminded him with her questions, dragging those memories back into his head—not that he minded them being there. They were just that: memories. But it irked him that she did not believe him when he said he was fine. Next thing, she would go and tell Dunka; then they would all start worrying and invading his privacy when he was, in fact, doing quite well and feeling very pleased with himself.

"What is it, Rit?" he said at last.

She blinked, snapping out of whatever reverie she had been lost in, and said, "The calendar is a good idea."

Panshak felt a warm glow of pride beam out from his center.

He tacked the calendar to the wall using some nails and a hammer he found in their father's glove compartment. He had noticed that Dunka was spending a lot of time around the truck. Nothing had really changed between Panshak and his older brother. The words that passed between them had never been much. As far as Panshak was aware, he had never sat with Dunka—just the two of them—and talked, whether surrounded by four walls, or sheltered by the branches of a tree, or just wrapped in the same pocket of air. Not even when they had lived in the same room. Never, to his memory, had he shared anything else with Dunka.

He barely slept that night. His mind spun with ideas about the things he could learn to do. The calendar was just the beginning. If he had the books, he could have taught himself. What if he built a small plane just large enough to carry them far away to another country, where nobody knew of them or the Grey and they could live normal lives? He could write a book about the Grey, so that if anyone came along years later, after they were all dead, they could never say that it had not happened.

As the new day broke, his eyes began to close. Just when they had finished closing and his mind had started slowing to a listless tranquility, a hand shook him back to wakefulness. Dunka's face, cupped by the sun's sleepy light, was hovering over his. In this moment, detached from all other moments, independent of all other memories, the Grey did not exist. It was too dark to see Dunka's eyes, and they could have been anybody's eyes. All that existed was his brother's face, so beautiful and serene that he wished everything would stay like this: he on his back, his brother's hand on his shoulder, his brother's face watching over him and dripping with tenderness.

"Pan, wake up."

"Hmm?"

"Wake up. It's me."

Panshak sat up. He blinked multiple times, trying to clear the sleep from his eyes. "What?"

"We have to go and look for her today."

"Who?"

"Panmun."

"What if she's dead?"

Dunka shook him so hard his head rattled back and forth. When he regained his bearings, his vision was perfectly clear. The sleep was gone. Now he could see the Grey inside Dunka's eyes again.

"The next time you say something like that, you won't like what I'll do to you."

Dunka paced the room for a moment, gathering his anger. At last, he said, "I want the other boy to come with us. The more of us there are, the easier it will be to find her."

After Dunka had left, Panshak got ready. He broke off a branch from the avocado tree and whittled it with a knife until its thickness was even along its entire length. He looked up into the tree. Its fruit had gotten worse in the two years since the Grey came, so he was not prepared for the size of the avocados he saw hanging off the high branches. They might have been in the sky, for all he knew. They were not yet ready for eating, but their promise startled him. Panshak's mind swiveled on Panmun, and he realized that he missed his sister powerfully. Of all his siblings, she had been the only one who had given him any attention when they were growing up. She helped him with his homework, played with him when he was lonely, even bathed him before he knew how to bathe himself. Something had changed after their parents had died. She seemed to have pulled herself into a shell, ignoring him, becoming less responsive to his attempts at conversation. He was still looking up at the tree, thinking about Panmun, when Dunka returned with Rit, Rit's boyfriend, and Tongrot in tow. Dunka went into the house to see if the girl was awake.

When he reemerged, she was with him. The skin on her face had been caressed by sleep. It was only the second time Panshak was seeing her, and this time, he was really seeing her. Though she had on a pair of sunglasses, it was obvious that the poor light of their kitchen had not done her justice. Long after she and Rit had embraced, Panshak continued to stare at the way beauty sat on her so casually, so effortlessly, that it seemed like an accident.

Panshak, Dunka, and Tongzum set out, heading straight into the bushes that began not far from the house. They stopped at the flame tree. Panshak touched the cross in the bark of the tree absently. Dunka suggested they begin there, since that was the last place they knew she had been. As he walked behind his brother, Panshak thought about that day. Nearly a week had gone by since. Had he really seen her? It had been partly dark in the back of the rickshaw. It could have been any other girl, someone else's sister. He wanted to turn back and return to his room. There was so much he had to do, important things, like completing the calendar. Besides, if he had really seen her, he would have told Rit and Dunka. Why hadn't he? Because he had not seen her, and she was dead somewhere, and it was best for them not to probe too hard, to remember her alive. He halted, suddenly horrified at the possibility that she might be dead. How could he think it so casually? What was wrong with him? The next second, Tongzum walked right into him.

Panshak whipped around and shoved him. "Can't you see where you're going?"

"I can. Can you?" Tongzum said.

Panshak gripped his staff hard and took a step back. He was going to have to teach this stupid boy a lesson. It was because of him Rit had abandoned her real home. Panshak remembered him from Nana Kanke's house. They had never spoken to each other. Perhaps it was the reason neither boy had said a word to the other about their time there. Tongzum had always been accompanied by his little sister wherever he went, with the girl preferring to hang around him instead of going with the other girls. It was then, as he was squaring up to the boy, that Panshak realized they had disappeared at a certain point after Nana Kanke's death, and he had not even noticed at the time. Tongzum raised his fists and held them in front of him, ready. Dunka stepped between them.

"What do you think you're doing?"

They glared at each other without responding.

"I don't have time for this," Dunka said. He was speaking to both of them, but he was looking at Panshak. "If you're going to act like this, you should go back. I'll look for her by myself."

Without waiting, Dunka walked on. Tongzum lowered his fists and went next. Panshak brought up the rear this time, keeping his distance. He paid no attention to where they were going. Dunka simply steered them through field and foliage. There was no plan. He seemed to be possessed by an unspoken drive. Sometimes he would stride so quickly that he would momentarily vanish from sight and they would have to hurry to catch up. They started up the side of a hill that was studded with groups of boulders. Each huddle of rocks revealed nothing new, only what they had seen before. Shade, grass, a small tree, a wild bush.

When they reached the top, Panshak could see the roofs of Pilam, silvery, reddish, faded green, or rusted orange in the glare of the day. It was hot, and the sky was a shockingly clear blue. Nothing stirred except the three of them, turning to look first one way, then another. Panshak leaned on his stick and waited for Dunka's next move. His brother turned to them.

174

"We should split up. I'll go that way. Tongzum, you go that way. Panshak, you go that way. Let's meet back at the flame tree in an hour."

"How will we know it's time?" Tongzum asked.

Dunka stood there, uncertain. None of them had a watch.

"Count to three thousand," Panshak said. "Three hundred seconds is five minutes. Three thousand seconds will be fifty minutes."

They both looked at him. Dunka nodded.

"That's close enough," he said.

As Panshak walked away, he began to count, matching each drop of his stick with a number. It felt fun and freeing. Twenty-seven, twenty-eight, twenty-nine . . . he wove his way down the hill, enjoying the tug of the descent on his legs . . . fifty, fifty-one, fifty-two . . . twirling the stick in his hand like he had seen a ninja in a movie do . . . one hundred and nine, one hundred and ten, one hundred and eleven, one hundred and twelve . . . stopping to swipe at a cluster of feather grass fingers that failed to explode the way he imagined they would . . . four hundred and twenty-five, four hundred and twenty-six . . . cutting through stretches of tangled elephant grass and stinging nettles . . . nine hundred . . . emerging onto the side of an unpaved road that was wide enough to carry two cars abreast.

He stopped counting and looked around, recognizing the spot he was standing in. Somewhere along this road five days ago, a group of rabid boys had chased a rickshaw. He had been one of them. He turned around and followed the road as it curved gently around the side of the hill, coming to the place where they had first heard the distant roaring of the rickshaw as it approached. How they had waited until the bright yellow-and-green vehicle appeared. How Panshak had felt like he was about to relive his nightmares all over again, all of them, even though it was just this particular one. Now Panshak wished he had taken that picture as he chased the rickshaw. He followed the road in the direction the rickshaw had gone that day. He counted his steps as he went. Why had he suggested that Panmun might be dead that morning? Did he really believe it, or had it just been a senseless product of his sleepiness? He was now ashamed that he had harbored such a thought. Now that he was looking for her, he realized that if anyone ought to hold out the hope of her being out there and safe, it should be him. He *had* seen her that day, no use in denying it.

The road was gradually tilting upward, rising along the side of a mountain that loomed immense in the distance. Its slopes shimmered with granite and brown grass that stood stiffly in death. At 2,340 steps, he stopped. He felt tired, and it was time to stop pretending. She may be alive, but she had abandoned them. Left without even saying good-bye. Now the only thing to do was abandon the search. She had walked out of their lives. She was not dead, but she was gone forever.

Back in his room, he pulled the camera out from the bottom of the drawer he had hidden it in. The battery had just a bar left. He checked the memory, just in case there were any pictures left, but it was empty. He had done a thorough job of deleting everything, including the awkward self-portraits of the man who had first owned the camera. Of all the pictures that he took and could have taken during those days, the one he longed for the most was that of the rickshaw as he ran beside it—the picture Goshi had been urging him to take, the picture whose absence had tipped the balance of their relationship, pushing them both into madness. He might have caught her face or some other part of her by accident.

Dunka entered without knocking, and Panshak hid the camera under his pillow just in time. He did not understand this need for secrets and private treasures, but it felt necessary, essential.

"Where were you?"

"I lost track of time."

"I thought something had happened to you."

Panshak looked up at his brother and saw how tired he was. He saw the burden he was carrying. Whether someone had put it on his shoulders or he had taken it on by himself, who could say? But it was there, and he was doing his best to carry it, and the Grey was not making it any easier.

"I saw Panmun."

Before that moment, it had never occurred to Panshak that a face burdened by the Grey could look any more desolate than it already appeared. The shadow of fear that slid across Dunka's features was instant and horrifying to witness.

"What?"

"Some days ago. I think she was with Zumji. He was driving."

Dunka sat down.

"Where?"

"The back road that goes up the mountain."

"Why didn't you say anything?"

"I don't know." Across the expanse of those three words, Panshak felt his voice trembling with emotion. Maybe it was the reason Dunka moved closer and touched his shoulder. He did not lift his hand afterward. Panshak relished the feel of it. He looked into his brother's eyes, forcing himself not to avert his gaze from the Grey. There was a buildup of something wet and sticky and substantial inside his head, and he felt that crying was the way to get rid of it. He wanted to cry. Now would be a good time to cry. But nothing happened.

"What's today?" Panshak said.

"It might be Sunday or Monday. But I'm not sure."

"How do you know?"

"I thought the day I went to Pishang was a Tuesday. I was trying to keep count. I must have gotten lost."

"If you don't write it down, you'll get lost."

Panshak did not want to be the one to show him the calendar. He was hoping Dunka would turn and see it splayed on the wall, marvel at the genius of it, tell him what a good idea it was, but Dunka stood up, spared one last smile, and left the room.

Rit brought meat that evening. She said that Tongzum had trapped the pig and she had killed it. She said it while she was standing in the middle of the room, her back straight and stubborn against Panshak's laughter. His voice rang out like a sound from another world, serenading the room. He remembered vaguely that they used to laugh a lot together. Or rather, he did more of the laughing, because he would tease her and she would huff about and threaten to report him or bring down brimstone on his head and he would press on and she would finally release the smallest of smirks as she realized her protests were of no use.

After she left, he stared at the plate of food on his knees. The slab of meat, charred and thick, took up most of the plate, leaving barely any room for the beans. His mouth filled with saliva, and when he swallowed, it instantly filled again. He bit into the fleshy chunk and had to pull in both directions—with his hands and with his teeth—before he came away with meat. Deep inside the layers of flesh, it was almost raw, and he tasted what he knew to be blood. There was a whisper of spoilage that lingered at the back of his tongue. It floated up into his nose. Before taking the second bite, he transferred the plate to the floor so he could use both hands without obstruction. He wrestled with the meat, each bite a match in its own right. It was not delicious; it had no appealing flavor or aroma to it. But who in their right mind would say no to meat?

He felt full after he had swallowed the last bite, but now he was scared of falling asleep. How long would he go on pretending that Goshi did not plague his dreams? When he closed his eyes, he still saw the older boy's mangled body and battered head. Lying on his back and pausing intermittently to wipe his oily hands on his trousers, he picked at his teeth with both tongue and nails as a distraction. The morsels were stubborn. Sometimes, he had to squeeze a jet of saliva between his teeth to dislodge the meat. Each piece that came away was a small victory, the pleasure of it so disarming and satisfying that when he was done, he closed his eyes and went to sleep.

17

RIT

Rit changed her mind about the beans and decided to cook something even better. She had seen a white-flowered galanji tree in the distance as she walked from her parents' house to Zumji's the day before. Now she took Tongrot to look for it. When they found it, Tongrot shimmied up the stem and tore off slender chunks of branches heavy with leaves. It would not hurt to make a decent meal, something befitting, as an introduction. She had to show this stranger that they were not starving, that they ate well and got along just fine without the help of her people. If Rit's mother had been here, she would have done the same. They went back home with laden arms and picked the tiny round leaves off the branches until their backs were sore and Tongrot was on the verge of tears. It took Rit nearly an hour to get the fire going. With her face and nostrils full of soot and smoke, a part of her was ready to call it a day, but she persisted until the fire sprang into being.

After the puk was ready, she measured out the maize powder and made the mun. She took extra care to let it cook properly and to stir the thickening paste until it dragged with delightful golden thickness. She took a bath and tied one of Panmun's colorful scarves over her head.

After they had eaten and saved some for Tongzum, they set out with the dished meals.

Dunka was still bent over the pickup when they arrived. He looked at Tongrot with a smile.

"Is this one of your friends?" he said.

"I'm Tongrot. Are you Uncle Dunka?"

"Yes, Tongrot. What's that in your hand?"

"It's mun. We made enough for all of you," Tongrot said, beaming.

"You must be very strong to make so much of it."

Tongrot bit her lip and said nothing more.

"Where is she?" Rit said. "She must be hungry." Her heart thumped unsteadily.

"She's sleeping," Dunka said.

Rit felt like a portion of her life was repeating itself, given that this was the same response Dunka had given the day before—the girl seemed to exist only in perpetual sleep. Dunka collected the bowl of puk from her and took it into the kitchen. They followed him inside.

"Where's Panshak?" Rit asked.

"In his room."

Rit left Tongrot with Dunka and went to Panshak's room. He was sitting with his legs crossed on the bed, a piece of charcoal in his hand. There was a large sheet of brown paper in front of him with lines drawn across it in a grid. He looked up at her with a bright face and launched right into an explanation before she asked.

"I'm making a calendar for us so we can keep track of time."

Rit pointed at the first square box.

"Is that today?"

"What's today?"

Rit blinked stupidly at her brother. "I don't know." It bludgeoned her, this realization. She did not know what day of the week it was, or the month. She knew only there had been a yesterday and there would be a tomorrow. She almost blurted out what she was thinking: that this calendar was a waste of time. What difference would it make what day of the week it was? Every day was the same day, repeated over and over again. They may grow older and something may happen tomorrow that did not happen today, but the slow drip of their lives would amount to nothing more than a puddle. Time would never change anything, and when it was ready, the Grey would welcome each of them into its arms. In some weird, warped way, Rit could not wait for that to happen so that it would all be over.

Despite all that, her brother's eager hands caressing the surface of the calendar and his beaming face that was a sun unto itself were all the reason she needed to tell him it was a great idea. His excitement seemed genuine this time, like his old energetic self was really returning, and she would have gladly pretended that black was white if it would bring him back fully. Still, she was not completely convinced that he was not hiding something. She stole secret glances at him, watching his hands move over the calendar, afraid that this side of him would disappear again at any moment, leaving behind the sullen, sad Panshak.

When she looked closely again at the sheet of paper, it occurred to her that it was the brown paper that was used as a ceiling in all the bedrooms. She looked up and saw a large hole that confirmed it. She recalled the day their father had brought the paper home. He had saved up money to buy it after so much time had passed without a ceiling in any of the rooms. The heat from the sun trapped by the metal roof fell in ceaseless waves, turning the rooms into ovens. They barely stayed indoors during the day, choosing rather to sit and play outside in the shade of the avocado tree. When the brown paper ceiling arrived, Panmun had grumbled, but Rit rejoiced because it seemed like progress and they no longer had to go and sit outside just because it was noon.

Dunka and Tongrot broke off their conversation when Rit stepped through the kitchen door. A part of her wanted to hang around and wait for the stranger to wake up. The fact that she slept so much was already beginning to grate on Rit. If she was going to live here, would this be her routine? Sleeping all day while the rest of them worked and served her?

"Greet her when she wakes up," Rit said as she and Tongrot left.

As they approached the other house, Tongzum came out to meet them. He was breathing hard, and there were knives in his eyes.

"I've been looking for you," he said.

"We went home," Rit said.

"Come with me. Tongrot, you stay here."

Rit exchanged a confused glance with Tongrot before turning to follow Tongzum as he led the way, walking and trotting intermittently. Not a word was said. Rit had to jog to keep up.

They arrived at a thicket that would have been lusher and wilder had the rains fully arrived. Now the bushes were crisp and brown from too much sun and dust—the rain that had fallen weeks ago had failed to give them life. Rit bent with her hands on her knees, sweaty and out of breath. She looked at the cluster of thorn bushes, bony shrubs, a bitter leaf tree, and a bush of yellow flowers. She heard it before she saw it, something loud and powerful shrieking and thrashing from amid the plants. Tongzum beckoned to her. Slowly, she drew closer and then, together, they stepped into the circle.

How could she have known that the grating, piercing screeches were coming out of a pig? A great dark hog trapped inside a deep, broad pit. A long wooden shaft stuck out of the ground nearby, pointing at the sky. It was longer than Tongzum's whole body. He pulled it out to reveal a sharpened, deadly point at the other end. Tongzum went around the edge of the pit to where the pig was making angry sounds. He aimed and plunged the spear into the back of the creature, but the pig tore off to the other end of the pit with a mighty squeal, where it remained.

Tongzum came up to Rit and extended the shaft of the spear. She looked from the spear to Tongzum's face. His beestings looked like they had always been a part of him.

"It won't stay still long enough for me to kill it. The hole is too big. You'll have to help me," Tongzum said.

Her mind swam through a dense fog as she took the spear in one hand. It was heavier than it looked, and she had to bring her other hand to steady it. Many years ago, she used to sneak out of the house to play in the fields with the neighbor's children. They would climb trees, chase goats, and throw stones at lizards. When she returned home with bruises and her clothes torn, her mother would be there waiting to berate her and remind her that she was a disappointment of a girl. What would she say if she could see her now?

"Do you understand?" Tongzum said. "We have to be fast."

Rit nodded. "What will you do?"

In answer, Tongzum picked up a long knife from among his hunting tools and slid down into the pit. He looked up at Rit.

"When it comes toward you, stab it."

He did not wait for her other questions. How did the pig get there? Why was there a big hole in the ground? How was she supposed to kill a giant full-grown pig when she was just a young girl? Tongzum crept toward the pig, trying to avoid going at it head-on, but the pig kept against the wall of the pit and swung around to face him each time he approached. He raised his knife and leaped; the pig shot across the pit and berthed right below Rit's feet. She stared down at the creature's back: it was thick and black and coarse with hair.

"Stab it!"

Tongzum was yelling at her, but his voice was not making any sense. The grunting of the pig was all she heard. Suddenly, her mind awoke and seized the reins of the moment. She lifted the spear and brought it down with a groan. The point struck the pig's hide and tore flesh, unleashing blood, but it did not stick. The pig charged toward Tongzum in blind panic, and Rit struggled in vain to pull the spear back up. She tottered on the edge of the pit, as if the pit itself were sucking her in. She released the spear at the last moment, but it was too late—she was already tumbling in.

She landed on her hands and knees and slid to a halt. The spear came to rest a few feet away. When she looked up, the pig was charging straight at her. She screamed and buried her head in her arms. There was panicked grunting and desperate breathing around her, of hog and human, in what sounded like an everlasting tussle. She looked up at last, and Tongzum and the pig were at the other end once more. It seemed the pig had taken a stand now, facing the boy down, daring him to strike.

Rit stood up. The sight of the boy facing off with the pig that was nearly twice his size, the boy with the knife in his hand that looked like a needle next to the pig, the boy who was determined to get them meat even if it killed him—the sight stabbed shame right through her heart. She picked up the stake. There was no knowing where the strength came from to hold it level, no time to wonder. The pig had cornered the boy and was bearing down on him. She charged with the spear held fore and strangely poised. Her hands did not shake. She drove the stake into the flank of the pig, drew back, watched in horror as the creature disintegrated into squeals of agony. Blood gushed forth and watered the ground inside the pit. Before long, death had stilled the pig, and long after that, the girl and the boy did not move.

After Tongzum had cut up the dead pig into manageable pieces, and after they had carted the dripping chunks of meat home, back and forth, multiple times, until the tiredness had seeped into her bones, Rit picked up a broken mirror she had found in the corner of the room they slept in. Her face was hidden behind a mask of congealed blood. Her eyes were two wet pools that shimmered in the light as she watched her reflection. She had grazes on her hands and knees where she had fallen on them. She put down the mirror and went outside. Tongzum had started a fire and was trying to smoke the meat. Tongrot helped him to drape the cuttings over the wooden slats. Her voice rang out excitedly as she asked question after question.

Rit thought her arms would fall off and splash into the well when she drew her first pail up. Every part of her felt sore and alien. When she had bathed and changed her clothes, she sat outside and watched as Tongzum worked into the night, tending the fire, turning the meat over, ensuring it got enough smoke.

The next morning, Rit woke up and found Dunka standing in the doorway of their room. She looked around. Tongzum was still stretched out, dead asleep. She did not say anything to her brother until they were standing outside. The smoking pit was covered with a giant sheet made from old pieces of plastic stitched together. She assumed the meat was under it. She and Tongrot had gone to bed at some point in the middle of the night, leaving Tongzum to carry on.

"I want to go and look for Panmun," Dunka said. "I shouldn't go alone."

Her mind churned with questions, but also with exasperation. What was he trying to prove? That he was the only one who cared enough about Panmun to look for her?

"But she left Pilam with Zumji. She said she would."

"You know I have to look for her, Rit. I can't just sit and do nothing."

"I want to come with you."

"Just me, Panshak, and Tongzum," Dunka said.

It stung, what he said and how he said it. Did he not know that she had killed a pig with her two hands? She was as good as any boy, never mind what their mother would have said. She had what it took to go on the search. But deep down, she really did not want to go. She knew it was futile. Whatever might have happened to Panmun, their sister was lost to them for good.

Rit went to wake Tongzum up. Soon they were all gathered in the backyard of her parents' house, waiting for Dunka to check on the new girl. Rit heard feet by the kitchen door and turned as Dunka came out. That was when she saw her, the stranger from the other side, the mysterious sleeper, the savior of their brother. She had on sunglasses. Her skin was dark like the bark of a mango tree and rich with life. Here before Rit stood a healthy girl, with flesh so full Rit wanted to reach out and poke it. She was not only healthy; she was beautiful too. Despite the slim black spectacles that covered her eyes, Rit could tell that she was. So beautiful that Rit was shocked by the twinge of jealousy that momentarily quivered in her chest. It reminded her of the way the pig's flesh had vibrated long after they had quartered it, even when no one was touching it.

When Arrit spoke, Rit noticed her chipped front tooth. Rit scoured the exposed parts of the beautiful stranger's face, searching for purpose, but there was nothing. No malice, no love. It was difficult to truly assess her without seeing her eyes. Why were they covered? Had she been crying? If there were any secrets to be dug up, she certainly would not unearth them by being cold. Rit decided to make her feel at ease, so she closed the gap between them and embraced her.

That evening, they made dinner and shared some of the meat with the others. After they had returned from delivering the meal, Rit and Tongrot went to bed while Tongzum remained outside. Rit lay beside Tongrot. It was the only way to get her to fall asleep, even if she was not ready for bed herself. When the little girl was breathing soundly, Rit got up again. Tongzum was where they had left him, on the steps outside the kitchen. Rit settled beside him.

"Did you dig that pit all by yourself?"

"Uncle Zumji already dug it. He laid the trap. I just found the pig."

Crickets were chirping from secret places around them, but Rit wanted to hear more than that. She wanted to hear all about Tongzum's day. What had happened when he went with her brothers? Had they hit it off? And she wanted to tell him about hers. About the girl from the other side and the way she seemed like she had always belonged in this world—how she, the newcomer, had led them around the village and opened their eyes to the possibilities that existed behind the closed doors of Pilam's empty houses. She wanted to tell him that her palms and knees still stung from yesterday's fall, and that she had absorbed the pain into her body, refusing to give it away. She wanted them to talk about the pig, about all that blood. They could even joke about the two of them being the worst hunters in the history of hunters. Then again, she sensed that Tongzum would not find that funny. He would consider it a failure of some sort, and then he would punish himself and force himself to work harder. She saw it all, the ways he was stretching himself beyond all that he was. He would never accept that the responsibilities he had taken on were a bit too large. That it was okay to fail sometimes and to laugh at oneself. What would it take to make him loosen up, to relax?

"I want you to stay," Tongzum said.

Rit looked at him, unsure of what she was hearing.

"I'm sorry I made you think I wanted you to leave and go back to your parents' house. I want you to stay here with me and Tongrot."

The idea dropped into Rit's head with a soft splash. It took control of her faculties. It took her entire body. She did not care what her mother would have said. She leaned into Tongzum and kissed him ever so gently on the cheek, right on one of his stings. She pulled back and watched him, even though her heart was pounding, deafening her in the process. Night had fallen, but she could tell that his face had lit up, as if she had reached out and flicked on a light. In the darkness, he turned his head in her direction.

She had often thought about the garden in the intervening days, how the basic sight of growing vegetables had taken her breath away and wrung tears out of her. She thought she had seen and felt it all; she thought that there was nothing left that was capable of surprising her in this world. But here she sat, confused under the stars, for something alive and untamable had taken root in her.

18

ARRIT

Arrit found a mirror with a long handle in the large suitcase. Her eyes had turned mercilessly black. She could not even see her pupils. There was a pair of sunglasses at the bottom of the suitcase. They would not cover much of her face, but at least they would hide her eyes. She put them on and stood there. Her terror had turned into laughter, which had now faded into silence, leaving behind a steadfast numbness. She did not know what to do.

Dunka knocked and entered. His brow creased at the sight of the sunglasses. Should she tell him?

"Everyone's outside. They're waiting to meet you."

She followed him out to the backyard. Panshak was the only one she recognized. There was a boy of about Panshak's age who wore a permanent scowl on his face; there were two girls. The younger girl seemed too small, while the older girl stood with her back very straight, as if her body were determined to announce it would never be defeated by anything. For an endless moment, they all stared at Arrit, and Arrit stared back. Then the older girl went up to Arrit and pulled her into an embrace.

"Thank you for saving my brother's life."

She guessed this must be Rit.

Rit looked up and beamed at her. It was when Rit pulled away that Arrit realized she had not returned the hug. It was too late for that anyway, because Rit moved away to stand with the others. Maybe she was offended by it. Arrit felt constrained by the knowledge that she was from the outside world. She also felt contaminated, like if she touched any of these children too carelessly, she might pass the sickness on to them. How could she have gotten it so quickly? Was it because Dunka had touched her, carried her from the flame tree to the house? She stood there in front of everyone the way she had stood in the room, without certainty or direction. She wished she could disappear from there, or cease to exist entirely. They all just kept looking. Mercifully, Dunka spoke.

"I'm going with Panshak and Tongzum to look for Panmun. Rit and Tongrot will stay here with you."

"Where will you look?"

"Everywhere there is to look."

She almost asked if she could go with them. An unfamiliar restlessness was building up inside her, threatening to break out through her arms and legs. She wanted to walk, run, flee toward nothing and from nothing. She remained silent and watched them leave. After they had gone, Arrit looked inside the metal bucket by the door. Her uniform was missing. Rit and Tongrot stood at a distance, watching her. Arrit really wanted to take the glasses off. On top of the fact that the world was now gray to her, the spectacles made everything blacker, darker. Her mind was becoming unmoored, as if she were dreaming and awake at the same time.

"You're Tongrot," Arrit said.

"Yes."

"You're Rit."

"Yes," said Rit.

"Nenrit?"

"Ritdirnen." It was Tongrot who answered. The little girl tilted her head to look at Rit with a proud smile. Rit ran her fingers through the girl's hair.

"Arritmwa?" Rit said.

Arrit smiled, nodding. She liked what they were doing. Tasting each other's names, attempting to kindle something warm and alive, perhaps a friendship, or a polite familiarity. They would see.

"I heard you know how to start a fire," Arrit said.

"Tongzum does it best. It doesn't always work for me."

Rit tapped Tongrot on her back. Tongrot entered the kitchen and returned with Arrit's uniform. The two pieces of clothing were neatly folded, one on top of the other. Tongrot gave it to Rit, who raised it to Arrit like an offering. Despite her new vision, she could still make out the bloodstains in the white fabric, now dark like faded mwir-pet stains.

"Thank you," Arrit said.

She returned to the room. She could hear the footsteps of the two girls behind her. When she placed the uniform on the bed, she turned and saw them standing in the corridor, framed in the doorway. They were watching her as if they had never seen anything quite like her before. She wished she could be alone, but she could not ask them to leave. Perhaps their company was a good thing for her. It helped that their gaze did not make her feel like an aberration. The curiosity so plain in their wide, gaunt eyes and their frail little bodies seemed pure, harmless. Would it change if they knew that she now also carried the sickness?

"Won't you come in?"

The two girls stepped into the room. Tongrot sat on the edge of the bed, her feet barely touching the floor. Rit remained standing.

"This used to be your sister's room?" Arrit asked.

"I used to be here too, before our parents died."

"When did she leave?"

"A few days ago."

"Where did she go?"

"Nobody knows."

"What do you do during the day?"

Rit looked at Tongrot and smiled. "We try to fix things around the house. We take care of the garden."

"You have a garden?"

"We can show you," Rit said.

Arrit followed the girls through the fields. It reminded her of the way she had come yesterday to get here. All those bushes. And that horrendous barricade. After she had burrowed her way beneath it, the whole time fearful that someone, perhaps Uncle Yilshak's ghost, might grab her ankles and drag her back to that house, she gazed up at the staggering structure from the other side and shuddered. How had this thing come to be? She had heard about it, glimpsed it from a distance, but seeing it like that brought her face-to-face with the sheer impossibility of it all. Yet there it stood before her, as real as her skin, glinting in the morning sun. She ran from it. The grass and bushes grew wilder as she went, reaching to her shoulders with dried hands, scratching her. She half expected some wild animal to leap up from the undergrowth and maul her.

Now, as she followed the girls, the wildness of her surroundings adjusted itself in her vision, taking on the shape of normality. Regardless, she still felt like she had been plucked from real life and dropped into this dreamscape that was peopled with stick-figure children—and now it was permanently tinted with the Grey. She had never been this untethered, free to do whatever she wanted. All her life, adults had marked the path she should take, telling her what she could and could not do. Every moment of her existence had been measured and accounted for by others, born of a desire not to protect but to control. But here she was, unbound and unsure of what to do with it. That restlessness stirred again.

They went up the driveway flanked by rows of cacti. A few trees grew on the sides of the path. Their branches formed canopies overhead that dappled the sunlight on the ground. They walked past the house itself, toward a portion of the fence that was draped with a curtain of creepers. Rit and Tongrot each grabbed a handful of vines and pulled them aside to reveal a doorway. Arrit entered and went around admiring the gestating vegetables. Some sat on the ground, rotund. Some pushed out of the earth with thick green tendrils. Others drooped from supports. The smell of earth was fresh and sweet in her nostrils, but everything remained a hopeless gray.

"My brother says we can start eating them soon," Tongrot said.

In Uncle Yilshak's house, if they needed vegetables or fruits, anything fresh, they went to the market and got it. The only plants they grew, apart from the flowers, were the herbs Aunty Pagak used for her business. Arrit and Bimorit had been forbidden from plucking any of them for cooking. Not even the waterleaf or spinach. There were other kinds of leaves too, but she did not know their names. All the plants were so heavily restricted that they were grown in a section of the grounds cordoned off by a low wall. Not even Polu, who did the gardening, was allowed to touch them. Matyin tended and watered them herself.

The girls took her toward the house and showed her the mud silos. An old motorcycle leaned against a wall, like an unwanted guest waiting to be invited in. Around the house hung the perpetual smell of meat that had begun to go off. The soil around a dead tree was dark with blood. Arrit turned around and came face-to-face with something black and alive. She froze. Through the shimmering, pulsating covering, she could make out snatches of a lighter shade, almost white. She realized the black thing was a massive swarm of flies. There was barely any room for them. They flew round and round and round, desperately trying to get in.

"What's that?" she said. Vomit was threatening to leap up into her throat.

Rit picked up a dirty rag nearby and struck the flies. They scattered in an explosion of furious buzzing, revealing the head of a pig. Its tiny eyes were frozen, its lips curled in a twisted grin. The head was resting on a dead tree stump.

They sat in the backyard, and Arrit tried to forget the pig's head and the flies. The girls tried to make small talk, but it mostly came out as questions.

"What's life like on the other side?" Rit said.

"Normal."

"Were you going to school?" Tongrot said.

"Yes."

"Was that your school uniform?"

"Yes."

"I used to wear a uniform like that. Will you teach me how to add and subtract?" Tongrot asked.

"Maybe," Arrit said.

There it was again, that stirring in her gut. She began to suspect that it was connected to the blood-soaked ground merely a few feet away; to the pig head and the tree stump and how sad they looked that way, one on top of the other, each having been once filled with life, now dead and separated from their original purposes; to the Grey that had now become a part of her. She looked at her big toe, the one she had stubbed last night—the blood had dried up, the cut now a tiny gash in her skin. She stood up, cutting off Tongrot, who was in the middle of saying something that made her face bright with excitement. Arrit had to do something with herself or else she might go mad.

"I want to look around," Arrit said.

The girls looked at each other, then back at Arrit. She had questions. She wanted to see. Her curiosity and her restlessness propelled her into Pilam, the other two dragged along by their confusion. How many families remained in this place? How many people? Had anybody bothered to take a tally of the dead? To write their names? Who remembered them when it was just children who were left behind?

The houses seemed ordinary as she passed them. Some had fences, most sat bare and exposed. Arrit pointed at one.

"Do you know who lived there?" she asked.

Rit shook her head.

"What about that one?"

She got the same answer. Randomly picking one that opened right onto the street, she skipped over the drainage trench in front of it and went up to the front door. She turned the handle; the door opened. She looked back at the street, where Rit and Tongrot stood, watching her. She remembered how their faces had carried their curiosity earlier as they stared at her through her bedroom door. Now the same faces carried fear.

Ignoring them and her own fear, she entered the house. It was dark inside, and she was standing in a sort of nexus that opened to other rooms. All the doors were closed. She pushed the first door; it contained a toilet. The next door was a bathing room with a drain in the floor. The next door was a tiny kitchen. There were still dishes flipped over on the draining board beside the sink. On the floor, there was an upturned pot. She looked inside, and it contained the rotted dregs of a long-forgotten meal—it seemed someone had been through here before her, perhaps someone like her who had also just tried the front door. She looked inside the cupboards, but there was nothing worth scavenging. Whatever condiments and ingredients there once were had been torn open and licked up, their containers discarded.

She turned and was about to leave when she noticed it on the edge of the countertop, as though it had been waiting there for her all this time. She picked up the small paper box and shook it. The sound of the matches rattling inside, something she had heard countless times before, was different this time. It seemed to her that it was the sound of mercy.

She looked in the rooms, but there was nothing there, just a stripped bed and a handful of old, worn clothes that would not have been of much use.

Emboldened, she entered the next house, a bungalow with a low fence. The gate stood wide open. This time, the girls went in with her. It was a long building, with the kitchen at one end. As they made their way through the house, they picked up a packet of candles, some kerosene, a half-used bar of laundry soap, a bottle of cooking oil, half a container of ginger powder, and more matches. The bedrooms were at the other end. As Arrit pushed open the door to the first room, a powerful, rancid odor assaulted her. Standing in the doorway, they saw the body entwined in the sheets. Tongrot screamed and ran several steps down the corridor, but Arrit only took a step back. She and Rit looked at each other. A special recognition passed between them then. Arrit felt like a covering had fallen away to reveal a kindred spirit in this girl who was standing next to her. No words were spoken, but as though with one mind, they both raised their collars to their noses and entered the room.

It was the body of a woman. Shrunken, like a dried raisin, with skin like sun-beaten leather and limbs like withered boughs. Her clothes, a pair of tight jeans and a colorless top, seemed fashionable, but what did Arrit know about fashion trends? All her clothes had been oversize hand-me-downs. It was difficult to judge the woman's age, but going by her clothes, she must not have been much older than Arrit. Her eyes were sealed shut. Arrit scanned the room. A suitcase bursting with clothes sat in a corner. A thick white duvet had slid from the bed to the floor. Cosmetics lined a vanity across the room. She had no desire to take anything. It now felt like stealing.

Back in her room, Arrit laid out the spoils of their outing on the floor. They no longer had that smack of victory because of the dead woman. There was something tainted about the objects, and a part of her wanted to return them. She looked at Rit, who studied the objects intensely. Was she thinking the same thing? Arrit turned to the door and found Dunka standing there. After they had greeted each other, he turned to go back outside. Arrit followed him. By the time they were under the sun, he had taken his shirt off. His bare shoulders glistened with sweat; his sculpted arms were like two thick iron rods. Something in her chest stumbled when he turned to face her, but she did not avert her eyes.

"Why are you wearing those glasses?" he said.

Arrit pretended not to hear. "Did you find her?"

"We looked everywhere. She's gone."

"What do you think will happen to her?"

"I don't know." He drew closer, looked at her more intently. "Are you also sick?"

It was unclear to her why she felt unwilling to admit that she was. Instead, she focused on the reason she had followed him out here. After she had explained, Dunka, without a moment's hesitation, pulled his shirt back on, picked up some digging tools, and followed her. She led him right to the body. He spread the bedsheet on the floor.

"Help me," he said to Arrit.

Against every proclivity, Arrit forced her body forward. Reached down and took hold of the desiccated wrists. They laid the woman on the bedsheet and pulled it over her until she was properly covered. Dunka carried the body outside and found a spot behind the house. Arrit watched him dig the hole, using the hoe and shovel interchangeably. She watched as he placed the white bundle gently inside the grave. She watched him cover it up. He wiped sweat from his brow when he was finished and looked at her. Of all the things he could have done then, what he chose to do was smile at her. The corners of her mouth rose until she was smiling back. They had just buried a long-decayed corpse, with the grave between them, and they were smiling at each other. Arrit's head spun at the incongruity of it all. There was a warm, tickling fullness in the pit of her heart that was spreading to other parts of her, imbuing them with energy. Was it right to feel such a thing, at such a moment, in such a place? She was sick with the Grey, and she could still feel this way. She stood there, holding the moment in her hands, afraid that any movement might scare it so far away that it would refuse to return.

Afterward, it was easier for her to examine the items they had found that day. There was no distaste on her tongue when she and the girls lit a candle just to watch the white fumes trail up to the ceiling and disappear. Or when they sprayed a bottle of perfume and basked in the zesty scent it produced. Or when they took a whiff of the cooking oil and came away with the faint trace of fried fish.

In her room, she waited until the house grew calm. The daylight had begun to fold away. When she was sure there was no one hanging around who might burden her with questions, she carried her school uniform outside.

Her first day in school, two years after she came to live with Uncle Yilshak, had been the happiest of her life. At the age of fourteen, she had never been inside the walls of a classroom before. Her life was about to change forever; she would become smart and make new friends and learn interesting things. But in time, school became its own nightmare. She came to hate it. She still did. Anything that reminded her of it, or Uncle Yilshak, or what she had done to him, had to be destroyed.

In the backyard, she moved as far from the house as she could. She ended up behind the blue pickup truck, a small, respectful distance from the grave. She doused her old clothes with kerosene and set them aflame on the ground. She watched as the flames licked them up. She could still see the dark stains on the white shirt. Blood that she had spilled. Whatever she might do, wherever she might go, would she ever outrun the sound of blood that was calling her name? She moved the clothes around with a stick, poured more kerosene when the fire threatened to go out. The pleated skirt, green only in her memory, turned even grayer and then black as it curled away from the fire. The white shirt, together with its bloodstains, was erased into ashes.

Back in the room, she took off the glasses and sat alone with the Grey. Before now, she had not had time to consider what it would do to her. But it was going to kill her, was it not? It would make her find something sharp and poke a hole in her body the way she had seen Dunka do to himself three nights ago. Three nights. That was all it had taken for everything about her life to change forever.

There was a knock, and she quickly put the glasses back on. It was Dunka. He came and sat next to her on the bed. He took off the sunglasses and placed them beside her. He held her gaze for a long time, looking nowhere but into her eyes. Now that he had seen her, now that he knew, now what? They would all die in the end.

As though in answer, Dunka pulled her into an embrace and held her. There came crying and shaking and shuddering, but it was not hers, for she still felt the same numbness. It was his, all of it.

19

DUNKA

As Dunka left Arrit's room, he wiped his tears away. He did not know what had come over him, crying like that. He went to his father's pickup truck and resumed his work of trying to revive the vehicle. He removed the carburetor and stood examining the object. It was clogged with dirt. He blew through it as though it were a pipe. He used a wire to poke around inside it. He would have to get gasoline if he were to make it any cleaner. Once that was done, he would have to figure out a way to charge the battery. And if the car still refused to start, he would have to look at the spark plugs. He would do everything he could to bring it to life. At a point, he went still. He was only deceiving himself. His mind was not here with himself and the vehicle; it was back in the room with Arrit, where she sat with the Grey in her eyes. Arrit had the Grey and it was because of him and she was going to die and there was nothing he could do to save her.

He had first suspected Arrit was sick when he saw her wearing the sunglasses that morning. They had become such a dead giveaway—sunglasses, a symbol of death hiding coyly under covers. It was the same way he had sensed that Panmun was also sick days earlier, when he last saw her in the living room as he set out for Pishang. The last time he would ever see her, planning it to be the last time so he could hurt her, but not realizing that it truly was the last time. Everybody around him was crumbling toward death because of him, and he had succeeded in dragging Arrit into the whirlpool of his failure. He had set out to save his siblings from the monster but had only ended up dooming one more person. He should not have escaped from Pishang alive. He should be dead and tucked away in assured darkness, where he would not be able to destroy anything again by his mere existence.

He had just leaned back into the entrails of the pickup when Rit walked up.

"I brought dinner," she said. "I left yours in your room."

Dunka nodded. He wanted to thank her, but the words felt heavy and strange—not because he was ungrateful, but because he was ashamed.

Rit did not go away. She had a determined look on her face as she continued speaking. "Did you speak to Panshak?"

"About what?"

"About what happened."

"Where?"

"At the house he was staying in."

"Nana Kanke's house?"

Rit nodded. She bit her lips as though trying to endure the moment.

"What happened?" Dunka asked.

"I think he killed someone."

Dunka raised his head and looked at her, but he did not say anything.

"I saw the body when we went to look for him."

"Who?"

"I don't know. I just saw the body."

"How do you know it was Panshak?"

"I asked him."

"He said he did it?"

"No."

Dunka's silence was his answer. He watched Rit's face as she deciphered the quiet, watched as a disappointed comprehension, then frustration, flooded her face. She stumbled over her words.

"I know it was him."

"Did you talk to someone at the house?"

Rit sighed. She turned her face toward the sky. It seemed to him she was arranging the words in her mind.

"When we reached the house, I asked a girl if she had seen him. She looked like she was afraid when I said his name. She looked first at something that I couldn't see; then she told me where his room was. Later, I saw the thing she was looking at. It was the body."

"But that doesn't mean Panshak killed anybody."

"You can believe or choose not to, but I've told you." A cool wrath had entered Rit's eyes and was coming out through her voice.

After she left, Dunka stood for a long time thinking about her words. It still crushed him that he was being fed by his little sister, when he should be the one providing for her. Now, with what Rit had shared fresh on his mind, his appetite had disappeared altogether. She had not given him concrete facts of how she came to that knowledge, yet he believed her. He understood how she could accept something that had not been said to her verbatim, something that she had only sensed. His little brother had become a murderer, and as with nearly everything else when it came to his siblings, the blame sat squarely on Dunka's shoulders.

He entered the house and stood in the corridor outside Panmun's room. Arrit's room. She was inside, behind that door, where he had left her not an hour ago. If he could see through walls, he would see her at that moment. What might she be doing now? Earlier in the day, she had brought hot water, undone his bandage, cleaned his wound, and bound it again with a fresh cloth. After that, he had stood in that same spot once or twice, asking himself whether he should knock on her door and go in. But he had run out of pretexts, including food. She was only ten paces away, but she and everything she touched, even the air she was breathing, seemed like a whole other world. He liked being suffused with that air. Going through that door would mean passing through a portal. He steadied himself and drew up to it, the portal. He knocked. The portal opened, and he stepped through it.

Arrit sat down on the bed after opening the door and turned her Grey-ridden eyes on him. Her bowl of food was on the bed beside her. She picked it up and raised it toward him.

"Join me."

Dunka shook his head and said, "Thank you." He realized his smile was too large and lingered too long. The shame of having cried in front of her was still heavy on him, and he was trying to pretend it did not exist. But how could he, when the Grey was there in her eyes and it was the reason he had cried in the first place, because he had brought it upon her? By some strange logic, to deny his shame of crying before her was to deny that he had been responsible for her misfortune.

Arrit continued with her meal. There was a rickety old chair against the wall. Dunka perched on the edge of the seat, wary of trusting it with his full weight. Something was hammering and pummeling his heart. Or was it his heart that was doing the hammering? He swallowed. "What's that?"

Arrit raised the dark slab that was sticking up over the edge of her bowl.

"It's meat. Didn't you get any?"

"I haven't eaten yet."

"Rit said she killed the pig herself."

"Rit killed a pig?"

While Arrit nodded, Dunka thought to himself dryly that his siblings appeared to have a talent for taking life.

"How does it taste?"

Arrit raised the meat and bit. After a moment's struggle, she lowered it back into the bowl, and they were both enveloped in the laughter that followed. Dunka allowed his gaze to linger on her after the last chuckle had faded. He noticed everything about her, from her chipped tooth to the few scars she had on her arms, even a small depression in her chin. Their eyes met. He had so many questions he wanted to put *to* her, *about* her. Like where each scar came from. Why she had released him. Why she had been covered in blood that day he found her under the flame tree. (To his eyes, the blood had been a blackish, ink-like substance.) Whose blood, when it clearly was not hers? Why was she here, in this room that was on the wrong side of that barricade, eating burned meat and bland food? It had been only two days since she had arrived, but her face looked leaner than it had when he first saw her in front of her uncle's house. And why had she burned her clothes? The whole time, he willed his eyes to stay locked to hers, even when decorum tried to lower them for him.

"I'm sorry," he said.

"For what?"

"For bringing you into this."

Arrit put her food down and said very gently, "You didn't bring me into this. I chose to come here. I'm not a small girl. For the first time, I feel like I can do what I want to do. Like I have a life. It's not your fault."

She smiled and picked up her food again. Dunka smiled back. He did not know what more to say. He went to the door. When he had opened it halfway, he paused. There was something else burning in his throat. She was the only person he felt he could speak to about it, the only person he wanted to ask. It took entering this room and standing there like a lost creature to understand that if Arrit had not been here, he would not have been able to speak to anyone else. She was the closest thing to a friend he had. None of his siblings even came close, and he felt yet another twinge of guilt. His failings as the eldest towered over him, threatening to crash and bury him alive.

"I just found out that my brother may have killed someone."

Arrit stopped eating and paused with the food in her mouth. As with the crying, he could not believe he was opening up in this way to someone who had been a stranger to him just a few days ago.

"I don't know what to do," Dunka said.

He had said it without looking at her. When he finally turned, she was staring at the floor. She remained like that for a moment. Her nostrils flared, and her breathing quickened while she searched for the words down there. She swallowed her food and looked at him.

"I killed someone too."

Dunka did not respond.

Off his blank expression, Arrit continued. "I did it because I had to. I don't have any siblings, but if I had a big brother, I would want him to believe that I wouldn't have done it if there was another way."

"He isn't saying anything."

"Nobody likes to talk about killing. If you want to talk about it, then you have to go to him. That's why you're the big brother. Because you're stronger and wiser."

Wisdom was not a quality Dunka would have associated with himself, that much he was ready to accept.

On his way to his room, he stopped outside Panshak's room. His old room too. They had once shared it. That was all he remembered of that time. What they had said to each other, what they had done with each other, if anything, was located in the blind spots of the past. They had moved to this house when Dunka was seven, the year Panshak was born. When the boy finally became old enough to have his own room, the only option was to share Dunka's. Panshak moved in and Dunka barely paid him any attention, coming home at late hours when his brother would already be asleep. There had been important things to do, people to see. All those things and people had since fallen away, clearing up like a mist. Now that he could see well enough, one of the things that remained was his little brother.

Dunka entered the room and found Panshak asleep. There was a plate with freshly chewed bones on the floor beside the bed. Panshak had oil stains around his mouth. As he stood watching him sleep, Dunka felt a surge of tenderness and an unspeakable desire to protect, neither of which he had any memory of ever feeling before. He wanted to reach out and undo, lay waste to anything that so much as hinted danger toward his siblings. He had left this house five days ago to find a cure for them, to save them. The truth was, there was no such thing as a cure when it came to the Grey. It did what it wanted, when it wanted, to whom it wanted. He knew that now. He would never be able to destroy it. But he was going to put up such a fight that by the time it was done with him, the sickness would know that it had vanquished a worthy foe.

20

PANSHAK

Early the next morning, Panshak got dressed and left the house. He carried his stick with him. Its roughness against his palm gave him a sense of purpose. Rather than take the shortcut that squeezed between buildings and cut across boundaries, he took the main road, the same road a car would have taken if it were driving from their house to Nana Kanke's. He saw a few others on the way, but everyone kept their distance. Even though he could not see their eyes from that distance, he saw the weariness that clung to the grown-ups' bodies and could tell that they were carrying the Grey. How long did Dunka have before something happened to him?

He did not keep track, but it felt like an hour had passed by the time he was standing in front of Nana Kanke's white gates. They were wide open. The house looked the same, which was no surprise. It had been only four days, after all. He made a beeline for the front door, not sparing anything else a second glance, and made a point of giving the great neem tree a generous berth. Once he was safely inside, he tried to close the lopsided door behind him, but it fell off its last hinge and clattered loudly on the floor. After the noise had ceased, he looked around the space on the ground floor. This, he did not recognize. Every piece of furniture had been dislodged from its place, upturned. He picked his way through the mess. This was where they'd had their lessons. The books were all on the floor, many of them ripped to shreds. A noise came from across the room, and a small scrawny man came out of the kitchen. Panshak raised his stick and waited, but the man was not interested. He turned and went back to whatever he had been doing.

Panshak went into Nana Kanke's study. Not much had been disturbed here. Her desk was still standing in its place, but the drawers had been pulled out and emptied on the floor. Panshak scoured through the papers, files, books, looking for anything that had a date on it. There were teaching notes, letters from Nana Kanke's husband, old receipts, and notes on expenditure. But there were no diaries or calendars.

Upstairs, he looked in the rooms that had been their dormitories and found the same thing in all three: beds and mattresses overturned. In Nana Kanke's room, her wardrobe had been cleared out, with clothes strewn on the floor. The large mattress that had once lain on the bed frame was leaning against the wall, the same mattress that Nana Kanke had died on. The bedside table was still in position. It was a miracle that the woman's photograph was right where he had left it, intact.

He picked it up and studied her face again. The wife of the brother of the man from Pitong. Yilamka. *You are not lost.* That was what the name meant. It struck him again, this time more forcefully, how young she seemed. She did not look much older than their Panmun. Her hair was parted in the middle, with each half curving down behind her ear and dwindling into a twist. He had not noticed before that she was smiling, with just one side of her face, one cheek raised, one lip corner curled as though around a secret. It was the way he had started to smile after he realized that using all of his mouth and all of his face made him seem too eager and, therefore, awkward. Not that there was much cause for smiling, anyway. This time, he placed the picture inside his pocket.

He pulled the drawer of the bedside table and riffled through its contents. There were more letters, most of them handwritten. He started to read one addressed to Nana Kanke. The date was so long ago that it was meaningless to him. He saw that her full name had been Kankemwa Gobum. After the first two lines, he stopped reading. It felt disrespectful.

At the bottom of the drawer, he found a notebook. It was the kind of exercise book he had used in school to take notes, about twice the size of his hand. Its cover had the image of a palm tree on a beach with a light blue ocean in the background becoming one with the horizon. One word was written in the space provided: *Timekeeping*. He opened it and saw two lines in Nana Kanke's impeccable, bold script:

The sickness began three days ago, on Tuesday. Mrs. Bijimrit told me her neighbor was the first person to get it. She said she went to his house on that day and saw him with black eyes. Her neighbor died today. He killed himself with his wife's gun. (His wife is a policewoman.)

The date above it was February 9. Since that time, Panshak knew that two rainy seasons had come and gone. He remembered from school that the rains usually started in March or April. The Grey had been with them for more than two years.

He flipped through pages and pages of entries. One caught his eye because there were two dates above it:

I'm losing track of the time. My phones have died, no electricity to charge anything. Today may be Monday or Wednesday, a date between 4th and 12th of May. I'm so forgetful.

He flipped again until he found the last entry:

I threw Goshi out today. I don't know where he'll go. If his parents were alive, they would have accused me of abandoning their son. But I think I tried. Maybe I just have to accept that he is a monster. I don't know what happened to him before he came to live with me many years ago. I always suspected it was something bad. Now I have other children here, and he is a bad influence. It is still painful because he is like my son. But I had no other choice.

After that were ruled lines of immaculate white space that would never know the weight of her pen and her memories. Panshak closed the book and stood up to leave, but then he heard the sound again. It had been there from the beginning, the type of sound you might hear and convince yourself you had only imagined it. Like the times he and his mother would sometimes be left alone in the house when the rest had gone to the market. Perhaps his mother was not feeling too well. He would be in his and Dunka's room, playing with his toys, or practicing his handwriting, and he would hear his mother's voice calling his name. When he opened the door to her room, he would find her fast asleep.

It was a sucking sound, so tiny and intermittent, coming from behind the mattress. He raised the mattress from its position against the wall and let it fall on the bed frame with a soft bump. On the floor with her back against the wall sat a woman with a baby in her arm. The woman's left breast was exposed, and the baby was suckling. In the woman's right hand was a large knife stained with blood. There was blood on her hand, blood oozing out of the wound on the side of her stomach, blood pooling on the floor. It was bright red, fresh, but it had not touched the baby.

Whether Panshak stood there for a moment, a minute, or a lifetime, it did not matter. It was all forever. Watching the lifeless body that was still giving life to the hungry infant, neither body aware of its position, both simply obedient to the demands of nature and fate. Neither was the boy who bore witness aware of any meaning to the moment or the spectacle. In the face of the multiple meanings that seemed to cross each other out like opposing parts of an equation, the boy's mind stopped processing information and simply saw a dead woman holding a living baby.

The baby began to cry. Panshak lifted it into his arms and it fell quiet, and its mother's arm fell away. He pulled the light blue hand-knit blanket closely around the baby. He could not tell whether the child was a week old or a month. By instinct, he smiled at the little face that was watching him with shiny black eyes devoid of motive. By instinct, he swayed, gently at first, then rocked steadily, until the dead woman and the upturned room and the Greying world outside fell away without a sound and all that was left, all that mattered, was this life he was carrying in his hands. When the child had fallen asleep, he laid it on the straightened mattress and faced the mother.

Panshak looked for a shovel in the backyard just outside the kitchen where the tools were stored, but there was none. His search took him to the lawn, and he found one lying near a freshly dug patch of earth. Confused for a moment, he looked around and spotted Nana Kanke's grave ten paces away, with the blank headstone he had erected. This grave at his feet was someone else's. Without thinking too hard, he knew whose. He gave silent thanks to whoever had dug it.

Picking up the shovel, he went a few yards away and began to dig. The ground was hard. Each shovelful required such an exertion of energy that he paused briefly between them, getting more tired each time. At some point, he sat on the ground, trying to catch his breath. As he got up again, he noticed a pickax lying in the dead brown grass some feet away. With the pickax, the work went faster. Even though he still had to pause a bit after every few strokes, he was pleased that he was figuring it out for himself. He stabbed the earth until it felt soft enough, and then he shoveled. Stabbed and shoveled. The hole he made was not large, nor was it that deep, but it had to do. All his strength had fled him.

He went back upstairs. The baby was still asleep. He took the knife out of the dead woman's hand. He decided the best way was to pull her by her armpits rather than her legs. It meant getting blood on him, but it seemed more appropriate. It was also more difficult because there was much less purchase for his hands. Corners and doors were a particular challenge. Still, he managed. He reached the top of the staircase and released the body, tired in every way. How should one carry a dead body down the stairs when it was nearly twice one's size? He bent again to lift the woman up, to drag both her and himself down, step by step, uncertain whether he had any strength left for it. He heard feet on the stairs and whipped around in panic. Dunka was coming toward him with a pained expression. Panshak ignored the questions he wanted to ask his brother, like what he was doing here and how he had known where to find him. They did not matter right now. What mattered was that he was here, and he had never been gladder to see him.

Panshak straightened up and drew back, watching as his brother hoisted the body clean to his shoulder and led the way out to the lawn. Dunka placed the body down gently on its back and raised the pickax.

"Get a cloth," he said.

Panshak rushed back into the house. The curtains on the ground floor were a pale yellow, decorated with the green tendrils of a vine that pirouetted around each other, swooping and swirling and looping. He grabbed the first one and tugged hard, ripping it off its rail. Outside, Dunka was succeeding in making the grave deeper, swinging steadily. As Panshak stood aside and watched, his brother's movements seemed so effortless.

On the way back home, Dunka carried his digging tools while Panshak carried the baby in one arm, his walking stick in the other. The child slept through it all. No one spoke.

Much later that evening, after everyone had met the baby and Arrit had confirmed that it was a girl, Arrit left the room to get something to eat for Panshak from what Rit had brought. While he waited for his food, he pulled out Nana Kanke's notebook and scanned through it. If even she had failed at keeping track of time, what hope did he have? What would they do?

Panshak put the notebook down and went to the calendar. The world outside Pilam had its own clock, and they would have theirs. They owed the world no obligation of keeping to its definition of time. Wednesday, Monday, Sunday—it made no difference. They only had to start somewhere. He marked the calendar as Sunday. The first day. The beginning of time.

He stretched out on the bed and listened for the infant's breathing, but there was no sound. He bolted upright and checked the baby's face. As if to assure him, a little squeak escaped the infant's mouth. He lay back down, moored with relief, and told himself that it had not been such a bad day after all. That was when the tears came.

21

PANMUN

They had already summitted the mountain by the time it was getting dark. While it was still twilight, they found a spot off the road among some flowering bitter leaf bushes and parked. Zumji told Panmun to lie in the back of the rickshaw while he insisted on sleeping on the ground, just as he had done the first night. She could hear a strain in his voice. It seemed like he was holding his breath even while he spoke, talking slowly, as if each word were too heavy to pronounce.

"Are you all right?" she said as she stretched out on the back seat and covered herself. He was climbing out of the vehicle slowly.

"I'm fine," he said. It was already too dark to see his face. He held her hand and squeezed it. "Let's sleep now so we can start early."

In the morning, she was up before him. She stepped out of the rickshaw. It was bright enough to see the individual blades of dead grass on the ground. They were damp with dew. The air itself was damp. That her vision had become a permanent monochrome was no longer strange to her. She simply saw things as she saw them. She stood over Zumji and called his name, but he did not answer. She called it again and still there was no answer. She bent down and shook him, but he did not move. She pulled away his blanket, revealing a crumpled old shirt he held over his waist. She took the shirt away and saw the wound. There was gray blood everywhere.

She looked at his face. His eyes were closed. She clutched his head with both hands and yelled his name. She was prepared to scream and scream his name until her voice deserted her and the mountain they were on crumbled and everything she cared about, including the child she was carrying, was dead and gone and nothing mattered because nothing did. But he made a sound that seemed to come from deep inside his belly, and so she did not scream to end all things.

He opened his eyes a fraction and closed them again. He turned his head from one side to the other. She said something, and he did not respond. She looked around at the gray rocks and gray grass and gray trees. She looked at the gray rising sun. She looked at the gray rickshaw. There were about ten paces between them and the vehicle. She tried to get him to his feet, but he collapsed right back to the ground. He released another groan. Some of his gray blood had gotten on her. She tried again, half carrying and half dragging him all the way. Something came down from heaven, or rose out of the earth, filling her with strength. She had to enter the rickshaw from the far side and pull him into it. She threw out everything in the back seat. She threw out the gray sacks and the empty gray jerrican and the gray watermelons. She leaned him back on the seat. The wound was leaking steadily, ceaselessly, like mercury. A pistol lay on the floor of the rickshaw. She looked at it once, then looked away and did not think about it again.

She sat in the driver's seat and stared out through the empty window. That was when she became still. Her hammering heart was an excruciating point in her chest. If her father were alive, he would have told her what to do; wherever he may have been, she would have sensed his counsel and known what to do. When she had gathered her senses and could see the road before her clearly, she turned her head and looked at Zumji. She looked at him as though he had just popped out of thin air before her very eyes. The fact of him, wounded and helpless, was fantastical, a figment of the cruelest, most far-fetched imagination. She looked down at the controls before her. Turned the key, just like he showed her. Released the lever on the floor with her left foot. Engaged the clutch pedal with her right foot. Pressed the ignition button. She did everything, though she was not certain it was in the order he had shown her. And she must have done it right, because the engine started.

When the rickshaw had become a rumbling, living thing in her hands, she willed it forward. She did not know how she was doing it. It bounced along the uneven ground, and she had to steer it around with all her might so that it faced the road. She kept glancing back to make sure he was safe. She drove slowly because she was afraid he might fall out if the rickshaw shook too much. The roughness of the road did not let up. She drove and drove while the sun climbed and then began to fall. It was too slow, she knew, but slower and steadier was better than throwing him out of the rickshaw and wounding him further. At a point she stopped glancing back at him, determined to keep the vehicle moving, to keep her eyes on the road, keep her focus unbroken because she had to get him home. She had to get him home to safety even though she did not know what would happen when they got there or if anyone would know what to do about the wound or how to stop the bleeding or how to save him. But everything would be all right once she got home, and she had to get home because nothing else mattered, and the rickshaw rumbled on along the road and the gray sun fell from the gray sky and dragged shadows across the gray earth and the road stretched on and on like a cruel joke that refused to reach its punch line and then she felt his head bump into her back and knew at once that the world had finally come to an end.

Panmun climbed into the back of the rickshaw and pulled him to her. She did not look at his lifeless face, but rather placed his head on her chest as night overtook them. By morning she was spent. Her eyes had soldered shut, because at some point in her unraveling, she had fallen asleep. When she came to, she refused to open them and just went on crying. She did not know what her body was lying on and she did not care. The sun's heat shone on her and remained there, as though attempting to console her, but went away when she paid it no mind. Evening came and then night and it got colder, and that she paid no mind either. Sleep took her and brought her back intermittently, in broad passages of time. She existed in gray dreams in which Zumji said words to her that made no sense and that she could not remember when she was awake. Her siblings were in those dreams too. They were happy to see her, telling her how glad they were that she had come back.

Why had she insisted on going back to Pilam when they had made a clean escape? When Zumji had insisted on pressing on? If she had listened to him, none of this would have happened. He would not have been hurt and they would have been somewhere else by now, alive, happy together. The insistent feeling that they would always be in danger if they were outside Pilam, the substantial guilt that accused her of deserting her family—even Dunka—these feelings that had gripped her throat and made her weepy and erratic and stubborn about turning back—she would gladly crumple them up and burn them. She would gladly forsake her family for him. She would gladly die for him.

Death. There it was, a way out of all this. And she had options. There was the gun, though she would have to figure out how to shoot it first. There was his knife, lying around somewhere too. Whatever would be quicker and less painful. She did not like pain. Would he be there on the other side, waiting to welcome her? Her mother and father? Would she be able to have her child there? If the child were never born here, would it exist on the other side? She did not care one way or the other. She recognized the dark, heavy sheet that now covered her. She had first felt it under the flame tree, and then a couple of times after. It was different from her grief, an addition to it. Unlike her grief, which was like a body of water she was submerged in, water that could either drown her or carry her, this was a giant flat rock, an entire planet, a great expanse of distilled despair, crushing the air out of her. It was the Grey, and it was telling her to end it all.

She had to use her fingers like levers to pry her eyelids open. She was lying on the floor of the rickshaw, squeezed between the front and back seats. Daylight stabbed her eyes as she groped for the gun. It was on the ground beside the rickshaw. She crawled onto the sand after it. When she had it, she had to use two hands to carry it, and even that seemed barely enough. Filling her hands like an oversized, misshapen rock, it felt cold and brutal and rigid against her fingers. If she could have carried it with one hand, she would have held it against her temple. It would have felt less frontal, less intrusive. She pointed it up instead and placed the cold muzzle under her chin. Her hands were shaking; she tried to will them to stop, but they shook on. She found the solid, unmoving outline of the trigger and placed both her forefingers on it, bracing herself for the power she knew pulling it would require.

Her mind was in a state of utter blankness when she pressed the trigger. She felt it give way, felt the gun come to life. But nothing happened after that. There was no blast, no pain, no freedom. She opened her eyes and saw the same pewter landscape. The sun had begun to go down again. She lowered the gun from the point where it was digging raw pain into her chin, looked at it. It was useless to her. She did not know how to make it work, how to unleash the death it contained upon herself. It seemed impregnable and unyielding, a complete mystery. She threw it away, placed her head between her knees, and willed herself on to death.

When she raised her head, and then her body, it was in the dead of night. She could no longer feel the Grey. The flat rock, the planet, whatever it was that had been crushing her, had lifted. Her head was quiet and clear. She felt her way toward the rickshaw and found him in the back seat. Positioning herself next to him, she laid her head on his chest, pulled his arms around her, and closed her eyes.

At first light, there was no change. He remained as still as before. She stood next to the rickshaw and waited for the light to grow stronger. There was a gentle breeze. It had rained somewhere. As she stood there, she realized that something like a pillar of steel had emerged from the floor of her being through the night. It was the thing that was holding her up so that she did not crumple and dissolve into tears once again. Finally, when it was bright enough, and every detail in every object in the world was laid bare, she stooped into the rickshaw and, for the first time in the nearly three days since he had died, looked at his face. She did not know what a peaceful dead face looked like. His eyes were closed, and his body was here with her. That was all that mattered.

She looked in the compartment behind the rear seat and found some folded clothes, including a large bedsheet. She covered him with it and arranged him in the back seat, ensuring he was as comfortable as she imagined he could have felt had he been alive. She started driving again. It felt easier this time. She knew no tiredness, no hunger—these had become lesser concerns.

Soon she began the descent from the mountain, snaking along the switchback, unaware that she was performing an act that had challenged even more experienced drivers. She came to the place where they had stood during their escape and stared out at the sunset, the place where he had wept in her arms and she had held him, the place where she had told him she was pregnant. She passed it without a second glance and descended into the valley that held her birthplace like a prisoner. She drove through Pilam without acknowledging anything, right up to the house with the rocks on its roof and the avocado tree in its backyard and the blue pickup truck that sat beside her mother's grave.

She drove the rickshaw into the backyard and stopped. When she got down, there was a girl who was not Rit standing outside the kitchen door. She had beautiful dark skin, and she was wearing Panmun's clothes, her sunglasses.

"Where is everyone?" Panmun said.

"Rit is in the other house. But I don't know where Dunka and Panshak went to."

Hearing the names of her siblings come so casually from this stranger's lips told Panmun that this had become her home too.

"I'm Panmun." A look of unrestrained pleasure came over what she could see of the girl's face.

"I'm Arrit," the girl said, before rushing forward and throwing her arms around Panmun. Panmun found herself putting her own arms around her, found that it was the natural thing to do. She came undone once again, this time by the simple contact with warm, living flesh. The pillar of steel that had held her up the last few hours gave way. They were no longer holding each other; it was only Arrit holding her. And then carrying her. Or was the carrying being done by someone else? Because she heard a male voice. Voices. She could have been held by her feet and swung like a pendulum, or thrown into a chasm to fall forever, or dropped inside a hole and covered with earth, and she would have been none the wiser. There were more voices. Talking. A squeal. And weeping that was not hers. Her name chanted like a blessing, or like a prayer.

When she came to, the world was still gray, but her siblings were gathered around her. All of them. There was Panshak standing by the bed with something in his arms, a bundle—a baby. Rit was on her left, between the wall and the bed, half lying, half sitting, her face shining with tears. Dunka was sitting on her left with his Grey-swaddled eyes, holding her hand. *Dunka* was holding her hand. There were others in the room too. A boy and a girl—Tongzum and Tongrot—standing at a respectful distance. Arrit was by the door, using her hand like a rag to wipe her face behind the glasses.

"We have to bury him," Dunka said. "Before night comes."

Panmun nodded and looked at the window. Daylight was already falling sideways into the room. When she went outside, she saw that Dunka had already dug the grave, a hole beside their mother's grave. The body, draped in the bedsheet, was lying next to it. Her heart squeezed with gratitude; it was a lovely gesture. But it was not the right place.

She took them to the foot of the flame tree and said, "Here."

In the six days since she had last seen it, more flowers had emerged among its leaves. They were nothing but dull, bloodless petals to her eyes. She stood by and watched Dunka swing and dig and sweat, knowing that it was wrong of her to make him dig another grave, but that the greater wrong would be letting Zumji lie in a place that he would not have chosen. She could see him, hear him say plainly that he should be buried under the tree he had marked with an *X* in the name of their love. It was only fitting that his grave be covered in a carpet of flaming red flowers at the height of the rains, even if she would not be able to see the scarlet.

When the grave was ready, Dunka brought the body and placed it beside the hole. He climbed down into it, then lifted the body and laid it on the fresh exposed soil at his feet. Panmun climbed the flame tree to the lowest branch and plucked a flower. She dropped it into the grave. Dunka began to shovel the earth back in. Panmun watched as it swallowed up Zumji's body. More tears took her, and someone had to hold her up.

They all stood around in silence for a long time afterward. When it was almost too dark to see, someone remarked that the baby should not be outside, so Panshak and Arrit carried her home. The others left a little after to go back to "the other house." Zumji's house. Then it was just Panmun and Dunka standing under the tree in the deep twilight, looking at the grave.

Sometimes, where wounds exist, words can be insufficient. Even an apology can be impotent. But a touch—as light as an arm around someone, as Dunka was doing with his sister. A gesture—as small as a head placed in trust on a shoulder, as Panmun was doing with her brother. These can heal.

When they were back in the house, Panmun went to Panshak's room. She wanted to see the baby. The moment he let her in, she could tell that he had been crying.

"Are you all right?" she said.

Panshak smiled and wiped his eyes.

The baby was on the bed, asleep. Panshak told her how he had found her, where he had found her. She wondered whether it was too soon to mention that she was going to have a baby, then decided not to do it today. She sat beside the baby and stared at her for several minutes. Panshak stood against the wall, not saying anything. When she looked up, she noticed the large paper sheet on the wall.

"Is that a calendar?" she said.

Panshak nodded. He pointed at the first box.

"Today is Sunday."

She hadn't known today was Sunday. She did not know the last time she had thought about what day of the week it was. But it seemed right that today should be Sunday. Food came and she still had no appetite, but she forced something down because she knew her body was running on fumes.

When she was lying on her mother's bed, sleep took a long time coming, despite how tired she felt. His face kept swimming inside her eyelids. She may or may not have slept, but she was awake first thing in the morning, and she got up and went out to the grave. As she left, she took care not to rouse Rit and Tongrot, who had both slept on the same bed with her.

The wind had picked up, and there were clouds so thick in the sky that the sun was blotted out before it had begun to truly sing. She watched as the leaves and branches of the flame tree shook. It seemed right that they should shake and scatter their flowers on his grave below, shake and scatter flowers for him. She stood there and listened to the rumble of thunder, and then the rain as it began to fall on everything, gently at first. The drops drummed like a thousand tiny feet on the metal roofs in the distance. They shattered against her skin, grew more insistent. Soon, she was drenched, cocooned inside their enchanting sound as they battered the ground. She felt safe in them. Safe and strong. Strong enough to smile at the scarlet petals that covered the grave.

22

DUNKA

Dunka rose before the sun. He got his digging tools from the back-yard and left the house as the sky was beginning to light up. The woman he had buried yesterday at Arrit's behest was the third person he had ever dug a grave for. The first had been his mother, the second Nana Ritdirnen. Something about digging the grave and gently laying the body of a stranger into the earth had filled him with purpose, as if he had found a new calling. Seeking the dead out wherever they lay, burying them.

It did not take him long to find the body on Nana Kanke's property. His eyes slid quickly over the head wound and the broken limbs. Panshak had done this. He draped the sheet he had brought with him over the body, hiding the face, determined not to see too much. Then he looked around for a proper place. His eyes fell on the unmarked gravestone. It had to be a gravestone, because the ground in front of it had no dead grass. He began to dig a spot beside it.

At some point, he paused to watch the pale, colorless sun as it peeked over the edge of the world. Its rays grew stronger and brighter, painting silvery light across the skin of the day. When the grave was waist-deep, he wrapped the sheet around the body and eased it down into the hole where he was standing. Before he shoveled earth back in, he stopped to think of what to say. It did not seem right to just bury someone without some special words, especially considering the circumstances of his death and Panshak's involvement and, by extension, Dunka's own. But he did not know this boy. He barely knew what he looked like. He held on to Arrit's counsel because it was all he had: his brother must have had no other option. With nothing to say, he picked up a handful of sand and tossed it on the body. And then he filled the grave back up.

As he turned to go, he saw Panshak crossing the grounds toward the house. He hoped his brother would not see him, but he did not try to hide. When Panshak had gone inside, Dunka stood in front of the house. It had been dark when he arrived—he had failed to notice how grand it was, with a stonework facade and stonework pillars that held up the porch roof. He waited, but when it seemed to him that Panshak had spent too long inside, he followed him in.

As they walked home afterward, Dunka stole glances at Panshak. He truly did not know him, and the blame was all his own; he did not know this boy who had killed another and was now carrying a baby in his scrawny arms. The sight would have drawn a laugh out of Dunka in prior days, prior years. It was a child carrying a child, after all. But there was true intention in Panshak's face, in every step he took. His little brother had become a man even while he was still a boy.

When they got home, Panmun was crying on the ground in the backyard while Arrit held her to stop her from hurting herself. A battered rickshaw stood there, missing so much, including its windshield and most of its hood. There was a dead body inside, and Dunka did not need to pry to know who it was. He watched his wailing sister as she railed with all her strength and with all her voice against nothing, against God. It was like she had emerged from a dream, materializing in the real world, with her tears and her dreadlocks. And though he could see her and hear her, he still did not believe that she was real until he lifted her from the ground into his arms, felt her weight. Carried her inside. Smelled the stink of sweat that rolled off her in waves, the dirt that covered her like a second skin. She had driven the rickshaw here from someplace out there. He had not known she could drive anything.

He laid her in their mother's bed and on she railed. He told Panshak to get Rit. Panshak handed the baby to Arrit and scurried off. Gradually, they gathered in the room, watching her, burdened by a strange cocktail of joy at the sight of her, sorrow at the spectacle of her grieving, and confusion about everything else she had brought. Rit lay beside her sister and also wept, but quietly. The baby started to cry too, and Arrit took it outside. When Arrit came back a little later, the child was asleep. Panshak collected it and remained standing.

Knowing they owed Zumji their lives, Dunka dug the space where their father should have been buried, beside their mother. It was the greatest honor he could think of. But later, when Panmun protested, he said nothing. More than any of them, this was her grief, and therefore her decision.

After they had buried him and the others had dispersed and it was just the two of them under the flame tree and he had curled his arm around her, she began to cry again, in a more contained way this time. Her body shook with the great gusts of her emotion, and his along with her. He did not let her go. He would never let her go again.

When he was back in his room and had made sure that Panmun had bathed and eaten and was now asleep, Arrit came to see him. He invited her to sit. This was her first time in the room: the awareness occupied his vision, pushing a flurry of thoughts through his head, including the question of what she would do if he kissed her. She was so close he could feel the heat from her body blazing toward him. He stood, crossed the room, and leaned against the wall, ashamed that he should be feeling things like that at a time like this.

"It's a girl," she said with what was almost a smile.

Dunka nodded. The question of the baby's sex had not crossed his mind.

"Where did he find her?" Arrit asked.

"In Nana Kanke's house. You don't know it, it's on the other side."

"What about her parents?"

"We buried the mother."

"She needs milk."

"Milk," Dunka repeated.

"Yes."

He went to the window and lifted the curtain. Digging four graves had taken its toll on his strength; now the day was gone, any chance of finding milk along with it. By all indications, this child would die too. Another grave to dig.

He kept awake all through the night. That had been the rhythm of his sleep since his escape from Pishang. One or two nights of patchy sleep followed by a full night without any sleep. He would sometimes feel the Grey like a hand groping around inside his soul, looking for a tender spot where it could hurt him. Then it would stop moving as suddenly as it had started. Since it had crippled him and caused his capture that day in Pishang, the day he met her, it had not come for him with the same animosity. Still, he waited for it every day, particularly in those moments when he was alone and all he could see was the starkness of his existence, which was being soaked up like water in sand. Moments like this.

When the night was in the deep passages of slumber, that stretch of time that is no further from dusk than it is from dawn, Dunka lit the piece of candle he had received from Arrit—she had distributed candles like medicine to everyone in the house, and even to Rit, Tongzum, and Tongrot in the other house. Raising his candle, he went outside. A breeze buffeted the flame, but it did not blow it out. He looked up. The stars pulsed like a million little heartbeats, stark and enchanting against the black sky. He was glad he had a candle tonight. If she happened to come out again and run into him, she would not think he was a ghost and flee. She would see his light, know it was him, stay. They would stand there and be dazzled together by the little points of light above their heads, by how immense and true they seemed in the absence of the lesser lights of human affairs.

What would he tell her? What would she say in return? Would she let him take her hand? And then what? She had said the baby needed milk. He did not know what to do about it. How many times had his siblings looked up to him, and how many times had he failed them? Instead, they had been saved by the kindnesses of others. He should have been more present when they lost their parents in quick succession. He could have done more for Nana Ritdirnen as the Grey ate her away. For the life of him, he could not remember where he had been when he was away from the house in the early days. He had walked a lot. Sat alone inside caves, under trees, thinking about his old friends, his dreams, and everything else the Grey had stolen from him—mostly time. Being angry a lot. But he had never really had a plan. He had wanted to be rich, but he had not figured out how to do that. He could have gone to the university like his mother had wanted or learned how to farm well like his father had wanted. He had really thought he had time.

His father had once told him that the rain, the sun, and the clouds must first agree before a rainbow could appear. Why they chose to agree at any given moment was not anybody's concern. What mattered was that the rainbow appeared. It had been said in a moment of anger. He knew that his father had been speaking to him about the difference between being a dreamer and a doer, about which produced results. Now the words took on a different meaning, a more convenient one. It did not matter what had happened before now, nor the things he had not done, nor the reasons why he had not done them. What mattered was that he was here now, that he was present.

A sound crept out of the kitchen door and into his ears: the sharp, needle-thin shrieking of an infant. Dunka followed it to Panshak's room. When he opened the door, his brother was pacing the room with the baby, looking utterly determined and utterly helpless. His face was contorted in pain on the child's behalf.

"She's hungry."

Dunka stood there, feeling just as helpless. Painfully aware that he was the adult here and ought to do something. He wanted to take the baby and see if he could quieten her, but what would he do differently that Panshak had not already done? Arrit swept into the room and took her. The crying did not stop, but it seemed to abate somewhat. She clutched the baby to her chest and rocked her back and forth. She seemed to be trying to grasp the front of Arrit's blouse in search of breast milk.

"You need to find something," Arrit said. She was looking at Dunka.

He swallowed the saliva that had collected around his tongue.

"Panshak, let's go," he said.

He left the room without waiting, propelled by the sudden and frantic need to know what he was doing, or at least appear to do so. He stopped by his room and pulled on a shirt. When he was outside and the sound of the crying baby was a distant wailing, he turned and found Panshak at his elbow. The next thing to do became clear to him then. He went to the pickup truck and rummaged under the front seat until he found a couple of old rags, chewed up into tired strips of cloth by the years. Next, he found their father's old hose in the back of the truck, and then the bucket in which he had found the burned pieces of fabric that he knew to be Arrit's school uniform. With his lips on one end of the hose, he pulled on air from the belly of the truck with a sharp sucking sound. For a moment, it seemed that all the gasoline had evaporated, but then there was the gentle swirl of liquid as it flowed out of the tank and into the metal bucket. Dunka was aware of the kerosene Arrit had found the day before, but that would be saved for cooking their meals.

He picked up Panshak's stick, which was leaning beside the kitchen door, wrapped the strips of rag around one end, and dipped it into the bucket of gasoline. When he held the dripping cloth to the candle, a bright white flame erupted into being, casting away the darkness. He snuffed out the candle and set out into the night.

"Where are we going?" Panshak asked.

Dunka's tongue had gone limp, his mind hollow. He did not feel like talking, but his limbs had a life of their own. They followed the light of the flame until he was walking down the aisle of cacti that led to Zumji's house. He knocked on the door at first, as a courtesy, but when no one came, he entered and made his way to the bedroom.

Tongzum was the only one sleeping on the large bed. He did not stir. Dunka shook him until he was awake.

When they were all outside, Dunka explained the situation. "Where can we get milk?" he said.

Tongzum looked at him with heavy eyelids, the sleep slow in retreating.

"Have you seen any cows in the area?" Dunka said.

Tongzum shook his head. "Uncle Zumji said cattle herders have been avoiding this place since they built the fence."

"What about goats? No goats?"

Dunka knew that most of the goats that people kept had escaped into the wild. Except for the occasional buck, it was rare to see a goat roaming the streets. They had all vanished among the rocks.

"I've seen some goats," Tongzum said.

"Where?" Dunka said.

"They move around."

"Haven't you tried to trap any?"

"Uncle Zumji said it's hard to catch them because they destroy the traps. But he showed me how to make a goat trap. I can try."

"No," Dunka said, "we have to catch one this night. Do you know where they sleep?"

There was a brief pause. In the eager, dancing firelight, Tongzum's face was hard and sad, gleaming like marble. He nodded slowly. "I think I know the area."

"Let's go back to the house and get more light."

As he said those words, Dunka felt useful, responsible. Like he knew what he was doing. Raising the light like a scepter, he led them in a single file back to the house. They ripped and bound and doused and lit; then each boy raised his torch above his head, and the circle of light that pooled at their feet grew wider until it spilled past the rickshaw and onto the dirt road that ran past the house.

"Keep the flame above your head," Dunka said.

They set out once more with Tongzum leading the way. The walk seemed to be without end. Every now and then, Dunka would steal a glance at Panshak, who kept swapping the torch from one hand to the other and back. Dunka knew his arms were getting tired. Passing through a cluster of baobab trees with the night chirping and hooting around them, they emerged onto a field. Dead, knee-length grass shimmered in the breeze like the surface of a pond, stretching away into darkness. Beyond all that, at one end of the sky, a pale light was slowly spreading across the length of the horizon.

"I saw them here a few times," Tongzum said. "I think they're in there."

He pointed to his right, where the outline of a small hill loomed thick and black. They went toward it, moving along the line of trees. They stopped at the foot of the hill, and he pointed up into the rocks that lay like scabs on the hillside.

Dunka looked around, trying to think of the next thing. Would they scare the goats off if they went among the rocks with their torches?

"We have to catch a female," Dunka said.

"How will we tell the difference?" Panshak asked.

"The ones with big stomachs," Tongzum said.

"Target the ones that have kids with them," Dunka added.

234

"Are we chasing them?" Tongzum said. "They can be fast."

"We'll have to be faster," Dunka said. "Go up and drive them out. We'll wait here to catch them."

Slowly, Tongzum turned and made his way up the hill. His shape and his light soon vanished among the rocks. The sky was growing lighter by the minute. Dunka looked at his torch—the wick was gradually shrinking into a glowing ember.

Panshak was staring at the ground. The torch was askew in his hand. He seemed to have forgotten he was holding fire.

"Are you worried about the baby?"

Panshak looked up. "A little."

"She'll be fine," Dunka said, wishing he could believe his own words. Feeling the sudden urge to do more, he stuck the end of his torch into the ground so that it stood straight. He went to where Panshak was standing, placed his hands on his little brother's shoulders, and looked into his eyes—they glinted with the light of the flame that flickered over their heads.

"The girl will be fine," Dunka repeated.

Panshak nodded and smiled a weak, lopsided smile. He looked tired and purehearted. Dunka saw a child's face, open and eager and trusting.

"She'll need a name," Dunka said.

"I have one."

"You do?"

"Yes."

"What?"

"Shwar."

Dunka smiled. "That's a good name." He returned to his torch and picked it up, still smiling.

As the light grew stronger, he realized the base of the hill stretched away on both sides of them. The goats could come down from any direction.

"We should spread out," Dunka said, and they went farther apart along the bottom of the hill.

As the flames grew weaker, the need for them also diminished. Dunka could see Panshak where he stood at the other end without raising his light. He was a dark shape, outlined by the pale light coming down from the sky. If he focused his gaze, Dunka could see the beginnings of his brother's face and the muted color of his red T-shirt under the jacket he wore. Panshak stuck his torch into the ground and squatted next to it. Watching him do that made Dunka feel tired too, and he remembered standing on Arrit's street eight days ago—though it had not just been eight days; it had been his whole life that had unwound between that moment and this. He remembered how his shoulders had been hunched against the relentless tiredness of that day, realized they were hunched in the same way now: he was perpetually steeling his body against the undying fatigue. And he could not squat or bend or betray his exhaustion.

Suddenly, Dunka snapped his head around to look at Panshak again. How had he known that his shirt was red? He squinted at it, saw the unmistakable flash of crimson. Panshak's torch was crowned by a bright yellow flame that was melting into a livid reddish ember. Then he heard the first bleat, and a single brown goat bolted out of the rocks. Buck or doe, it was hard to tell. Before he had finished making sense of the fleeing creature, a cacophony of bleats floated down to him from behind the rocks. As though they were climbing out of every hiding place on the earth, the goats emerged in streaks of black and brown and ochre. There was color everywhere. Dunka threw his burned-out torch aside and spread his legs instinctively like a goalkeeper, realizing how stupid he must look. The goats were fanning out as they rushed down the hill, terrified. Far behind them was Tongzum, waving his torch and free arm wildly.

When the first goats reached him, Dunka grasped blindly, trying to grab anything—a horn, a tail, an ear—but they slipped around his legs, bleating small clouds of hot air into the morning and escaping into the field. Ignoring the pain in his forearm, Dunka whipped around to give chase and froze. Half of the rising sun had crested the horizon, splashing liquid yellow light across the brown grass and setting it ablaze. The goats became like golden rivulets in the glare. The world had gone from black and white to full living color. It was like every possible shade in the spectrum had been squeezed into the vista before him. Dunka blinked suddenly, returning to the moment and realizing what was happening. Panshak and Tongzum were beside him, gaping at the sunrise too.

"They're getting away!" Dunka shouted.

They all scrambled after the goats. As Dunka ran through the grass, his legs seemed to grow longer, taking him farther with each stride. His body was waking up, every pore yawning, taking in every sensation. Dew leaped off the disturbed grass and blessed his toes. Delicious cold air wafted into his mouth and lungs in long drags. Light reached into his pupils, and then deeper into some other place inside him, pulsing through each cell until he felt like his spirit was light itself. He could have stood in the center of Pilam at night and lit up the whole place. He could have joined the sun in the sky right then and become one with it, or floated up to heaven like some winged god. But the baby needed milk, and he was gaining on the goats, and Panshak and Tongzum were there, running beside him. Someone whooped, and Dunka whooped back. It made sense to whoop. He laughed out loud as he thought of the baby and her new name. Shwar. *Laughter.*

A brown doe with glorious, large udders came into focus. She was being followed by a small black kid. The kid could barely keep up. As Dunka caught up to it, he bent and scooped it into his arms. The mother picked up speed, charging forward. Dunka stayed with her, cradling the bleating kid under his left arm, reaching for the mother's hind legs with his right hand. His heart was beating so hard he thought it would burst. If he could just get some milk for the child, because all that there was, all that existed, was the goat, the milk, and the baby.

Goat, milk, and baby, goat, milk, baby, goat, milk, baby goat milk baby goat milk baby—

His hand closed around the doe's leg and he slammed his heels into the ground, skidding on the slippery, dead grass. She was too heavy to lift clean off the ground, but he had her at last. She wailed with a voice so human that his skin tingled. Tongzum was struggling with another goat a few feet away. When Dunka drew closer, dragging the doe behind him like a sack of maize, he saw that it was a large buck, more than half the size of the boy's entire body. The creature tried to butt the boy with its horns, but Tongzum kept an arm fastened around its neck and carefully avoided the two sharp points. A strong, musky scent rose from the two of them, adding a deep flavor to the fresh air. All around them, the sounds of bleating. Most of the animals, sensing that the chase had ceased, had stopped running and stood in the distance. Some were facing the sunrise like statues carved in its honor, others had begun to nibble at the dead grass. A little farther ahead, Panshak was making his way toward them, lugging a kid.

"We should have brought rope," he said when he reached them. His face broke into a broad grin at the sight of the complete catch. It was aglow with some ineffable joy that Dunka shared.

Dunka carried the buck and Tongzum the doe. They both slung the animals across their necks. Panshak took the two kids, which were small enough to fit under one arm each. There was deep rumbling in the sky, and when Dunka looked east, he saw a thundercloud forming.

When they reached the house, Dunka resisted the urge to go right inside, where he could look in his shard of mirror. Panshak found a rope, and they tied the two adult goats to the tree. They placed a pot under the doe. The black kid drew up to its mother and tried to suckle.

"You'll have to hold it," Dunka said to Panshak.

He lowered his head below the goat and tried to grab her udders, but she jerked and pulled away.

"Tongzum, hold her head for me."

"I think you should wash your hands," Panshak said.

Dunka drew a pail of water from the well and washed his hands. With the goat secured, Dunka cupped the udder in one hand and squeezed a little, but nothing happened. He took hold of a teat the size of his thumb, pressed it gently. A weak stream of milk escaped, dribbling over his fingers. As his fingers pinched and held the teat where it protruded from the udder, he sensed that this was the way to go. Below that point, the teat had become distended with milk like a balloon. He remembered the bulbs of sweetened cow's milk that were sold to them as kids, secured tightly inside transparent plastic bags that jiggled and threatened to burst when you pressed too hard. Dunka squeezed with the rest of his fingers and a powerful jet of milk shot out, hitting the bottom of the pot with a zing. He brought his free hand to the second teat and did the same thing. After three or four squeezes, he found his rhythm.

Twenty minutes later, the pot was nearly full. The sky had turned black with clouds that were turgid with rain. The wind was getting stronger. Dunka carried the milk into the house and rummaged through the drawers until he found a black plastic bag. He had wanted the kind their mother had used to wrap balls of mun, the same kind in his memory of sweet milk bulbs, but this would have to do. He blew it to clear it of debris, then poured some milk in. He tied the bag's mouth in a knot so that the liquid inside made the surface of the bag bulge, like a full cheek. Tongzum and Panshak flanked Dunka as they went down the corridor. The door to Arrit's room was wide open. Inside, he saw that the girls had gathered and were all splayed out on the bed, each curled against the next. The baby was stretched out on Arrit's chest. Panmun was not among them.

Rit, who had her eyes open and faced the door, saw him first. She saw the black thing in his hands and shook Arrit awake. Arrit sat up, cradling the baby. Tongrot slept on. Dunka watched the baby's limp body. He was waiting for someone to explain, to state in plain terms that the baby had died, but no one spoke. When Arrit was seated on the edge of the bed, she looked at the black ball, and then she reached for it.

Dunka met the question in her eyes.

"Goat's milk," he said.

Arrit's eyes filled up and popped with surprise as she looked at him, like she was noticing something about him for the first time. But she said nothing. She raised the tip of the black bulge to her mouth and bit. Beads of milk squeezed through the tiny opening, baptizing her hands and the baby's clothes. As the bag met the child's lips, a sucking sound filled the room. Dunka released a great breath he had not known he was holding. They all stood around the baby, listening to the sound—bearing witness to the miracle—of her sustenance. When Arrit broke the feeding so she could stand up and put the child in Dunka's arms, the little girl released a shriek of protest. Making sure he held her with his good arm, Dunka took the milk in his free hand and resumed the feeding. Holding the child like this, Dunka felt large, overgrown. Like any move he made would hurt the baby because she was so fragile, and he was so big. He stood as still as he imagined a strong tree would stand, like the avocado tree outside, like the flame tree guarding Zumji's grave. Shwar. And suddenly, everything else seemed significant. Tongzum's dirty face as he looked on, and Tongrot, stirred awake by the suckling, and Rit, who sat on the bed wearing a proud smile, and Panshak, leaning against the wall, watching too, but in a serious, brooding manner, as if making sure that everything was proceeding accordingly. All of them pieces of his family, old and new together, here in the same room, witnessing glory. And Arrit. She was not just watching him—he felt like she was witnessing him too, witnessing his eyes. As if their eyes had become people in themselves, seeing each other, acknowledging each other. The rain began to fall. He wondered whether Panmun might still be asleep. The sound became heavy and full and steady, filling the house with a constant, comforting din.

Later, after Dunka had laid the sleeping Shwar back on the bed, he went to his room. Before he could find the broken mirror, he heard footsteps behind him. It was Arrit, holding another mirror. He recognized it, a small round pink mirror with a long handle. One of Panmun's mirrors that she had often left lying around the house. Arrit raised the mirror in front of him. The eyes that stared back at him were not the same eyes he had been wearing for what felt like his whole life. They were brand-new eyes. Arrit also had new eyes. They heard footsteps and turned to see Panmun coming in from the rain, drenched to her bones and dripping water all over the floor. She seemed animated and bursting with words. Her eyes looked the same as theirs: pristine, white, save for the irises and pupils, which were dark and rightly so, because that was what irises and pupils were. Apart from that, there was no trace of speck or stain. The Grey was gone.

Acknowledgments

Before the idea for this book was even conceived of, these dear friends demonstrated a persistent, unwavering, confounding faith in my talent over the years: Ulan Garba Matta, Sa'ada Metteden, Anja Wallace, and Cristin Williams. Thank you for the books, the words of encouragement, and your friendship across time and distance.

Aishat Abiri, Miracle Adebayo, Oluwabambi Ige, Ulan Garba Matta, Hon. Nengak Apollos Nden, Ifeoluwa Nihinlola, Olakunle Ologunro, and Cristin Williams read the novel at various stages of its evolution and provided invaluable feedback. I remain forever grateful.

To Enajite Efemuaye—thank you for your demonstrated faith in this story, for letting me know I wasn't wasting my time, for asking for more. My thanks also to everyone at Kachifo (Farafina)—especially Kelechi Njoku—who championed this book.

To Selena James—the love you have demonstrated for this story has been humbling and empowering. Thank you for giving it a home. To the team at Little A who worked tirelessly to bring this book to life—I am deeply grateful.

Thanks to Lota Erinne for that final fresh pair of eyes and the extra push to keep honing.

My thanks also to Nancy Adimora, who went out of her way to help this book along on its journey.

My deepest thanks to David Godwin and Andrea Somberg. Without your faith, enthusiasm, encouragement, and persistence, this book would not have found a home.

To my family—my mother, Esther Turaki, and my sisters, Azara and Maryam Turaki—thank you for putting up with me and my stubborn ways in the name of art.

I started writing this book before I met my wife, Tongriang, but I would not have finished it without her encouragement. She stooped to pick me up between rejections, urging me to write on, to send that email, to never give up. She prayed with me, read drafts, brought me tea in the middle of the night, and cracked her whip if I was being lazy. Along the way, a little person called Sarkhinen arrived, bringing so much light and peace, and proving to be the charm that brought this project home. For their love, companionship, and magical support, I remain immensely grateful.

About the Author

Photo © 2021 Nyam Abok

Umar Turaki is a writer and filmmaker whose work has been short-listed for the Miles Morland Scholarship and long-listed for the Short Story Day Africa Prize. For more information, visit www.umarturaki.com.